BLUSHING AT BOTH ENDS

'You're not going to – to *spank* me?'

'Oh, but I am, my dear. I most certainly am. I'm going to do just what your own father sadly neglected to do: that is, put you across my knee, take down your knickers, and then –' Matthew's voice slowed, and he gazed almost hypnotically into Susie's eyes, gauging her reaction to his words '– and then, Susie, I shall spank you – spank you very, very soundly indeed on your soft bare bottom. Spank you lovingly, long and hard, just as you deserve; spank you until every inch of your pretty young bottom is blushing rosy red; spank you until you wail and plead for mercy; spank you, Susie, until your sweet bottom is scarlet and tender and burning hot and you're very, very sorry for what you've done.'

With each reiteration of the word 'spank', Matthew's hand lightly slapped Susie's rear end, making her plump cheeks quiver through the thin fabric of her trousers. Now he smiled at her – a smile of great warmth and kindness, full of a sense of coming joy.

'That, my dear Susie, is what's about to happen to you. As I said, you have a beautiful bottom: full and soft and round, the kind of bottom that's absolutely made to be spanked. More's the pity that nobody's done so – until now.'

BLUSHING AT BOTH ENDS

Philip Kemp

This book is a work of fiction.
In real life, make sure you practise safe, sane and
consensual sex.

First published in 2008 by
Nexus
Thames Wharf Studios
Rainville Rd
London W6 9HA

www.nexus-books.com

Typeset by TW Typesetting, Plymouth, Devon

Penguin Random House is committed to a sustainable future for
our business, our readers and our planet. This book is made from
Forest Stewardship Council® certified paper.

MIX
Paper from
responsible sources
FSC
www.fsc.org
FSC® C018179

Printed and bound in Great Britain by Clays Ltd, St Ives plc

ISBN 978 0 352 34107 5

Contents

Acknowledgements

Some of these stories originally appeared in *Janus*, *Februs*, *Privilege Club*, *Stand Corrected* and on the Shadow Lane website.

1

Room Service

'*Ah merci, monsieur. Bonsoir.*'

The hotel porter pocketed his two euros and departed, leaving Charles Kenyon to survey his room at the Hotel de la Poste.

It was all much as Mme Hubert had led him to expect. Plush, nineteenth-century comfort, a touch shabby, but solid. At least he would sleep well; none of those intrusive voices through paper-thin walls that he'd suffered from in swisher, more modern establishments. Good sleep was some consolation for four days in a town where he knew nobody. Nobody, that is, except Mme Anne-Giselle Hubert, née Carignac – known to history as La Giselle.

Mme Hubert was a find: one of the last living links with the fabled Paris of the 1920s. While yet in her teens she had been the friend, and probably the lover, of Picasso; the lover, and possibly the friend, of Hemingway; the intimate, in different ways and to differing degrees, of Braque, Cocteau, Modigliani, Colette, Jean Renoir, Scott Fitzgerald, Josephine Baker, Gide, Ravel, Diaghilev – you name them, La Giselle had known them, had shared their joys and their sorrows, and very often their beds. And now she was old, very old, long since retired back to her native Arles, and Charles was determined to interview her for his book on that glittering era before she departed, as she soon surely would, for the great salon in the sky.

She had replied to Charles's letter in a touchingly shaky hand. Yes, she would be happy to see Monsieur Kenyon: but she hoped he would understand that, at her age, to talk for more than an hour would tire her greatly. If he would be so kind as to extend their conversation over a few days? And, alas, her apartment was small, she regretted she could not offer him hospitality. But the Hotel de la Poste was a *bonne vieille auberge* with a sound *chef de cuisine*. For the rest, she would do all in her power to make his visit worthwhile.

Mme Hubert was right about the hotel chef. Charles enjoyed an excellent, if solitary, dinner before retiring to his room. Once in bed, he picked up the novel he had bought in London just prior to departure: the fifth in Eve Howard's 'Shadow Lane' series, invitingly entitled *The Spanking Persuasion*. For several minutes he lost himself in Howard's cool, sensuous prose, in her seductive world of pretty provocative brats and stylishly dominant men, of sweet soft female bottoms lovingly bared and yet more lovingly spanked to a hot stinging blush; then he turned out the light, brought himself to a fast rippling climax and fell contentedly asleep.

The next day Charles returned to the hotel around six in an excellent mood. The first session with Mme Hubert had gone swimmingly; hesitant at first, the old lady had become increasingly fluent and animated as the memories returned to her. The years seemed to drop away and Charles could glimpse the kittenish charm that had so enchanted *le tout Paris*. The little apartment – shared, she explained, with her granddaughter who was out at work – was crammed with souvenirs, letters and other invaluable stuff that Monsieur Kenyon was welcome to borrow as he wished. His book, Charles happily realised, would be hugely enriched. To cel-

2

ebrate, he treated himself to a superb lunch, washed down with a fine Aloxe-Corton, in one of Arles' Michelin-starred restaurants and spent the afternoon exploring the town, its ancient stones mellow in the late autumn sunlight.

His room had been tidied, the bed neatly made. Eve Howard's novel lay where he had left it, on the bedside table; Charles had meant to stow it discreetly in a drawer, but it had slipped his mind. But his bookmark now lay beside the volume and another, of a different colour, peeped from the pages. What on earth – ? Intrigued, he opened the book and found a brief note, in a neat feminine hand:

Monsieur, Do such things interest you? I too. I am off duty at 5.00 p.m. If you would wish to talk with me about these matters, please leave a reply in same place. Most respectfully, Claudine, your chambermaid.

Charles's heart leapt. Could this be a hoax? But if not . . . That morning, leaving his room, he had glimpsed a chambermaid along the corridor. At a distance she had seemed young and shapely, and Charles had been pleased to see she wore the old-fashioned maid's uniform of short pleated black skirt, white frilly apron and black stockings, that Alan Bennett once so aptly termed 'spanking costume'. But whether she would appear as attractive close to, or whether indeed this was the mysterious Claudine, was another matter.

Still, the possibility was too good to miss, and in any case what had he to lose? The next morning when Charles left to see Mme Hubert, another note lurked in the book.

Dear Claudine, I am amazed by your impertinence, and I think we should certainly discuss it. Kindly

3

come to my room at 5.15 p.m. precisely. Do not change from your hotel uniform. Yours sternly, Charles Kenyon.

That day Mme Hubert was on even better form, and it was as well that Charles had brought his trusty cassette recorder, since he had trouble concentrating on her lively and colourful memories. Images kept distracting him – images of a short black skirt to be lifted, of lacy knickers to be lowered, of rounded white globes that bounced and jiggled and took on a rich roseate glow beneath stinging spanks. In the afternoon he again tried to distract himself with the sights of Arles, but impatience got the better of him and he was back at the hotel soon after four. His note was still in place, but a few words had been added.

Monsieur, I have indeed been most impertinent. I am sure you will know how to reward me as I deserve. *A bientôt.* Contritely yours, Claudine.

In a fever of anticipation Charles settled himself to wait. Another chapter or two of Eve Howard would put him in the mood, he thought, but he couldn't settle and found himself constantly glancing at his watch. Slowly, slowly the hands crept round to 5.15. No Claudine. By 5.30 Charles felt like kicking himself with disgust. Of course it had been a hoax, how could he have been such a fool as to think otherwise?

He had all but decided to go and find consolation in a friendly bar when there came a shy tap on the door. '*Entrez!*' called Charles. And she did.

As a teenager, Charles had harboured a crush on Leslie Caron, seeking out such films as *Gigi* and *An American in Paris* to lust wistfully after the actress's gamine appeal. Far more than Bardot, with her blatant sexiness, Caron had always seemed to him the epitome

4

of sensual French allure. Her dark-haired beauty, her full mouth, her dancer's grace and her figure, at once petite and delectably curved, had fuelled many of his secret adolescent fantasies. Now, gazing at Claudine, he felt himself transported back to those hot randy nights of fervent masturbation. This girl could have been the young Caron's sister. Something else about her was familiar, too, though he couldn't think what.

'Oh, monsieur, I am desolated to be late.' Her voice was husky and musical. 'There was *une crise* – I could not get away sooner. Please do not be too angry with me.'

After closing the door, she came and stood before him, her hands clasped behind her, the picture of obedient submission. She was a delicious sight. The old-fashioned uniform fitted her perfectly, emphasising her pert breasts, the slimness of her waist and the lush swell of her hips.

Charles became aware that he was gaping, and recalled himself with an effort. 'Ah – yes, Claudine, your lateness will be taken into account,' he said, adopting a tone of stern reproof. All day he had been mulling over the words of a speech to initiate this little piece of theatre, and now they recurred to him. 'But it's your impertinence that we must talk about first. Is it normally your practice, mademoiselle, to pry into the books in guests' rooms – let alone dare to leave them provocative notes?'

'Oh *non,* monsieur! Never before have I done such a thing. I am desolated – I beg you to forgive me!' Claudine hung her head. Everything in her posture and expression conveyed humble contrition, but she couldn't quite conceal the mischievous sparkle in her eye. This girl, Charles realised, knew exactly what game she was playing – and was enjoying it hugely.

'Forgiveness is all very well, young lady. But before you can be forgiven, I think you deserve to be punished. Don't you?'

5

'Punished, monsieur? But how?'

'Well,' said Charles, as if mulling deeply over this difficult question, 'I suppose I really should report this to the hotel management. I'm sure they wouldn't be amused. But I would hate to put your job at risk. So I think, all things considered . . .' He paused, savouring the moment, watching as the girl shifted uneasily from foot to foot. 'All things considered, Claudine, I think it would be best if I put you over my knee and gave you a good sound spanking.'

'A spanking, monsieur?' The young woman looked convincingly shocked, for all the world as if such an idea had never occurred to her. 'You mean . . . to smack me on my bottom?' She pronounced the last word with an equal stress on each syllable – *bot-tomm* – as if to emphasise the roundness and ripeness of that part of her anatomy.

'I do indeed. Very hard – and very thoroughly.'

'Oh, but, monsieur – I am not a child! I am twenty-two years old – much too old to be spanked on my bot-tomm!'

'Do you think so, Claudine? Well, you're about to learn otherwise.'

The maid pouted, swaying her hips mutinously. 'But it will *hurt* me, will it not?'

'Oh, I expect it will,' responded Charles happily. 'In fact I'm sure it will. Especially since I intend to spank you on your bare bottom, young lady.'

Claudine's brown eyes widened in well-simulated dismay. 'On my bare bot-tomm? Oh, *non*, monsieur, that would be shameful! Please, I beg you, do not offend my modesty! Spank me on my *culottes*, *je vous en prie* – see, they are only light.'

Turning, she bent forwards slightly and flipped up her skirt at the back, presenting to Charles's gaze a heavenly prospect: beautifully rounded twin globes jutting enticingly towards him, their ripe curves hugged by cream silk drawers discreetly trimmed with lace.

Gulping almost audibly at the alluring sight, Charles reached out to pat the proffered roundnesses. The silken fabric felt enchantingly soft. The plump mounds over which it was stretched felt softer still.

'Very pretty,' he murmured. 'So pretty, in fact, that I would hate to risk damaging such an exquisite garment. No, my dear, we must remove it from harm's way.'

So saying, he slowly eased the silk drawers down over Claudine's rearward curves, revealing pale flawless bare bottom-cheeks that trembled charmingly at being robbed of their last protection. As she felt the drawers descend, Claudine uttered a reproachful little 'Oh, *mais non!*', but made no move to prevent him.

Taking the girl by the hand, Charles drew her towards him. 'Time for your spanking, young lady,' he said gently. 'Across my knee with you, now.'

Claudine gazed at him appealingly. 'Oh, monsieur, please – you will not smack me too hard?'

'No harder than you deserve, my girl,' Charles retorted as he arranged her face-down over his lap in the time-honoured position and turned back her brief skirt. 'And no harder than you can bear. This pretty bottom is very nice and plump; I think it's quite well uphol-stered enough to take a good sound spanking.'

'Ah, cruel!' murmured the maid, but she lay submiss-ively across his thighs, making no attempt to escape while Charles stroked and squeezed the lovely orbs of her naked *derrière*, relishing their succulence, savouring the exquisite moment of anticipation.

'You have a superb bottom, my sweet,' he told her, 'absolutely made to be spanked. I've only one criticism: at present it's rather too pale for my tastes. But we'll soon change that.'

Joyfully Charles raised his hand and brought it down hard on the pouting bare bottom, connecting with a crisp juicy smack. The girl caught her breath as it stung her defenceless flesh, and gasped again as a second spank, equally sharp, stung the other cheek. Charles paused to admire the matching pink handprints that now adorned the creamy mounds, then settled down to spanking her with a steady rhythm, gradually increasing the force of his smacks, distributing them across every inch of the glorious rump placed so invitingly at his mercy.

He hadn't exaggerated; Claudine's bottom was truly made to be spanked. Full and peachy, the sweetly rounded globes swelled provocatively upwards, begging to be smacked; the pale sensitive skin coloured readily, and the whole target area was soon suffused with a becoming blush that deepened as her punishment progressed. At each spank Claudine gasped and wriggled, kicking her black-stockinged legs and causing the frothy tangle of her drawers to descend from knees to ankles until, catching on one of her high heels, they were sent flying, like a tiny silk parachute, into a corner of the room.

Charles was no novice at this game, but rarely had he had the joy of punishing so fetchingly pretty and delectably spankable a girl. Nor did he feel any compunction in spanking her long and hard; for all her feigned distress, it was clear she was enjoying the experience no less than he was. Her breathless little cries of 'Oh – oh – oh!' sounded not so much plaintive as ecstatic, and as the heat built up in her nether regions she ground herself shamelessly against his thigh. So he took his time, relishing every stroke and feasting his eyes on the lively dance of her bouncing bottom-cheeks. For fifteen minutes or more his hand rose and fell, turning the soft quivering globes from warm pink through rich rosy red to a glowing scarlet.

Finally he paused and helped the girl to her feet. There were tears in her dark eyes and she stood pouting at him reproachfully as she rubbed her blazing curves, but her eyes were sparkling and the hint of a mischievous smile played around her lips. 'Oh, monsieur, you spank a poor girl so terrible hard,' she murmured. '*Oh mes pauvres fesses*! How shall I ever sit down tonight? It is cruel of you to spank me so hard!'

'Is it now?' retorted Charles, grinning wolfishly. 'Well, that's just too bad, young lady, because we're not through yet. We still have the small matter of your lateness to deal with. Were you not ordered to be precisely on time?'

'Oh, but, monsieur,' protested the maid, 'that was not my fault!'

'Maybe not. But it's your bottom that will pay for it, *ma chérie*. Go to the dressing table and fetch me that hairbrush – and keep your skirt well raised. I want to admire my handiwork.'

Claudine pouted mutinously again, but obeyed, and Charles was treated to the delicious spectacle of her rosy well-spanked bottom-cheeks trembling and undulating as, holding her skirt high above her waist, she sashayed to the dressing table on her high heels. She picked up a black wooden-backed hairbrush, brought it back to Charles and held it out doubtfully.

'You will not spank me with this, monsieur? It will hurt most fearfully!'

'I'm sure it will,' said Charles calmly. 'Now, back across my knee with you, Claudine.'

'Oh please, monsieur, no more,' she pleaded, but still let herself be drawn back down into the classic position. Once again, her ripe young globes lay invitingly across Charles's lap, plump and defenceless but now yet more beautiful, adorned as they were with an opulent glow. Enchanted, he stroked the radiant cushions. They felt fiery hot and even softer than before, twin tender targets perfectly prepared for the hairbrush's burning kiss.

Charles rubbed the broad wooden back of the brush across the girl's rosy mounds, making her wriggle with apprehension. 'You were fifteen minutes late, my sweet,'

9

he reminded her. 'So you're going to get four hairbrush spanks for every minute of tardiness – sixty spanks in all.'

'Oh *non*,' wailed Claudine, wriggling in alarm and causing her lush, roseate curves to tremble exquisitely. '*Sixty* more spanks? It is too many, monsieur!'

'Any more argument from you, my girl,' said Charles happily, 'and I'll double it.' Raising the brush, he took careful aim, and . . .

'*Aïeee!* Ou-ou-ou-ou-ou-ou-ou-ou-ou-ou-ou-ou-ou!' squealed the girl, her body jerking as much from surprise as from pain.

Charles had changed tactics. Where his hand-spanking had been steady and measured, he now applied the hairbrush in a rapid fusillade of crisp hard smacks, making the girl's bottom bounce and wobble so fast it seemed like a scarlet blur. Claudine's dark mane of hair tossed wildly and her legs flailed as the merciless high-speed assault built up the heat in her bottom so fiercely she felt as if it must surely burst into flame.

Though Charles had promised her sixty spanks, it was impossible to keep accurate count at such a rate. But, being a conscientious man, he was determined not to fob her off with short measure. The squirming young beauty must have received near on a hundred stinging swats before he finally stopped and contemplated the richly reddened globes with the sense of a job well done.

Gently he caressed the scarlet mounds. 'OK, my sweet, you've had your punishment, and you took it very well.' Helping the girl to her feet he hugged her warmly, and for a few moments she sobbed on his shoulder while his fingertips strayed over her soundly spanked rear. When she lifted her head there were still tears in her eyes, but she gave him a sweet, tremulous smile.

'Oh, monsieur, thank you! It was a lovely spanking. I never imagined an Englishman could spank a girl so beautifully.'

10

Stroking his hair, she pulled his mouth down to hers and their lips met in a long passionate kiss. Charles's hand slid round and explored between her legs. Her cleft was creamy and swollen with lust, and she moaned deep in her throat at the touch of his fingers.

In turn her hand stroked his groin, unzipping him and releasing his engorged prick. She caressed its hot hardness, then sank to her knees and took him in her mouth. Her agile tongue licked and flickered around the head of his penis, while her fingers teased his shaft and balls, tickling his scrotum and tugging deftly down on his foreskin. Within seconds a spectacular orgasm seized and shook him, and he spent copiously into her willing mouth.

A true gentleman, Charles returned the favour as Claudine lay back on the bed with her legs well parted. Her pussy was sweet and fragrant, and he licked deep into her before tonguing and nibbling her clit. His hands squeezed her still fiery bottom-cheeks, one finger slipping between them to explore the puckered rosebud of her anus. She too was quick to climax, writhing on the bed with full-throated groans of joy. (Thank heavens for thick walls, thought Charles.) Then, after swiftly stripping off, they dived together beneath the covers.

Some hours later Charles awoke. It was dark, but the curtains were open and enough light came from outside to reveal that he was alone in the bed. He switched on the bedside lamp. A note was propped against it.

Mon anglais chéri, Your naughty impertinent thanks you for her lovely spanking – *et pour tout le reste.* My bottom yet glows deliciously and I think of you each time I sit myself down. I leave a little something for you to remember me by. *Bons baisers de ta méchante Claudine.*

11

His book lay where he had left it, but again the bookmark had changed. His place was now marked by a pair of delicate cream silk drawers. Charles held them to his nose and, with a sense of ecstasy, inhaled deeply.

The next day was his last in Arles. In the morning he had his final session with Mme Hubert before taking an afternoon plane back to London. It was tempting – very tempting – to prolong his stay and seek a further rendezvous with the enchanting Claudine. But it would involve an exorbitant additional airfare – and, besides, how could any repeat performance, however delicious, be quite as intoxicatingly sensuous as last night's? Best, surely, to leave it as a perfect glowing memory.

Mme Hubert was on fine form, happy to prolong their talk beyond the allotted hour, and Charles's cassette recorder reaped a last rich harvest of anecdote and reminiscence. In every way it had proved a superbly successful trip, and as he rose to leave he thanked the old lady effusively.

'Believe me, monsieur Kenyon, for me also it has been a pleasure. I love to revisit these ancient ghosts, and with your help I have recaptured much that I thought lost for ever. If I live so long, I shall be enchanted to read your book, and I am glad if I have aided you a little in the creation of it.' She smiled, and there was a hint of some secret laughter in her eyes. 'I trust that my granddaughter too has contributed to the pleasure of your stay in Arles?'

Charles stared. 'Your – granddaughter?'

'But of course; my little Claudine. She works at the Hotel de la Poste – as a chambermaid.'

As realisation dawned, Charles's eyes strayed to a photo of Anne-Giselle, all of seventeen years old, strolling arm in arm with Picasso on the Pont des Arts. Of course! No wonder Claudine had seemed somehow familiar. 'Then – then you knew?'

'Oh, monsieur Kenyon!' The old lady was laughing openly now, but not unkindly. Once again the years seemed to drop away, revealing the mischievous gamine who had captivated Paris all those decades ago. La Giselle smiled. 'At my age there is little one does not know. And besides – did I not promise to do all in my power to make your visit worthwhile?'

2

Blushing Bride

There she stands at the altar, my lovely Jenny, my golden girl, the close-cut ivory satin wedding dress outlining her superb figure, its sleek fabric hugging the curves of her beautiful bottom. And there beside her stands . . . someone else entirely. Not me.

Do I feel bitter? No, not now. Not since last night. Because I know a few things that fat oaf standing beside her doesn't know, maybe never will. And one of them is that his blushing bride, not twelve hours ago, was blushing far more vividly, and in a very different fashion . . .

I read Jenny's letter on a scruffy little Greek steamer somewhere in the further reaches of the Aegean. I'd picked it up from *poste restante* at Piraeus the evening before and thought I'd save my pleasure in reading it until the next day, relaxing on deck with a glass of rough raki in my hand. So I opened it against an idyllic backdrop of impossibly blue sea, soaring gulls and tiny deserted grey-brown islets.

Jenny and I had been together four years, since I was twenty and she two years younger. My golden girl, I called her. Long honey-blonde hair, skin that glowed like sun-warmed stone, a sensuous mouth, liquid brown eyes and the kind of body men dream about. The only reason she wasn't with me now, exciting lecherous glances on a Greek beach, was that she had her final exams to finish. The letter, I assumed, would tell me how they went.

'My darling, beloved Paul,' it began, 'I don't know how to tell you this . . .' and ended three pages later, 'My sweet darling, please, please forgive me.'

In between came the dagger stroke. She'd dropped me. To marry – my howl of fury panicked the gulls – Leslie Porchester.

Leslie Porchester. A fat, balding slob – I speak, of course, quite objectively – with no redeeming features whatsoever. Except that his father, some pompous City pinstripe, was stinking rich.

The nickname 'golden girl' bore an ironic side-meaning. Jennifer had a fatal weakness – for money. She'd been comfortably brought up – 'spoilt rotten' was my taunting version – despite her dad's heroic attempts to pour his wife's fortune down his throat. She liked to be comfortable, and a bit more than that. And she knew – we both knew – that I'd never be a good steady provider. We'd had plenty of discussions and more than one row about what I called wanderlust and she called irresponsibility. A few settled months, and I got restless. I'd take off, travelling light and sleeping rough, wherever the fancy took me. I wasn't, as Jenny's mother would put it (and often did) – ideal husband material.

So now Jenny – nudged, no doubt, by dear Mummy – had made her choice. And *what* a choice. I aimed a few further curses at the innocent gulls and headed into more raki. Lots more raki. By the time the boat dropped anchor at Amorgos I was stinking stupid drunk. Gathering from my boozy ravings what afflicted me, the Greek crew, with infinite compassion for the lovelorn, carried me ashore and bedded me down in a room above a tiny taverna, where I awoke the next day to a Wagnerian hangover.

* * *

When I got home the card was waiting for me – stiff, embossed, gold-edged. Rather like the people it came from, in fact. 'Mr and Mrs James Cunningham request the pleasure . . .' The fuck you do, I snarled, hurling it into the wastebin. But later I reconsidered, retrieved it and sent my acceptance. Maybe I can show up pissed, I thought, and puke all over the wedding cake. Childish? Sure. But then, jilted lovers aren't known for their mature restraint.

The next few weeks I moped, growling and licking my wounds. There were one or two girls who might have been ready to console me, but I wasn't ready for consolation. Not just yet.

On the eve of the wedding I set out on a solitary pub crawl, but my heart wasn't in it. After a couple of pints I dropped the idea, and started to wander aimlessly. Guess where my feet led me.

The house stood well back from the street, and as I approached it I could clearly hear Jenny's dad. Unlike me, he'd evidently had no trouble sinking a few. Then, at an upstairs window I knew well from the inside, a white-clad ethereal figure. My lovely, faithless Jenny – trying on the wedding dress, no less.

I'm not sure what I planned, or if I had anything as coherent as a plan in mind, but before I knew it I'd circled round to the side door. It was locked, but I'd crept surreptitiously in, and out, too often for that to present any problem. I dug the key out of the geranium tub, let myself in and listened.

James's slurred bray and Isobel's contemptuous contralto echoed faintly from the sitting room. They enjoyed their rows – it was the only activity they'd shared for years – and would be at it for hours yet. I made for the stairs and had just reached the landing when a door opened and a slim teenager came out. She started when she saw me. 'Paul! What on earth – why are you . . .?'

Felicity, Jenny's seventeen-year-old sister, was as dark as her sibling was fair. We'd always got on well – in fact, I think she rather fancied me, as girls often fancy their big sister's bloke. Now she gazed at me, half-alarmed and half-gleeful at my inopportune presence. 'You shouldn't be here. What if someone sees you?'

'It's OK. Your mum and dad are well into one of their screaming matches – they won't surface for ages.'

Felicity gave a mischievous grin. 'Unless I tell them.'

'Don't you dare, Flicky! Look, here's a tenner to keep quiet.'

She took the note, still grinning. 'And if I do all the same?'

'Then the next time I catch up with you, young lady, I'll turn you over my knee and spank you till you can't sit down for a week.'

'Oooh!' said Flicky, her eyes sparkling. 'That might be rather fun.'

'Don't bet on it,' I said grimly. 'And don't think I wouldn't do it, either.'

'I bet you would, you sadistic beast. But don't worry, I won't tell. You go and tell my stupid dumb sister where she gets off – it's the least she deserves. Oh, Paul!' Her eyes suddenly filled with tears. 'How *could* she? Leslie Porchester – *yeuucch*!' To my surprise, she suddenly threw her arms around my neck and kissed me full on the lips. 'Oh, Paul, I wish it was you tomorrow!' she whispered, and vanished down the corridor.

Moving quietly, I approached Jenny's bedroom door and pushed it gently open. Though she was facing me, she didn't see me. Her wedding dress was over her head, and she was easing it carefully off to avoid creasing it. Knowing its rustling would drown the noise, I closed the door behind me and locked it, dropped the key in my pocket, then sat down in an armchair and crossed my legs.

'Hello, Jenny,' I said.

There was a muffled shriek from under the dress and Jenny's face, slightly flushed and totally horrified, appeared abruptly from beneath it. 'Paul! What the hell are you . . .? You shouldn't be here! Suppose someone finds out! It's my wedding tomorrow!'

'I know. Dear Mummy sent me an invite, remember? Probably saw it as a twist of the knife, the old bat. But I thought I'd like one last look before you turned into Mrs Leslie Porchester. So here I am.'

Jenny looked flabbergasted. She also looked gorgeous. Her slip had come off with the dress, leaving her in just a white lace-trimmed bra, matching white silk knickers, tan stockings and white high-heeled shoes. Her tousled honey-blonde hair had fallen loose in sweet confusion down her back. She had never seemed more desirable. Lust rose in me, along with anger.

'You've got to go,' she exclaimed frantically. 'I can't talk to you now, you know that.' Her expression softened slightly. 'Oh, Paul, I'm sorry, really I am. But it was the only way. You never offered to marry me, did you? And anyway you'd have made a lousy husband.'

'Maybe so. But did it occur to you to find something better than that lump of rancid sheep's turd you're shacking up with tomorrow? How did you think I'd feel, imagining him running his greasy fat fingers over your body, sticking his slimy little dick into –'

'How dare you!' Furious, Jenny hurled her wedding dress over a nearby chair. 'Who the hell are you to say who I can or can't marry, you . . . wastrel? What do you know about Leslie, anyway?'

'I know you don't love him. You don't even like him. You wouldn't so much as tolerate him and his sweaty pawings if it wasn't for his dad's money!' I stood up, seething with anger. 'Shit, Jenny, you always had your mercenary side, but I never thought it went this far. You really are just a greedy, callous, spoilt little bitch, aren't you?'

18

Her eyes blazed. 'I don't have to listen to this! Just fuck off, why don't you? Get out now – or I'll scream for help!'

'Go ahead, no one'll come. Your parents are squabbling downstairs, they'd never hear you.'

'Flicky's in her room – she'll hear me.'

'Sure she will, but she won't do anything about it. She knows I'm here; I met her outside on the landing.'

'I don't believe you! What did you do – bribe her, threaten her?'

'Both, since you ask. I gave her a tenner, and told her if she said a word I'd spank the living daylights out of her. And I will, too, if she does. Although, come to mention it, my girl –' for a glorious intention was rising like the sun in my mind '– I can think of someone who deserves a damn good spanking far more than young Flicky. And it would relieve my feelings no end to dish it out.'

Horrified realisation dawned in Jenny's face. 'No! You wouldn't dare! I'll scream!'

'Too right you will,' I said, advancing upon her. 'And before I'm through with you, young Jenny, you'll have plenty to scream about, believe you me!'

'No!' she shrieked and turned to flee, aiming to take refuge in her bathroom. But high heels are treacherous things, and she teetered off-balance just at the opportune moment.

Grasping her wrist, I sat down on the bed and with a sharp tug brought her sprawling across my lap, face-down in prime spanking position. She kicked and struggled wildly, calling me every obscene name under the sun, but I captured both her wrists in my left hand and held them out of the way, while with my right hand I tugged the silken knickers down over her ripe curves, well clear of the target area.

And what a target area it was. Full, white and shapely, Jenny's glorious rearward curves swelled

19

delectably upwards, bare and rounded and lusciously spankable. Her struggles made the tender flesh quiver enticingly – as well as providing further stimulation for my already rampant erection. With joyful anticipation I stroked and squeezed the smooth plump globes; they felt deliciously cool and soft. 'Such a gorgeous bottom, my sweet,' I told her, 'it fairly begs to be spanked. And it's going to be, too – hard and very thoroughly. Because a damn good bare-bottom spanking is the very least you deserve for being such a spoilt mercenary brat. And, since I'll probably never get the chance to do this again, I'm going to make the most of it now.'

'No! Help! Let me go, you bastard! Help!' yelled Jenny, writhing indignantly. 'I'll kill you! Don't you dare!'

'Oh, I dare, my sweet. In fact, it'll be a pleasure. A very special wedding present, from me to you with lots of love – the finest spanking of your young life!'

'Ooooooh!' wailed Jenny apprehensively as I raised my hand and, with a feeling of sheer sensual delight, brought it down with stinging force on the lush curve of her right bottom-cheek. I was rewarded with a loud yelp of protest from Jenny, followed by another as I smacked the left cheek just as vigorously.

'Owwww!' yelped Jenny, wriggling desperately. 'Stop it! That bloody well *hurts*!'

'I should bloody well hope so,' I retorted. Strangely enough, the thought uppermost in my mind was 'Why the hell did I never do this before?' And who knows, maybe if I had, things might have been very different.

But, meanwhile, there was a job to do, and I had every intention of doing it thoroughly. So, taking a firm grip on my struggling perfidious darling, I administered several more ringing spanks to her ripe young bottom, while her language grew steadily more unladylike. It's always good to have your work appreciated, and Jenny's squeals and shrill invective were a pleasure to hear.

'Owwww! Shit! I hate you, you fucking bastard!' she yelped. 'Stop it! Let me *go!*'

But I hadn't the least intention of letting her go, not for a long time yet. For a start, I was enjoying myself far too much, relishing the feeling of my palm smacking down on those tender trembling cheeks; the ringing sound of each spank, and the gasps and yelps it drew from the wriggling victim; and, above all, the supremely erotic sight of the warm pink blush that was beginning to enhance Jenny's squirming, bouncing flesh-cushions. Already, after only a couple of dozen spanks, a rosy glow suffused every inch of her beautiful bottom, contrasting delectably with the whiteness of her back and thighs.

'I always said you had a sexy bottom, my love,' I told her, still smacking her hard and steadily, 'but you know what? It looks even sexier when it's all nice and red. And it's going to be much, much redder than this before I'm through, my sweet. Brides are supposed to blush, aren't they? Well, you'll soon be blushing like no bride's ever blushed before!'

'Owwww!' wailed Jenny, her blonde mane tossing and her long legs kicking frantically as the heat built up in her spank-warmed rear. 'Help! No! Stop it, you bastard! I'll – yowwww! – *kill* you for this! Help! Mummy! Daddy!'

True to her word, she yelled at the top of her lungs as my vengeful hand continued to crack down across her squirming rump, each spank ringing round the room like a pistol shot. For all my confident assertions, I was a little worried that somebody might hear. But no one came. Poor Jenny, the moneyed comfort she so enjoyed had become her trap. So large was the house, so opulently solid its doors and walls, that no sound reached the ground floor. Young Flicky was in earshot, of course – gleefully listening at the door, I guessed. But no hint of the punishment being meted out reached the ears of Jenny's parents – not the sound of a merciless male palm smacking rhythmically down on soft pampered female bottom-flesh, nor the desperate yelps and squeals of the owner of the reddening jiggling bottom in question.

So how could James and Isobel Cunningham, bickering sterilely in their luxurious drawing room, have guessed that Jennifer Anne, their beloved elder daughter, the lovely blonde bride-to-be, was no longer as they imagined, coolly admiring the image of her shapely self in all her wedding finery? That, instead, to her great surprise and indignation, the nubile young beauty now found herself turned ignominiously over her disreputable boyfriend's knee – humiliatingly bare-bottomed and face-down across his lap, her knickers down around her knees and her luscious rear end squirming and blushing beneath the stinging strokes of the first real spanking of her young life?

No, there was no help for poor Jenny. No Seventh Cavalry, no protective father or adoring mother riding gallantly to her rescue. It gave me an intoxicating sense of power to know that this delicious young creature was wholly at my mercy. I could go on spanking her just as long and as hard as I liked, working off all my anger, grief and jealousy on those soft, smarting bare bottom-cheeks.

So I took my time, spanking her steadily and deliberately, pausing to let the sting of each smack sink in to her quivering rosy mounds. For a good ten minutes I spanked Jenny to my heart's content, smacking alternately left and right, taking care to cover every inch of her peachy twin globes and paying special attention to the sweet soft undercurve where bottom meets thigh. With every smack the blush deepened on her bouncing flesh-cushions, until every inch of her ripe rearward curves was mantled with a sunset glow. She was still kicking and squirming at each spank, but no longer made any serious attempt to escape, and her indignant yells gradually gave way to gasps and wails and increasingly tearful pleas to be let off.

And when at last I finished – for I had to stop sometime, if only because my arm was getting tired – Jenny lay sobbing and gasping across my thighs, the trembling mounds of her soundly smacked bottom glowing like ripe tomatoes. I stroked the crimson curves gently, then slipped my hand between her legs. Her cleft was dripping wet, and she groaned at the touch of my fingers, writhing round on my lap and lifting her tear-stained face to mine.

'I hate you, you bastard!' she whispered fiercely. 'I hate you! I hate –' as our lips met in a passionate kiss.

Much later, as we lay together in a warm post-coital haze, Jenny murmured, 'Paul?'

'Mmmm?'

'You know – Leslie's father sends him away on business a lot . . .'

'Mm-hmmm?'

'Well – I still think you'd make a lousy husband – but you're not too bad as a lover.'

'Thanks a bundle . . .'

And, still later: 'Paul?'

'Mmmmmm?'

'You were a rotten bastard to spank me so hard.'

'You deserved it, my sweet.'

'No I didn't! Well – maybe I did. But it still hurt awfully.'

'Should damn well hope so.'

'Beast! But, you know, if you didn't do it *quite* so hard . . .'

'Mmmm?'

'I think I might – almost – get to like it . . .'

So here we all were in church, watching Jenny and the gross Leslie plighting their troth – no other term could encompass such an overblown affair. Choir, brides-maids, ushers, grey toppers, morning suits – and a bishop, no less, officiating. The full caboodle. Trust Isobel Cunningham to go for broke.

Gazing at the white satin that hugged the curves of Jenny's glorious rear end, I got a mental image of that delicious bottom as I'd seen it last night – bare and blushing beneath my punishing palm. Were those lovely cheeks still smarting a little? I wondered.

I couldn't suppress a chuckle at the thought. Flicky, fetchingly kitted out as chief bridesmaid, caught the chuckle and the direction of my gaze and flashed a conspiratorial grin, miming the rueful rubbing of her behind. Just as I thought, the little minx *had* been listening at the door. And enjoying every minute of it, I bet.

But then, so had I. And from what Jenny had said it seemed I might have the pleasure of spanking her, and bedding her, pretty often in the future – if I wanted. The prospect had its attractions, that was for sure. But, then again, did I really want to be Mrs Leslie Porchester's bit on the side?

No hurry to decide. In the meantime, I realised joyfully, a weight had fallen from my heart. Last night's little escapade had cured me; the pain Jenny had caused by jilting me was revenged in the pain I'd inflicted on her bottom. There was still an ache in my heart for her, and probably always would be, but I was free of my obsession – free to look elsewhere. At the thought I glanced involuntarily round and caught Flicky's eye again. This time, there was a definite hint of encourage-ment in her smile. Maybe because she wasn't wearing her usual baggy T-shirt and jeans, I noticed the once skinny teenager had filled out very pleasingly in all the right places and promised to be just as pretty as her sister.

Well, why not? And just think how that would infuriate dear Mummy . . .

But first things first. The bishop had droned his way to the punchline, the organ was pealing out corny old Mendelssohn, the bridal procession was filing out of church. Now for the reception, and the crowning moment of my secret vengeance – the joy of publicly assuring Leslie Porchester, in the presence of his newly wedded wife, just how lovely she looked as a blushing bride.

3

'Reader, he spanked me': the Missing Chapter from *Jane Eyre*

Many readers of Jane Eyre *must have suspected there was more than met the eye in the relationship between Jane and Mr Rochester. On his part, all that tyrannical striding about and slapping his riding crop; all those sly, almost cheeky, retorts from her. Then there's Rochester's evident love of role-playing: at one point he gets into bondage gear, with fetters on his wrists; another time he disguises himself in drag. Just what* was *going on?*

The recent discovery, in a disused potting-shed at Haworth, of a bundle of forgotten manuscripts casts revealing light on the matter. Among them was a chapter evidently intended as part of Jane Eyre, *which Charlotte Brontë decided – or perhaps was persuaded – to omit on grounds of delicacy. From the context, it may originally have stood between the present chapters 17 and 18. The Camden Institute for Disciplinary Studies is privileged to have been granted first publication rights to this revelatory document. Brontë criticism, it's safe to say, will never be quite the same again.*

That night I was restless, and could not settle to sleep. Mr Rochester's look, and that half-uttered sentence, so strangely truncated, preyed on my mind. What could he have intended?

I had heard the stable-clock strike two, and sleep was at last stealing upon me, when a strange distant sound reached my ears. I roused myself in my bed and listened more intently. It seemed – indeed, it surely was – singing. No words that I could distinguish, but a female voice intoning a melody full of wildness and yearning, and of far-flung lands lost and longed for. There was an infinity of desolation in that voice, and I felt my own heart touched by it.

Whose voice could it be? Surely none of Mr Rochester's guests – cool, poised Blanche Ingram, chattering little Amy Eshton – was capable of such poignant tones. Besides, their rooms were situated in another wing of the house, far from earshot.

Consumed by curiosity, I rose, donned a robe and ventured out into the gallery. The singing, though still some way off, now sounded more distinctly; it came unmistakably from that gloomy third storey that Mrs Fairfax had shown me when I first came to Thornfield Hall, and where I had heard the strange laugh.

Quietly I ascended the stair and entered the low-ceilinged corridor. The voice seemed very close now, as if its anguish could reach out and touch my cheek, and candlelight gleamed from below one of the heavy oaken doors. But, as I cautiously approached, careful to make no sound on the uneven floorboards, the voice seemed to recede, and the light with it, almost as though the singer had sensed my presence and withdrawn into an inner chamber.

Very cautiously I tried the latch. It yielded, and I entered the room. It was indeed empty, though there was a sense – and a scent – of some recent presence; an air of something languorous, and musky, and strangely exotic. I felt at once disappointed and relieved not to have discovered the singer; for though her song was eloquent there had been an uncanny, even dangerous, quality about it too, as if the mind from which it issued were not in true balance.

Yet there remained a mystery: whither had she fled, the singer of the night? No other door was visible save that whereby I had entered. The window was ajar, and for one brief eerie moment I could fancy she had changed to a bird, and taken wing. Then I recollected my better senses; Jane, I told myself, this is sad nonsense. The singer was human, even if deranged; and human beings require doorways to pass from room to room.

One wall of the chamber was hung with tapestry. I walked over and lifted it, and the mystery was solved. Two doors lay concealed behind the hanging. One I tried; it was locked, but the latch was warm, as if a hand had touched it but lately. The other opened to me – and revealed a treasure-house of many hues.

Dresses and undergarments – finery such as I had rarely seen, even on the backs of the elegant ladies who visited Thornfield – filled the closet to overflowing, and billowed forth as I opened the door, as if craving liberation. Bold bright colours, like the plumage of birds from some tropical forest; sumptuous fabrics, fine silks and organdies, muslins and velvets, tricked out with brocade and lace; and all imbued with that same warm drowsy scent that spoke to me of rich spices on far shores, and of dark eyes that sparkled in the dappled shade.

I know not what imp of perversity possessed me, but as if under some strange compulsion my hand reached out to these priceless trappings. Deep within me there spoke a saner voice, saying, 'Jane, such as these are not for you; there is danger and the taint of luxury in the very weave of them. Touch them not; shut the closet; leave.' But I could not; the desire was too strong for me. Disregarding the voice of prudence, I lifted out from its hanger a corset of rose-pink silk frothed at the bosom and hips with snowy Brussels lace, such as might have graced the figure of a king's courtesan.

Nearby, there stood a looking-glass, dusty and crazed with age, but yet clear enough to serve its purpose. I stepped to it and by the refracted light of the full moon held the capricious garment up against me. My likeness, in my borrowed plumes, gazed back at me transfixed. 'Can this be I?' it seemed to ask, incredulous.

Before I knew it, I had slipped off my plain sleeping-robe and donned the frivolous confection. It was fashioned for a woman a deal taller than I, and of fuller contours; but such was the craft of its designer that it fit me more than well enough, imparting to my figure an outline of unwonted voluptuousness, narrow of waist and rounded both above and below. I turned, glancing over my shoulder to consider the rearward aspect of my novel garb, and caught a glimpse of pale seductively exposed hemispheres. Jane, thought I in disbelief, had you but been endowed with a wardrobe such as this, even you may have been tempted to turn wanton.

Moving as if in a dream, I returned to the closet and once more plunged my arm into its depths. This time my trophy was a dress of emerald-green shot-silk, a wondrous creation that fell like a waterfall in layer after layer of gathered flounces. The queen of some remote sea-girt isle might have sallied forth clad in such a shimmering verdant glory.

Once again I turned to the glass with my latest adornment, holding it to me by the shoulders and waist. The transformation was yet more startling. With my face shadowed in the oblique moonlight, and my loosened hair flowing to my shoulders, I might almost have been the belle of some colonial ball.

Such was the lustre of the dress, it seemed to glow in the half-light, and as I gazed at my image in the glass it was as if the illumination in that low drab chamber had imperceptibly increased. I must have become lost in a reverie, for it was only after some moments that I realised that the room was indeed growing lighter; and that the source of this alteration was not the dress I held, but the glow of a candle-flame approaching along the corridor and nearing the open doorway. A spasm of alarm seized me; I stood rooted and unable to move, or even to turn myself around, as a dark broad-shouldered figure armed with a riding crop loomed in the aperture. I was discovered in my flagrant misconduct – by Mr Rochester.

I expected to see anger on his visage; but, as he raised the candle to throw light on me where I stood with my back to him, I was amazed to see his expression in the glass was one of horror, as if faced by some doppelganger, or a revenant from a long-lost past. At this I turned to confront him, and as the light struck my face his gasp turned to something between a growl and a chuckle.

'What! Jane!' he exclaimed, regarding me in my purloined finery. 'What the devil are you doing here? And rigged out like this!' He examined me more closely, seemingly more amused than wrathful. 'You surprise me, Jane,' he observed. 'You harbour more capacity than I had imagined for vanity – and for mischief.'

Mortified by the hint of mockery in his tone, I could only hang my head and blushingly murmur my contrition. 'I am sorry, sir,' I said. 'It was inexcusable, I know. I was carried away by curiosity.'

'So I see,' he responded. 'As for sorry, Miss Eyre, that we may come to. But for the moment you had best return these draperies to the closet. No, stay –' as I started forward. 'Better you retain the corset, and resume your night-robe over it. Then replace the dress whence you found it.'

He considerately turned his back while I effected these changes. In my confusion I had wholly forgotten my half-clad state; and my blush deepened as I realised that my posterior nakedness must have been visible to him on his entry, and then in the looking-glass throughout our colloquy. Hearing me shut the closet, the emerald silk once more incarcerated in its depths, he turned.

'And now, Jane,' he said, offering his arm, 'I think it as well that we quit this place, and its associated temptations. Allow me to escort you back to your room, where we may discuss this night's escapade in privacy.'

Our removal passed in silence; from shame on my part, while Mr Rochester seemed musing on how best to requite my transgressions.

Once we gained the seclusion of my chamber, he sat down on a chair and gazed broodingly at me from beneath his heavy brow. 'Well, young lady,' he remarked at length, 'what am I to do with you?'

'I fear you must dismiss me, sir.'

'Dismiss you – for such a peccadillo? No! But you have been miscreant, no question of it, and your curiosity might have brought dire consequences upon you, and on others too. You are habitually so grave a person, Jane, and so sagacious beyond your years, that I often forget you are yet scarce more than a child in years; not yet nineteen, indeed. Tonight you regressed; what you did was no more than the thoughtless naughtiness of an inquisitive half-grown girl, and I feel it can be most fittingly requited as such. Come here, Jane.'

With this he reached out, grasped my wrist and drew me to him. At first I was uncertain what he intended; and, by the time I knew it for certain, it was too late to utter more than an incoherent gasp of protest. The next moment, to my great disconcertment, I found myself prostrated face-down across my master's lap.

Reader, he spanked me.

I blush to recall it; though not so vividly, perhaps, as my defenceless posteriors blushed beneath his punitive palm. Yes, defenceless; for, prior to executing my chastisement, Mr Rochester lifted back the hem of my robe, tucking it up beyond my waist and exposing, to my inexpressible shame, the naked orbs of my hinder parts.

Now was I amply requited for my vanity. The frivolous corset, designed at once to flatter and to tantalise, not only left my bottom quite bared and unprotected, but also plumped it out, enhancing its natural curvature and disposing it, I doubt not, the more temptingly as a target. Mr Rochester evidently relished the sight, for he stroked the tender globes – causing me to tremble as much at the intimacy of his touch, as from apprehension of the discomfort that this same hand would soon, I feared, inflict upon the parts it now caressed.

'Once more, Jane,' said he, 'I must confess you surprise me. So meek and sober is your everyday garb, I had not thought it to conceal such voluptuousness of form. Rarely have I seen a bottom more perfectly shaped to receive a sound spanking. For a sound spanking is what you deserve, young lady, do you not?'

If I demurred, would he remit my punishment? I suspected not. In any case, I could not find it in me to dissent. The sentence was just, even lenient, inexpressibly humiliating though it was to be turned over Mr Rochester's knee like an errant child, and to have my bare posteriors exposed to his eye and punitive hand.

Yet at the same time there was a strange delight in feeling myself held and controlled so masterfully by a man to whom I was not indifferent. Also I sensed that there was affection behind his sternness; that he would not have chosen so intimate and parental a form of punishment had he not cared for me a little.

Accordingly, I replied, 'Yes, sir. I have transgressed, been thoughtless, and a chastisement is the least I deserve. But I beg you will not be overly severe on me, or hurt me too much.'

'Fear not, Jane, I shall be merciful. It will sting; of course it will; what would be the use of a spanking that did not? But I shall not hurt you more than you can bear. Tomorrow morning you may feel the need to seat yourself with a trifle more circumspection than usual, but it will be no worse than that. And now, young lady, enough talk. Your punishment begins.'

So saying, he raised his hand high in the air. A keen thrill of fear and excitement ran through me. The next moment I could not forbear to gasp as a crisp smack stung my rearward mounds, swiftly followed by another; then by countless more, spank raining down upon ringing spank, until all my hinder parts seemed suffused by a fiery flagrant glow.

That this glow of warmth was matched by the heightened colour of the spanked cheeks I could have surmised for myself, but my chastiser took cruel delight in appraising me of the visible effects of his attentions to my unlucky person. 'I am gratified to see, Jane,' said he, even as he continued his assaults upon my trembling flesh, 'that already you begin to blush for your misdeeds – and very prettily too. But I fear you must come to blush more vividly yet, before you have been fittingly requited for your wanton curiosity.'

At this, he increased the force and frequency of his strokes, igniting fresh fires in my anguished nether regions. Since I acknowledged the justice of my punishment, I had intended to endure it in stoic silence, but in the event it was more than I could do to prevent myself crying out.

'Oh sir,' I cried, 'pray spare me! Oh! Ah! No more, I beg you! Ow! My bottom is aflame! Ah! Did you not promise me mercy? No more, for pity's sake! Ow! Oh! I am truly sorry!'

Abandoning all thought of stoicism, I writhed and squirmed on his lap, trying desperately to escape the stinging slaps that seared my ever more tender *derrière*. But my pleas, and my contortions, were equally in vain. Mr Rochester's powerful left arm held me fast by the waist, while his no less formidable right arm rose and fell in a steady rhythm, administering merciless punishment to my smarting hindquarters.

'Sorry, are you, young lady?' he muttered. 'Aye, no doubt you are, and shall be more so yet. I warrant you'll sleep face-down tonight, my inquisitive Jane.'

But at length he paused, and I thought my ordeal was over. He released me, and I regained my feet – shakily enough, in all conscience. Alas, there was further torment yet to come: to my horror I saw Mr Rochester reach for the riding crop where it lay idle on the bed. I found I could not speak; my breath came in convulsive gulps, close to sobs; but my eyes and my posture must have spoken eloquently of my dismay, for he smiled – a smile strangely compounded of cruelty and tenderness.

'We come now to the finishing touch, Jane,' said he, 'a measure intended to impress this lesson most in-eradicably upon your . . . memory. Kneel over the bed, please, and present your bottom for the crop.'

I stammered some form of protest, but he merely gestured impatiently to the bed, flicking the crop in a way scarcely calculated to allay my fears. Nonetheless, I obeyed, feeling myself wholly subjected to his will and, moving as if in a dream, assumed the posture he had specified. One small portion of my mind objected indignantly, demanding whether I had not taken leave of my senses, but so drained was I of all energy by the spanking I had undergone that resistance was quite beyond my capacities. Nor could I conceal from myself that there was a wild perilous sweetness in such utter submission.

So I knelt there as he bid me, meekly presenting myself for further chastisement, and felt him once more lift back the robe to expose my glowing posteriors, whose hue, I suspected, must now surpass that of the ill-fated corset that moulded them so invitingly. I trembled with apprehension as Mr Rochester laid the cool thin length of the crop across my heated flesh: glancing over my shoulder, I saw him take a pace back, raising his arm high in the air.

'Six strokes, Jane,' came his voice. 'Take them well, and it will all be over.'

The next instant it was as if a bar of white-hot steel had seared across my ill-used hinderparts. A scream pierced the room, and it was a moment before I realised that it was I who had uttered it. Tears welled in my eyes, and in my agony I had but one consolation: that my bedchamber was sufficiently removed from those of the Hall's other residents to be beyond their earshot.

Five more times the dreaded crop whistled down, and five times I shrieked in anguish. But somehow I maintained the recipient posture, desperately though I longed to leap up and clap my hands to the afflicted parts. Then – oh blessed moment! – I felt Mr Rochester's arm raise me up and enfold me to him, and I sobbed out my pain and penitence against his manly bosom.

'Well done, Jane,' he murmured, gently stroking my hair. 'You took your punishment in exemplary fashion. It's all over; the account is settled. Let this night's doings remain a secret between us.'

It was some minutes before I could respond; but at last the sobs abated, and I disengaged myself from his embrace and stepped back. 'Thank you, sir,' said I, though my voice still trembled. 'I deserved correction, and you have dealt with me justly. I hope you will always do so.'

'No resentments, Jane?'

'None, sir.'

'Good; then I shall take my leave.' He paused, and added with an ironic look, 'But before I go, perhaps you had best divest yourself of that corset and entrust it to my keeping. Now that your secret weakness is known to me, I shall consider it my duty to shield you from temptation as far as may be.'

Once more, he discreetly turned his back while I doffed the incriminating garment, rueing the moment I

35

set eyes on it and heartily wishing I might never see it again; I resumed my sober night-robe and handed Mr Rochester the corset. He took it, briefly caressing its roseate silk, then bade me goodnight.

'Goodnight, sir,' I replied. 'And rest assured, I shall never again presume to touch the garments worn by your late wife.'

Mr Rochester paused in the doorway. 'By my late wife?' he enquired. A strange indecipherable smile played over his saturnine features. 'By my late wife?' he repeated. 'Oh no, my dear Jane, you misapprehend. By *me*.'

4

In the Red

'I've come to see Mr Daniels, please,' Susie Redwood told the bank clerk. 'I've got an appointment.'

It wasn't an appointment she was at all keen to keep. In the two years since Susie had moved to London, her financial affairs had slid ever closer to catastrophe. It wasn't that she was poorly paid – anything but. Her work at the advertising agency earned her a handsome salary, with – since Susie was good at her work – generous bonuses. As a single girl she had no dependants or commitments. In theory, she should have been able to live well, indeed, very well, and still save a substantial part of each month's salary.

But living and working so near to the fabulous fashion stores of the West End was, for someone like Susie, a fatal temptation. She'd developed a serious shopping habit, and the wardrobes in her smart Regent's Park flat were crammed with items she'd just *had* to have – and had then worn maybe once. Expensive items, too. Susie had excellent taste but – in financial terms – terrible judgement. As her bank balance, now deeply in the red, and her monthly credit-card statements showed all too clearly.

It didn't help that Susie had grown up the only child of indulgent parents who had denied her nothing. Though too sweet-natured to be described as a spoilt bitch, she'd certainly got used to feeling she was entitled to have anything she wanted, without question. But since the sudden death of her father two years earlier, and the downturn in the stock market, that reassuring parental back-up was no longer available. Susie, however, kept right on behaving as though it was.

And now things had reached crisis point. She was several months behind with her rent – flats overlooking Regent's Park didn't come cheap – and the monthly interest on her credit cards was mounting horrendously. And then had come the letter from her bank. Had Miss Redwood noticed, it enquired politely, that she was now more than £3,000 overdrawn – an overdraft which she had neglected to pre-arrange with the bank?

Of course, thought Susie – the bank! Why hadn't she thought of it before? She would ask the bank for a loan! That was what banks were there for, after all, wasn't it?

But the bank, when she applied to them, proved strangely reluctant to advance her the £10,000 she asked for, not without further discussion. It wasn't, the young woman she spoke to patiently explained, quite as simple as that. Perhaps she would care to make an appointment with the manager, Mr Daniels?

So here Susie was, fetchingly turned out in a frilly blouse and a skirt that stopped just short of her dimpled knees. The effect was charming, if just a touch girlish. This was deliberate. Susie looked young for her age, but she wasn't naive, and she'd noticed that a hint of girlish helplessness worked very well on men somewhat older than her – as, she imagined, this Mr Daniels would probably be.

She was right about that. Matthew Daniels, it turned out, was probably around fifty – a sturdy well-built man, with a distinguished hint of grey about the temples. He received her courteously, with a friendly smile, but there was something steely in his glance that told her she had better be honest and open with this man. He wasn't, she suspected, someone it would be at all wise to lie to.

So when he asked her what precisely she wanted her £10,000 loan for, Susie abandoned all her planned fictions about 'business opportunities' and confessed she needed the money to pay off her debts. And very soon she found herself telling this calm fatherly man with the shrewd eyes and friendly smile just how she'd accumulated those debts, and how whatever she did she seemed quite unable to get them under control. And then, utterly to her surprise and humiliation, she found she was starting to cry.

Matthew Daniels pushed a box of tissues tactfully in Susie's direction (for bank managers, like therapists, always need to have tissues to hand), then sat back and studied her as she blew her nose and dabbed at her eyes. What a pretty, appealing, self-indulgent little girl she was. For in many ways she *was* still a little girl, proceeding heedlessly on her way with no thought of the consequences. She reminded him of his youngest and prettiest daughter, Jilly – but Jilly at fourteen, not the bright, independent 23-year-old she now was.

With her father's help, Jilly had learnt self-discipline. And perhaps, using similar methods, he could help the lovely Miss Susie Redwood learn the same lesson. It would certainly be very pleasant indeed to try . . .

As Susie composed herself, Matthew leant forwards and spoke seriously. 'Well, Miss Redwood, I'd like to thank you for being so frank with me. In return, I'm going to be equally frank with you. There's no way, I'm afraid, that the bank can lend you £10,000.'

Susie gazed at him, wide-eyed with dismay. 'Oh, but – but –' she stammered.

'I'm very sorry, but how can we? Against what collateral? A wardrobe full of designer outfits and a mountain of debt? Why, my directors would have a fit at the very idea. No, it's out of the question.'

He sat back and let the bad news sink in. Susie sat dejected, her bright hopes punctured.

'However,' he continued, 'that doesn't mean nothing can be done for you. This bank's been around for a long time – two hundred years or more – and we didn't survive by abandoning our customers to their fates. Even when –' he gave her an ironic grin '– those fates were largely self-inflicted. I'm sure we can help you put your affairs in order.'

Susie brightened visibly. Though there was little physical similarity, this man reminded her strongly of her father in his reassuring confident manner. Throughout her childhood, her daddy had always been there for her, always able to put things right.

'Two things to begin with, Miss Redwood,' Matthew proceeded. 'All these fabulously expensive designer clothes you've been splashing out on – most of them, you say, worn no more than once. They must still have considerable resale value. I have a friend in the fashion world. I suggest that you let her help you slim your wardrobe down by say eighty per cent, and get you the best possible price for those you relinquish.

'Second, that apartment. It sounds delightful – but right now it's way beyond your means. With luck, the sale of the clothes will pay off what you owe in rent. Once that's done, and you've found somewhere less extravagant, we can start considering how best to pay off your credit-card debts – and the bank's overdraft, of course.'

Poor Susie looked about to weep again. 'But where shall I live?' she wailed. 'Anywhere in central London's bound to be expensive – and if I move further out, my travel costs will be terrible. I'll *never* get it all paid off!'

Matthew looked pensive. 'Hmm, that is true. Still – now I wonder . . . Miss Redwood, would you kindly excuse me one moment? I have an idea, but first I must make a phone call.'

40

Left alone, poor Susie contemplated the horrors of living in the dreary dreaded dead-zone of London's outer suburbia. Names flitted across her mind – Croydon, Cricklewood, Hounslow, Ongar, Surbiton – dim distant stops at the far end of tube lines. 'Oh, I *can't*!' she groaned.

How her friends, her smart young colleagues at work, would snigger. 'Coming for a drink, Susie? Coming to the party? Oh no, you can't, can you? Got to get home to – where was it again – Dagenham? Oh yuck! Crudsville!'

Matthew returned, smiling encouragingly. 'Well, Miss Redwood, I've a possible solution to the accommodation problem. I just spoke to Helen, my wife.'

'Your wife?' echoed Susie, bewildered.

'That's right. You see, we've got quite a large house in Highgate. Really too big for us now, since all our daughters have found places of their own. The youngest, Jilly, left only a few months ago. And I must admit, the house does seem rather empty without them. So here's the idea. If you like, you could come and live with us as our guest until you've got your affairs back in order. You'd have your own room, your own bathroom, at the top of the house, plus another room to use as a sitting room – almost like a self-contained flat. We wouldn't need any payment, so you'd be living rent-free – that way, you'll be able to pay off your debts a lot faster. All we'd ask in return is that you follow our house rules while you're living under our roof.'

Susie could scarcely believe her ears. It was all too good to be true. In Highgate, too – as desirable an area, or even more so, than Regent's Park! How right her instincts had been; just like her father, Matthew Daniels was magically able to put things right.

So the very next day, Susie travelled up to Highgate to meet Helen Daniels, a charming elegant woman with a warm smile, and to see the cosy well-furnished rooms at the top of the rambling old Victorian house that would be her home for the next few months. A week later her wardrobe had been drastically slimmed down, and with the proceeds she had paid off her rent arrears and was even left with a little cash in hand.

Late one Saturday afternoon, a taxi deposited her and her possessions outside the Highgate house where Matthew and Helen were waiting to greet and welcome her. To Susie, it really did feel as though she'd found her second home. 'I'll be happy here, I know it,' she thought to herself.

She was right about that – although perhaps not quite in the way she imagined.

At Matthew's insistence, Susie had brought a folder containing all her credit-card statements, bills and other records of her financial transactions over the past two years. He beamed as she handed it over to him. 'Thank you, my dear,' he said. 'We'll start going over these after dinner in my study, and we can decide then the best way to deal with your problems – and how to make sure you never get yourself into such an embarrassing situation again. Now get yourself settled in, and then come down and join us for a drink before dinner.'

Upstairs, Susie showered in her neat little bathroom, then changed into something that she felt would strike the right note of tasteful simplicity: an embroidered white linen blouse with loose sleeves and well-cut black trousers that moulded themselves fetchingly to her shapely figure. Then, feeling happier than she had for months, she trotted downstairs for dinner.

'Oh, what a beautiful view!' she exclaimed as she entered the dining room. The wide windows looked straight out on to the wooded green sweep of Hampstead Heath.

'Yes, isn't it charming?' said Helen. 'And if you look right round to the left, you can just see Highgate Ponds.'

Obediently, Susie moved over to the window and leant on the sill, peering out. Her position, as she leant forwards, displayed the tempting curves of her ripe young bottom to their fullest advantage. Matthew's eyes gleamed, and Helen shot him an amused glance of complicity.

Susie, though, was not aware of any of this as the three sat down to dinner. Helen was a fine cook, and Matthew's taste in wine was impeccable. Susie displayed a healthy appetite, and Helen beamed maternally at their pretty young guest.

'Oh, my dear,' she said, 'you know we're so pleased to have you here. Matthew especially – I know how much he misses the girls. He's always been such a good caring father; a little old-fashioned, perhaps – aren't you, my dear? – in his attitudes, but none the worse for that. So it's really like having a daughter in the house again. No formality, please; call us Matthew and Helen, won't you? And may we call you Susie?'

After dinner, as Helen started to clear away, Matthew said, 'Right, Susie, I think it's time we started going over those accounts.'

He led her into his study and sat down at a handsome rolltop desk, indicating that she should stand next to him. He began to go through the bills, credit-card slips and other documents, putting his arm round her waist and encouraging her to draw near and scrutinise them with him.

Gradually, as the evidence of her reckless financial imprudence built up, Matthew's hand slipped down until it was resting on the ripe swell of her bottom. At each new extravagance that came to light he gave a sharp intake of breath, a muttered 'Tsk, tsk!' or 'Oh, Susie!', accompanying each comment with a light slap on her rear. Though little more than affectionate pats, much too light to hurt, these slaps made the soft flesh of her bottom-cheeks wobble, causing her to tingle with a strange anticipation. She found herself embarrassingly aware of the plumpness of her bottom, emphasised as it was by the close-fitting black fabric that hugged its lush full curves.

Finally, Matthew completed his audit and swivelled his chair round to face her. 'Well, young lady,' he said, 'you've been rather naughty, haven't you?'

Susie nodded, shamefaced. 'Yes.'

'Imprudent, spendthrift and thoughtless, with no consideration for others – in short, totally lacking in self-discipline. In fact, Susie, discipline is what you lack, isn't it?'

Susie nodded again, uncertain what he might be getting at.

His hand was still resting on her rump. Now he lifted it and brought it down in a slightly harder slap that made her cheek quiver. 'Well, now, my dear, while you're living here with Helen and me, we must see what we can do to make up for that lack. Now, what sort of discipline would be most appropriate, do you think, for a scatterbrained young lady like yourself?' He gazed at her quizzically, a half-smile on his lips. 'Mmmm?'

'I – I don't know,' Susie stammered stupidly.

Matthew raised one eyebrow. 'Really, Susie? No idea? Well, we've agreed you've been naughty, haven't we? And what's the time-honoured punishment for a naughty girl?' He patted her behind, squeezing it gently. 'Especially for a naughty girl who has such a very lovely bottom?'

Idiotically, Susie felt herself blushing. She felt a terrible sense of foreboding, a tingle of fear that seemed to run right through her bottom-cheeks. Surely he couldn't mean . . .?

Matthew smiled, his eyes twinkling. 'Would I be right in thinking you were rarely spanked as a child?' he asked quietly.

'No – never.'

'As I thought. And has anyone spanked you as an adult – a brother or a boyfriend, say?'

'No! Certainly not!' said Susie, bridling at the question.

'So this lovely young bottom has never yet been treated to a spanking? A great pity – it might have had a very salutary effect on your conduct. Well, my dear, that's going to change – starting now. Because, while you're here, you'll be living with us as though you were our daughter. Now our three daughters are all sweet lovely girls, and I love them dearly. But, you know, when any one of them was naughty, or wilful, or extravagant, as teenage girls so often are, I never hesitated to do what any loving father should do for his errant daughter.'

'You – you used to spank them?' asked Susie faintly.

'Oh yes indeed, dear Susie. Whenever any of them misbehaved, she knew exactly what to expect. I would put her across my knee, lower her knickers and spank her soundly until her bottom was burning hot and she was a very sore and sorry young lady indeed. An old-fashioned remedy, but most effective. And, you know, all of them were the better for it, as they'll be the first to agree.

'So what you're about to experience, Susie, is what your own father sadly neglected to supply – an extremely hot, sore and well-spanked bottom. And I firmly believe it'll do you a great deal of good.'

Susie could hardly credit what Matthew was proposing. She, a sophisticated young woman of 21, to be turned over a man's knee and smacked on her bottom like a naughty child? There was no earthly reason why she should submit to this: she should protest, refuse, walk out of the house. Yet there was something so authoritative, so masterful about Matthew, with his calm smile, sinewy frame and greying temples, that what was meant as defiance came out as a tremulous plea. 'You're not going to – to *spank* me?'

'Oh, but I am, my dear. I most certainly am. I'm going to do just what any good father should do for the guidance of his wayward but much-loved daughter: that is, put you across my knee, take down your knickers, and then –' Matthew's voice slowed, and he gazed almost hypnotically into Susie's eyes, gauging her reaction to his words '– and then, Susie, I shall spank you – spank you very, very soundly indeed on your soft bare bottom. Spank you lovingly, long and hard, just as you deserve; spank you until every inch of your pretty young bottom is blushing rosy red; spank you until you wail and plead for mercy; spank you, Susie, until your sweet bottom is scarlet and tender and burning hot and you're very, very sorry for what you've done.'

With each reiteration of the word 'spank', Matthew's hand lightly slapped Susie's rear end, making her plump cheeks quiver through the thin fabric of her trousers. Now he smiled at her – a smile of great warmth and kindness, full of a sense of coming joy.

'That, my dear Susie, is what's about to happen to you. As I said, you have a beautiful bottom: full and soft and round, the kind of bottom that's absolutely made to be spanked. More's the pity that nobody's done so – until now.

'So this will be your first ever chastisement – the first of many. Just think, young lady, of all those spankings you've missed over the years; those spankings you so richly deserved, that this lovely bottom was so ideally shaped to receive, but that the men in your life were so sadly remiss in administering to it. This is a seriously underspanked bottom, my dear, and we have a lot of catching up to do.

'You remember what I said about house rules, my dear? Well, this is one of them: that any naughty girl living here shall be soundly spanked whenever she deserves it. Now, of course, if you're not happy with that rule, you're at full liberty to leave, just as soon as you like. Right now, if you wish. But, as long as you choose to remain here with us, Susie, you will be spanked regularly and often. Every day, more than likely. Even twice or three times a day, if I feel you deserve it.'

Matthew paused and smiled kindly at Susie. His voice was calm and friendly; he might have been discussing the weather. 'Now tonight, my dear girl, since this will be your first ever chastisement, I shall let you off with no more than a hand-spanking. Later, we'll see what more might be needed. There are many implements that can be used to raise a fine blush on a pretty pair of cheeks like yours – straps and hairbrushes, paddles and tawses, belts, wooden spoons, even the humble kitchen spatula. Over the next few weeks, this beautiful bottom –' another pat '– will become intimately acquainted with all of them.'

Susie had listened to this recital with mounting dismay. 'But – but you can't!' she burst out.

'Oh but I can, my dear. And I shall. Now come over here, please.'

Taking her by the hand, Matthew rose from his desk and led her over to a leather sofa against the opposite wall. Sitting down on it, he smiled calmly and affectionately at her. 'Good. Now kindly unzip your trousers, please.'

As if in a trance, Susie found herself doing as she was told. Then Matthew was taking her by the hand, and gently but firmly guiding her to lie face-down across his knee, her head to the left and her plump young bottom uppermost over his lap. Then her trousers were being eased down to her knees, to reveal twin globes of soft white flesh, their ripe curves only partially concealed by lacy pale-blue nylon knickers.

'Comfortable?' Matthew asked gently.

It seemed an odd question, Susie thought, since he was evidently about to make her anything but comfortable. Still, there was something unexpectedly reassuring and, yes, even comforting about lying across the lap of this mature handsome man, waiting to receive at his hands what even she had to admit was a well-deserved punishment. So she murmured, 'Yes, thank you.' She almost found herself adding 'Sir'.

'Good,' said Matthew, as he proceeded to the final preparations. He loved these preliminaries to a spanking, regarding them as a key part of the exquisite ritual of spanking a pretty girl, and never hurried them if he could help it.

So now Susie felt her blouse being pushed out of the way above her waist, and her knickers were drawn slowly but inexorably down, well clear of the target area, to hang in a fetching tangle around her thighs. 'Oh please, no!' Susie breathed, as she felt the last protection being peeled away from her now utterly defenceless rear end, but she seemed powerless to resist.

Enraptured, Matthew gazed at the delectable prospect before his eyes, stroking the girl's bare bottom-cheeks, patting and squeezing them gently. They felt cool and deliciously soft, trembling and rippling beneath his hand. He hadn't been exaggerating: Susie really did have a most exceptionally spankable bottom, shapely and well rounded, full fleshed without being fat, tender yet resilient, the skin flawless and creamy white. A clearly defined crease marked the point at which the sensitive undercurve of each cheek (always his favourite spank spot) met the top of the thigh. How beautifully, he reflected with delight, these luscious globes would blush as he spanked them, how prettily they would wobble and quiver at each stinging smack!

And this nubile young beauty was his to punish whenever he wanted, his to put across his knee and spank as often and as hard as he liked, for weeks and months to come. For, though it seemed she had never realised it before, Susie clearly had a strong submissive

48

streak. Despite her horrified reaction, she had made scarcely any protest and put up very little resistance to being turned over his knee. When she felt her knickers being taken down, she had uttered a tremulous plea, but had made no move to prevent him, nor even placed a protective hand over her vulnerable mounds.

And, having once submitted, how could she refuse on subsequent occasions? She would soon become used to resigning herself obediently to frequent regular chastisement. Her financial affairs were in such a muddle that it could take months to straighten them out – months that could easily be extended, since the management of the whole business lay wholly in his hands. And, all that time, Susie would be here in his house, at his mercy, his to punish. Here to be spanked to his heart's content, as often as he liked, as hard as he liked, as long as he liked – spanked with hand or strap, with hairbrush, paddle or tawse – spanked on this beautiful bare bottom that no one had ever smacked before. It was a breathtakingly delicious prospect.

Face-down across Matthew's lap, Susie wriggled nervously. What on earth was he waiting for? She knew he must be admiring her bare bottom, feasting his eyes on its voluptuous curves – and that was flattering, for she knew it was an attractive rear, even if (she had always felt) a little on the plump side. But what an undignified spectacle she must present – draped humiliatingly over the lap of a man she scarcely knew, with her knickers down and the soft full mounds of her bottom upraised and bare, ready for his punishing hand.

But was he really going to spank her, she found herself wondering – for if he was, why hadn't he started yet? Perhaps it was all an elaborate joke and in a moment he would release her scot-free. And, even if he was going to spank her, she thought hopefully, how bad could that be? He was only going to use his hand, after all. *That* couldn't hurt much – could it?

A moment later, she gasped out loud.

Susie's gasp was as much from surprise as pain. Until that moment, she'd had no idea how much the impact of a hard male hand, descending with pitiless force, can sting the soft pampered flesh of a bare female bottom. Now she knew – and how!

Her second gasp was closer to a yelp. Only two smacks – and already both cheeks were smarting vividly. When it came to the spanking of young ladies, Matthew, she realised, was an expert. He had given no indication how long this, her first ever spanking, would last, but Susie suspected it wouldn't by any means be brief. And, if her bottom smarted like this after just two spanks, what on earth would it feel like by the time he finished?

'Oh please,' she begged pitifully, 'not so hard! It *hurts*!'

'That, young lady,' said Matthew cheerfully, 'is the idea.'

Ten more times his hand rose and fell, each spank ringing round the walls of the room, echoing like a pistol shot – and each eliciting yelps, gasps and frantic protests from the pretty young blonde squirming bare-bottomed across his lap.

After a dozen spanks Matthew paused, admiring the effect of his efforts so far. Susie was clearly going to be every bit as enjoyable to spank as he had hoped. Hers was the kind of pale delicate skin that coloured readily – already a fetching pink blush suffused the trembling mounds. And she was proving a pleasingly responsive spankee, gasping and yipping at every stroke, writhing and kicking, already begging for mercy with her punishment scarcely started. Some spankers demanded that their victims stayed stoically silent, but not Matthew. To him, there was no more exquisite music than the squeals and wails of a naughty girl receiving a sound bare-bottom spanking, her cries harmonising perfectly with

50

the crisp rhythmic smack of palm on soft bare female bottom-flesh. Such music, after all, no less than the ever-deepening blush on the bouncing cheeks, provided gratifying proof that his chastisement was having its full desired effect.

So with a sense of delight he resumed Susie's spanking, smacking now this side, now that, on her soft squirming globes and taking care to cover the full expanse of the luscious target area.

Matthew believed in taking his time; to spank slowly and deliberately not only prolonged his pleasure but also increased his victim's discomfort. So he spanked the lovely girl hard and steadily, pausing after each smack to let its sting sink in before administering the next one. And from time to time he indulged in a longer pause to stroke the yielding well-warmed flesh and feast his eyes on the vivid blush that steadily deepened on Susie's glorious bottom, turning it from warm pink to rosy red to fiery crimson, until the radiant mounds contrasted deliciously with the whiteness of her back and thighs.

At one point, much to Susie's alarm, the door opened and Helen came in. But, mortifying though it was to have someone else see her in this ignominious position, she felt a surge of hope; surely the other woman, astonished and outraged, would put a stop to the proceedings? But Helen merely smiled calmly, as if it was the most normal thing in the world to find her respectable husband with a pretty young girl lying half-naked across his lap. 'Ah, I see Matthew's taking good care of you, my dear,' she observed. 'That's wonderful. It'll do you so much good, you know.'

Helen kissed her husband warmly on the lips, then leant down and patted Susie's roseate mounds. 'Such a lovely bottom, my dear,' she said, 'just perfect for spanking. And I'm sure Matthew will do it full justice. He's a wonderful spanker, isn't he? So skilful and confident. I'll never forget the spanking he gave me on our wedding night. I was just about the same age as you. What finer way for a young girl to start out on married life – face-down across her handsome young bridegroom's knee, having her soft bare bottom spanked hot and crimson? You can think yourself lucky, my dear. Matthew doesn't spank just any girl, you know.'

She patted Susie's bottom again, squeezing it lightly. 'Oh yes, beautifully hot and tender – just the way a naughty girl's bottom should always be. But I think she can take a bit more, darling, don't you? Anything you need – hairbrush, a nice paddle? Oh, you're keeping them for the next time? Yes, that's probably the best plan. Well, then, I'll leave you both to it. See you at bedtime, dear child.' Another serene smile and she was gone.

With a sigh of satisfaction, Matthew resumed Susie's punishment. The brief pause had given time for the sting to sink in yet more deeply, and on her now exquisitely tender and ultra-sensitive bottom it felt to poor Susie as if he were spanking her harder than ever. An experienced spanker, he'd had good reason to ask if she was comfortable before her chastisement began. He wanted to be sure that nothing, not the least little thing, would distract this sweet girl's attention from the fires he was kindling on her lovely bottom. And in this he was wholly successful. All Susie's consciousness, all her quivering nerve-endings, seemed to have rushed to her outraged hinder parts. Her skin was aflame and her nether globes felt like two blazing fiery mounds, as if swollen to twice their normal size.

Helpless across his lap she yelped and wailed, squirming frantically as spank after spank assaulted the tender trembling masses of her bouncing bottom-flesh. She would never have believed that a mere hand-spanking could hurt so much – or that it could go on for so long! And the indignity of it! Never before had anyone so much as raised a hand to her; and now here she was face-down across a male lap, wriggling and squirming, with her knickers round her knees and her trousers round her ankles, having her defenceless bottom-cheeks soundly spanked until – as she didn't need Matthew to tell her – they must be blushing red as ripe tomatoes. Oh, how it hurt! How sore her soft bottom was! 'Oh please, Matthew,' she begged, 'that's enough! I'm so, *so* sorry! Oh please, won't you stop?'

But Matthew was in no mind to stop. This was Susie's first ever spanking, and he was resolved to make it a memorable experience. Besides, she was such a joy to spank that he couldn't resist continuing to his heart's content. So plump and well fleshed a bottom, he knew, could take a long hard hand-spanking with nothing worse than temporary discomfort. And of course it was always good to start as you meant to go on. Amazing as it was that such a pretty, flighty girl, with such a delicious bottom, should have reached age 21 quite unspanked, it did mean that Susie would have no idea how severe a typical spanking should be – how hard it should be applied, nor how long it should last. A good long bottom-smacking session now would set a fine precedent for all those to come.

So for a good thirty minutes Matthew's hard hand remorselessly rose and fell, steadily deepening the rich crimson blush that now mantled every inch of the succulent target area. Poor Susie squealed at each smack, pleading tearfully for mercy, writhing and kicking desperately as the punishment built up the smarting heat in her defenceless cushions. Once she tried to protect her flaming cheeks with her hand, but Matthew simply captured her wrist in his left hand and held it out of the way.

'No, no, my dear,' he murmured, continuing to spank her. 'No interruptions, please. You must take your punishment like a good girl. Otherwise I'll have to get out my hairbrush – and you won't like that, my sweet, not one little bit. But, meanwhile, young lady, I'm afraid that act of disobedience has earned you another hundred good hard spanks.'

'Oooooh!' wailed Susie, but Matthew, true bank manager that he was, never overlooked a debt.

After a few more minutes of crisp steady spanks, he paused and said, 'Right, my dear, we're nearly through. But now for that extra hundred I promised you.'

'Oh no,' Susie yelped, but, even before the words were out of her mouth, Matthew, with a startling change of pace, had unleashed a tornado of fast stinging spanks, delivered so rapidly that it seemed he was smacking both her blazing wobbling cheeks at once. The hundred spanks were administered in less than a minute, searing her tormented flesh. Poor Susie squealed desperately, her blonde hair tossing and her legs scissoring wildly.

And then at last it was over, and Matthew was lifting her up from off his lap, cuddling her, kissing away the tears, telling her in that calm warm fatherly voice that she was a good girl, she'd taken her punishment very well, and that now it was time for bed. And Helen was there cuddling her too, rubbing soothing cool cream on the fiery mounds, congratulating Matthew on having done such a good job. Together they helped Susie upstairs, undressed her, washed her, dressed her in pale-blue pyjamas and put her to bed – lying face-down, of course. Matthew sat down on the bed, stroked her hair and kissed her forehead – for all the world like a strict but fond father saying goodnight to his naughty but much-loved daughter.

And Susie, to her utter amazement, found herself taking his hand – the hand that had so mercilessly assaulted her tender bottom – kissing it and thanking him. 'I know I deserved it,' she whispered, 'but now I've been properly punished, haven't I?'

Matthew smiled, kissed her forehead again and gently patted the plump mound of her bottom through the bedclothes. 'Yes, of course you deserved it, dear Susie. And I'm glad it had such a salutary effect on you. But I hope you don't think, my dear, that two years' flagrant irresponsibility can be requited with one little spanking?'

'*Little*?' thought Susie incredulously.

'Oh no, young lady – that was just your first spanking, and a very mild one at that. You'll be getting another one tomorrow, *and* the next day – and every night for many weeks to come.' He smiled his fatherly smile. 'And of course if you're naughty in any other way, the punishment for that will be additional. Now go to sleep, my dear.' A final pat on her upturned rump and he was gone, switching the light out as he left.

Susie lay there, face-down in the darkness of a strange bedroom. Her bottom was still very sore, but the pain had transmuted into a deep warm glow that seemed to radiate all though her nether regions. Unbidden, her hand crept down inside her pyjama trousers, seeking the hot wetness between her legs – a wetness she had been humiliatingly aware of even while she was still across Matthew's lap. (Still worse, she suspected *he* had been aware of it too.) In no time at all her questing fingers brought her to a gasping shattering climax more intense than she had ever known before.

She drifted down towards a deep sleep. One small part of her mind, the modern rational part, was yelling at her, telling her she must be utterly crazy. If Matthew meant what he said (and not for a moment did she doubt it), then the next few weeks would see a sustained assault on the tenderest portion of her anatomy. No doubt those other implements – the paddles, hairbrushes and tawses he had spoken of – would soon be brought into play. They would *hurt* – hurt like hell! Sitting down in comfort would become a distant memory. A vision arose of herself pinioned face-down over Matthew's broad lap, kicking and squirming, her all-too-plump and spankable bare bottom blushing scarlet beneath his merciless spanks. She must leave this house *tomorrow*, first thing, insisted Susie's rational mind.

But its protests became a faint squeak and then faded out altogether. For an older, deeper, more powerful part of her told her that this was where she truly belonged – in this house, across Matthew's knee. This, or something very like it, was what she had been unconsciously seeking all her life. Tomorrow, she told herself as she drifted away, I'll be spanked again. And the next day, and the day after, and the day after that. Every day, without fail. And if I'm naughty (and somehow I think I shall be), then I'll be spanked some more. Lots more. And that's right. That's the way it should be.

And, with a contented smile on her face, Susie slept.

5

Motivation

If anyone starts telling you how glamorous Hollywood is, it's a fair bet they've never worked there. Because, believe me, Hollywood is mostly frustration, bullshit and hard graft – especially if you're trying to get a movie project off the ground. And all the more so these days, when most of the studio 'executives' are jumped-up, slick-suited young know-nothings who think movie history began with *Star Wars*. OK, maybe one or two of them – the brighter ones – have just about heard of Hitchcock. But mention Hawks, Lubitsch or Capra, and watch their eyes glaze over with ignorance and indifference.

You'll have gathered I don't much like Tinseltown. In fact, if it was up to me I'd never set foot in the place. As a Brit film director, I've enjoyed a fair-to-moderate career making movies my side of the pond where the bullshit level – though still high – is at least tolerable most of the time. But this latest project I was working on needed a bigger budget – some $35 million or so. And to raise that kind of money, you generally have to get into bed with one of the major Hollywood studios.

So here were Don, my producer, and I in La-La Land, pitching our project and hoping for a break. We'd been in LA a week, and things weren't going too badly; both Universal and Miramax seemed tempted to bite. But it would need at least another couple of weeks pitching, and already I was nauseous from the crap I was having to talk. With my last meeting of the day over, I headed thankfully back to my bungalow at the Château Marmont (hell, if you have to do LA, you might as well do it in style), looking forward to a quiet evening. There was a cocktail party up Laurel Canyon where some good contacts might be made, but I decided to leave that to Don. He's far more of a party animal than I've ever been, and schmoozing comes naturally to him. Anyway, what else are producers for?

I'd just settled into the jacuzzi with a long cool drink when the phone rang. That'll be Don, I thought, telling me what a great party it is and how I *must* come right over; so I let it ring. But then I heard the answering machine kick in, and a soft husky voice said, 'Leo? Pick up if you're there, sweet friend and mentor. It's Luci.'

Dripping, I lunged for the phone. 'Luci! How did you know I was in town?'

'Oh, word gets around, my love – you know how it is here. But how come *you* haven't called *me*? Darling, I'm deeply hurt.'

I gave a short laugh. 'Honey, take a reality check. A lot's changed in three years. You're now stratospheric; Keira snarls at the mention of your name. Me, I'm still a hack Brit director. I wouldn't get past your assistant PA's assistant PA.'

'Oh crap, Leo, cut the humble bit. *You* can always reach me any time; you know that.'

'Well, sweet of you to say so. And I'd love to see you, my darling. Shall we do lunch? How's tomorrow?'

'Oh, Leo,' she said. There was that little sad catch in the voice I could never resist. 'Leo, couldn't I come over now? Please?'

I had to pinch myself. This was Lucinda Lee, one of the biggest, highest-paid movie stars in the world, asking – no, *begging* – to be allowed to come over. To see *me*. Things must be serious.

'Luce, what's the trouble?'

'Oh, Leo, it's this new film. You know, *Angel's Kingdom*? I just can't get into it.'

I'd heard about it – an *Indiana Jones*-type romp, with Luci top-billed as the female adventurer. 'Sounds right up your street. Is the script bad?'

'No, the script's fine. It's the director.'

'Jed – whatsisname – Gassner? A first-timer, right?'

'Yes. He's a sweet guy, but he just can't give me what I need. Oh, sweetheart, you know what that is, don't you? What I always did need? What you could always give me?'

I knew, all right. 'Motivation?'

A happy sigh wafted down the line. 'Oh, Leo, honey, I *knew* you'd understand.'

'Come on over,' I said.

Three years ago . . .

'Lucinda Lee?' I asked incredulously. 'The super-model? You serious?'

Don leant back in his chair and grinned. 'Leo, you're a snob. Supermodel doesn't automatically equal bimbo.'

'Not automatically, no – just usually. And, even if she's not, what makes you think she can act?'

'See for yourself in a minute. But, first, think through the logic. With Hugh's fee taking up such a chunk of the budget, we can't run to a big-name co-star. Now Lucinda *is* a big name – but as a model. As a first-time actress, we can get her cheap. Clever or what?'

'Not clever at all, if she's a crap actress. Hugh'll walk. And then where will we be?'

'OK, wiseguy. Watch this tape, then tell me to go fuck myself.'

There were four commercials on the tape. I'd vaguely noticed them before, but now I paid close attention.

Lucinda looked beyond lovely, of course, everyone knew that, but now I realised something else: the camera adored her. Then came – oh crafty Don! – a screen test.

When it finished, I glared at him. 'Without saying a word, huh?'

He shrugged, all innocence. 'You were busy. It was just a hunch, and I didn't want to bother you. Well – so?'

'Yeah, OK, you win. She's got something. Whether it's enough is another matter. But let's call her agent.'

Don's grin widened. 'I already did.'

A week into the shoot, I knew Don and I had made the biggest, dumbest mistake of our careers. If we still had careers. Oh, Luci had potential, all right – but bringing it out was another matter.

You see, she *wasn't* dumb. That was half the trouble. She'd prepared for her big break by swallowing a stack of books, and she'd overdosed on Stanislavsky. Now the Method is fine for a lot of actors – but not if you're a natural. Which Luci was – or would have been, if only she'd let herself. Instead, she was making herself hopelessly self-conscious, blocking off her own instincts. 'What's my motivation here?' she kept asking.

I felt like telling her what Spencer Tracy said when faced with some young Method-addled type: 'Listen, son, I'm too old, too fat and too goddamn rich for this shit. Just play the fucking scene!' But something told me it wouldn't go down too well. So I tried to coax her out of it . . .

Without success. Spooked by her own inexperience, she reacted badly, complaining about minor details of costume or lighting, demanding retakes or added close-ups, generally getting on everyone's wick. 'Who's she think she is?' I heard one disgruntled grip ask another. 'Julia sodding Roberts?'

To make things worse, she was a hopeless timekeeper. An eight o'clock call, to Luci, meant 8.45 – if we were lucky. I suspected that her years as a supermodel, with everyone kowtowing and deferring, had spoilt her. Maybe in the rag trade they don't mind that kind of thing so much. But in the movies delay can do horrendous things to your budget. You've got actors and technicians stacked up in holding patterns, all highly paid, and the costs are ballooning by the second. So at the end of the first week I took her aside and tried to explain this. She tossed her tawny-blonde head with an 'Oh what a *fuss*' sigh, and muttered something offhand about the traffic.

'Come on, Luci,' I retorted, 'don't give me that shit. There's a limo waiting for you at six thirty every morning, and Jim's one of the most reliable drivers in the business. If you're late, it's not the traffic, it's *you*.'

She looked at me with those beautiful grey-green eyes as if I'd crawled out from under something unsavoury. With an effort I held my temper. 'OK, Luci,' I said, 'enough already. From now on you're here at eight on the dot every morning, OK?'

'Whatever,' she said, and swanned off.

Monday morning. Eight thirty came, and nine . . . and still no Luci. To fill in we started rehearsing the takes scheduled for after lunch, but everyone knew what the trouble was. I glimpsed Hugh, a professional if ever there was one, raising one sculpted eyebrow in exasperation. Any moment now he'd be calling his agent, wanting out – and then we really *would* be in deep doo-doo.

Finally, just before nine thirty she showed. Looking – just to make it all the more infuriating – drop-dead gorgeous.

'Sorry,' she said airily. 'Overslept.' She shot me a sidelong glance as if to say, 'And just what do *you* intend to do about it, lowlife?'

That did it. 'OK, everyone, break till ten,' I announced. 'Luci, I'd like to see you in my office, please. *Now*.'

Two minutes later she was sitting across from me on the couch, those lovely long legs crossed, one impeccably moulded kneecap pointed at me like the muzzle of a pistol. Her attitude radiated disdain, but underneath I sensed insecurity and need. For all her outward sophistication, I reminded myself, she was only 23.

'OK, Lucinda,' I began. 'First off, let me make one thing clear – you're not indispensable to this movie. Not by a long shot. You may be numero una in the rag trade, but here you're just another first-timer with no track record. Time enough to act the prima donna when you've earned it. As it is you're in gross breach of contract, and I'm well within my rights to fire you right now.'

'You can't,' she protested. 'I've shot all those scenes. You'd have to –'

'Reshoot them all with another actress? I know. But I'll be happy to do that. In the long run it'll be less hassle and, assuming she's more professional than you – which ain't difficult – probably quicker. We'll wrap the movie OK, don't you worry. But your film career, Luci, will be down the pan. When it gets round how you behaved on this shoot, no reputable production company will touch you with a ten-foot boom. It's back to the catwalk for you, my girl.'

By now she was starting to look worried. 'But I want to act – I really do! And I know I can! You wouldn't believe how boring modelling is! Look, Leo, I'm sorry I've been such a useless bitch. I'll really try from now on – and I won't be late again, I promise. Honest!'

'Yeah, I've heard that one before.' I paused, letting her dangle, then added, 'Still, against my judgement, maybe I can offer you one more chance.'

Relieved, she began to get up. 'Hold it!' I snapped. 'No one said you were getting off scot-free.'

She sat back down, looking puzzled.

'Here's the deal, Luci. Either I fire your ass off the picture, or –'

'Or what?'

'Or, young lady, I put you across my knee here and now and give you a damn good spanking.'

Her mouth fell open. 'A spanking? But you can't!'

'Want to bet?'

'I – I'll call my agent!'

'I just did, ten minutes ago. And I told Brendan exactly what I proposed to do. Want to know what he said?'

Luci nodded, still aghast.

'He said, "Good on you, Leo. She's a lovely girl but spoilt as hell. A well-tanned arse is just what she needs."'

'I don't believe you!'

I shrugged and handed her my phone.

She dialled frantically. 'Brendan? It's Lucinda. It's unbelievable! Leo's threatening to ... What? You ... But I ... But he can't ... Oh.'

She put the phone down and gazed at me in dismay. All the surface sophistication had drained away, and she looked like a little girl who knows she's in deep dark trouble. In fact, she looked so distressed and appealing, and so beautiful in her distress, that I almost opened my mouth to let her off. Almost. Instead I just waited in silence. Finally she dropped her eyes and whispered, 'All right.'

'All right, what?'

'I'll ... take the spanking.'

'Good girl,' I said. I came and sat beside her on the couch. 'If it's any consolation, Luci, you won't be the first young actress to spend time across my knee. If I told you the names of some of the girls whose bottoms I've warmed in the cause of good movie-making, you'd be amazed.'

'Like who?' she asked, genuinely intrigued.

'Oh no. That's strictly between me and them – just as this will be strictly between you and me. I'll tell you this much, though – a touch of old-fashioned discipline did their careers no harm at all. But enough talk; time's wasting. Over my knee with you, young lady.'

Taking her by the wrist, I drew her down into position. She gave a little gasp as she found herself face-down in the classic spanking posture, but she put up no real resistance, and her slim lovely body fitted perfectly across my lap. Reaching down, I lifted the hem of her short black dress.

Lacy black panties covered rather less than half the expanse of Luci's lush creamy bottom. A decade or so back, when models were all skinny clothes-horses, she'd have stood no chance in the profession; but the advent on the catwalk of Naomi Campbell and other black girls, and later of Sophie Dahl, had changed the parameters – and all for the better. Now it was reckoned OK for models to have female-shaped rearward curves – and Luci had those, all right. She was no J-Lo, but her bottom was peachy, pouting and beautifully rounded. This girl would be a delight to spank.

As if reading my thoughts, she twisted round on my lap and gave me a rueful grin. 'You're going to enjoy this, aren't you, you kinky bastard?' she said.

'Enjoy it? You bet I am. Who wouldn't? You've got a lovely bottom, Luci, but it's a bottom that's badly in need of a good sound spanking – on the bare, too. So before I start we'll just have these sexy panties down.'

'Oh no,' she breathed, but continued to lie submissively over my lap as I peeled the skimpy black garment halfway down her thighs. Then, after pushing her dress well back above her waist, I surveyed the prospect.

It was a ravishing sight. The sweet tender mounds of Luci's bare bottom swelled upwards over my thighs, begging to be spanked. I stroked the luscious globes; they felt cool and deliciously soft. She squirmed apprehensively at my touch, making her bottom-flesh quiver in anticipation.

'Oh please, Leo,' she whispered, 'not too hard?'

'No harder than you deserve, my girl, for screwing up my shoot and playing merry hell with the schedule. In fact, think yourself lucky I don't take a hairbrush to you. Next time, maybe I will. But, for now, I think you'll find my hand can make quite an impression – especially on a spoilt young bottom like yours.'

So saying, I raised the hand in question and brought it down hard on those ripe young curves. Luci yelped with pain and surprise, and her long legs kicked wildly as I proceeded to deliver a couple of dozen more swats, hard and fast, to her bouncing cushions. Her pale, delicate skin coloured readily, and a pretty pink blush soon suffused every inch of the sweet target area, rendering it even more beautiful. I paused to admire the results.

'Oww!' gasped Luci, wriggling. 'Leo, that really hurt! I won't be late again, I promise!' She made as if to get up, but I held her firmly in position.

'Oh no you don't, young lady,' I told her. 'You don't think you get off that lightly, do you? We've barely started yet. This is going to be a spanking to remember.'

'Oh please, no!' she wailed, but her appeal was in vain. I'd taken quite enough crap from this conceited young beauty, and I intended to make sure she got all she deserved . . . and then some. Besides, spanking Luci was proving even more enjoyable than I'd imagined. Her soft bare bottom, bouncing and wriggling beneath my palm, felt utterly delicious, and her gasps and yelps were music to my ears.

So I resumed her punishment, steadily increasing the force of my strokes until each one, laid on full force, rang out like a pistol shot. From the way they stung my palm, I knew they must be stinging Luci's sensitive rear far more sharply; and her squeals and tearful pleas for mercy were ample testimony to the effectiveness of what, I strongly suspected, was the first real spanking of her young life.

I wasn't keeping count, but by the time I finished she must have had well over a couple of hundred spanks and that glorious bottom was blushing like a peony. I lifted her to her feet and she clung to me, sobbing and shuddering, as I stroked her hair and gently caressed her burning curves. 'OK, Luci,' I murmured, 'it's all over. But remember – if you're late again . . .'

She detached herself and gave me a tremulous smile. 'I know – even harder, and with a hairbrush. I bet you would too, you rotten bastard.' She leant forwards and kissed me. 'But thanks, Leo, I deserved that. It hurt like hell, but I think it's what I needed.'

I left her alone for ten minutes to compose herself, then we resumed shooting. It was a good day, the best we'd had yet.

Not that the rest of the shoot was problem-free, of course. What film shoot ever is? And Lucinda didn't reform overnight, either. She was late once or twice more – and each time, as promised, she found herself back across my knee for a double dose: a good hard hand-spanking by way of warm-up, followed by the application of a wooden-backed hairbrush to her already rosy and very tender bare bottom. It made her yelp and wriggle beautifully. It seemed to work, too. By the time we wrapped, Luci's time-keeping had improved out of all recognition.

Now and then she started in on the prima donna stuff again, throwing tantrums, demanding to know what her motivation was. But that never lasted long. I'd lean over and whisper in her ear, 'Your motivation, young lady, is that if you don't cut out this shit I'll turn you over my knee right here and now in front of everyone.'

She'd blush and grin, and play the scene as good as gold.

We finished on time and under budget, and celebrated with a party. Afterwards, Luci and I enjoyed our own private celebration. On principle, I never sleep with actresses I'm working with; I find it makes direction damn near impossible. But once the movie's over, that's another matter. I suspect Luci felt the same way, because as we left the party she whispered, 'Honey, I think we've been good long enough. Your place or mine?'

'Mine's closer,' I said, treating her to a sound smack on the bottom. 'And when we get there I think I'll put you straight over my knee for being such a forward little minx.'

Luci pulled me close for an ardent kiss. 'Is that a promise?' she breathed.

She was a sweet lover, tender and passionate. We were together for the best part of two years – during which time she got spanked a lot. She always protested eloquently while across my knee, and afterwards would pout reproachfully and call me a 'rotten sadistic beast'. But, oddly enough, she never failed to give me a good excuse to spank her again very soon.

That debut movie of hers performed pretty well and established her as an actress. Her next one did only so-so and then – as you know – came *To Hell with Heaven*. It was the smash-hit British rom-com of the year, went down huge in the States, and suddenly Lucinda was the hot new young Brit actress. Inevitably, Hollywood beckoned. Tearful parting, promises of staying close that neither of us believed, and off Luci went to become a megastar in the Tinseltown firmament.

I watched her glittering career from a distance, with affection and fond memories. We'd had great times together, and the past was past. Or so I thought . . .

Until now, and this phone call to the Marmont. As I waited for Luci to arrive, I wondered if I'd dozed off in the jacuzzi and dreamt the whole thing. Hollywood does strange things to your sense of reality – and, anyway,

Luci had been on my mind. How could she not be, when I saw that lovely face and fabulous figure displayed twenty-times-lifesize on every other billboard in town?

The phone warbled. 'Mr Winton?' said the desk clerk. 'Miss Lucinda Lee is here to see you.' It takes a lot to impress the staff at the Marmont, but I thought I could detect a faint note of awe in his voice.

'Oh fine,' I drawled, cool as you like. 'Have her come over, would you?'

A few moments later there came a gentle rap at the door.

'It's open,' I called. 'Come on in.'

And there she was – as beautiful as ever, or maybe even more so. Somehow the legs seemed just a little longer, the curves a touch more voluptuous, the smile a hint more bewitching. But then Hollywood can do that too – even without plastic surgery.

'Oh, Leo,' she said, and then we were in each other's arms. I kissed her passionately while reaching down to fondle that glorious bottom. It felt just as soft and spankable as ever, maybe even – *gracias*, Hollywood! – a tad more so. I lifted my hand and administered a crisp swat. 'Oooh-mmm,' said Luci, growling deep in her throat, and ground her loins into mine. 'Sweetheart, can I stay?' she murmured in my ear.

'Stay for breakfast, my sweet,' I responded. 'If you're eating breakfast these days, that is.'

She gave me a wicked grin. 'Oh, I'm sure I can find something to nibble. But before you take me to bed, honey, you know what I need, don't you?'

'Sure,' I said. Taking her by the hand, I led her over to the couch. 'Come here, you bad girl, and get yourself across my knee. You've been acting altogether too sassy, young lady, and you're way overdue. What you need is some old-fashioned strict discipline – on your bare bottom.'

She gave a little shiver. 'Hey, that made my stomach drop. You know no one's talked to me like that for three years?'

'High time they did, then.' Sitting down on the couch, I drew her gently down to lie gracefully over my lap, the lush ripe contours of her bottom curved invitingly upwards, imploring my attention. She was wearing loose-cut silver-grey shantung slacks that slipped down easily, revealing the briefest of black silk thongs bisecting that peachy *derrière*. At the sight my heart missed a beat. Of all the girls I'd had the pleasure of putting over my knee, none had ever been quite such a sweet delight to spank as Luci.

Gently I stroked the soft cool mounds. At my touch Luci trembled, then twisted round to grin at me over her shoulder. 'OK, my favourite director,' she said, 'motivate me. Motivate me good and hard.'

'It'll be a pleasure,' I said, raising my hand high in the air with a sense of fierce erotic joy. 'Lights – camera – and . . . action!'

6

Gone with the Wind – The Lost Spanking Scene

No one knows just what treasures lie hidden away in the vaults of the great Hollywood studios. Dusty, long-forgotten scripts for brilliant films that never got made; piles of rusty cans, dented and mislabelled, spewing out reels of rotting celluloid that never saw the light of a public movie-house; suppressed scenes, or even whole lost movies, dating back to the fabled silent era. Somewhere in those cobwebby corners may lurk all ten hours of Erich von Stroheim's towering melodrama *Greed*, as it was before a panicky MGM chopped it down by 75 per cent; or the original director's cut of Orson Welles's masterpiece *The Magnificent Ambersons*, so crassly mutilated by RKO.

The vaults are guarded jealously: who knows what skeletons might emerge? But now and then a film historian or movie buff, more persistent than the rest, may bribe or cajole a way in and prowl around, with luck to emerge with some revelatory gem of lost movie history clutched in grimy fingers. And it seems to have been on one such unofficial trawl that a dog-eared file was found, containing letters and a few pages of script that throw unexpected light on one of the most famous films ever made: David O Selznick's great Civil War drama *Gone with the Wind*.

It's well known that even Selznick, foremost of the independent Hollywood producers, had to struggle to make *GWTW* the way he wanted. For at that time there was one man in Hollywood more powerful than Selznick, more powerful even than Louis B Mayer, the boss of MGM; and his name was Joseph Ignatius Breen. Ultra-conservative and ultra-Catholic, Breen was the head of the Production Code Administration (often called the Hays Office), and it was his task to ensure that no film shown in the USA 'should lower the moral standards of those who see it'. Which, most of the time, meant no onscreen sex – or precious little.

Scripts had to be submitted to Breen's blue pencil in advance. Out went profanity, innuendo, overt (and often even covert) eroticism. *GWTW*, despite being a big-budget, prestige production with the weight of Selznick and MGM behind it, was subjected to the same process. Breen objected to Rhett Butler's dalliance at the local brothel, to his colourful language, and even to the famous 'Frankly, my dear, I don't give a damn'. Above all, he objected to the notorious 'husbandly rape' scene when Rhett, driven beyond endurance by Scarlett keeping him at arm's length, sweeps her up bodily and carries her upstairs. Cut to Scarlett the next morning, luxuriating in bed, a satisfied smile on her face.

But now, the contents of the recovered file reveal, it seems there was even more to that scene than any of us guessed . . .

Joseph Breen to Val Lewton (Selznick's story editor), 9 January 1939: '*Spanking in itself, as a form of marital discipline, we do not object to, providing it not be overly prolonged. But it must be very carefully handled to avoid any hint that the man, and still less the woman, is deriving sexual enjoyment from the process of chastisement. In particular it would be unacceptable and morally suspect to suggest, as seems to be the case here, that the spanking is serving as an erotic prelude to sexual intercourse.*

'*I need scarcely add that Scarlett must remain chastely attired throughout. Spanking on the bare buttocks, or even on light underwear, is wholly contrary to the principles of the Code, especially in the context of a bedroom.*'

Breen to Lewton, 12 January 1939: '*Your suggestion that the spanking should take place downstairs in the dining room, prior to Rhett carrying Scarlett upstairs, fails to meet our objections. Indeed, it could make things worse, as the inference might be drawn that Scarlett finds herself so aroused by being spanked that she submits to being carried to the marital bed.*

'*As an alternative, could I suggest that you have Rhett spank Scarlett in the dining room, then stride out into the night, leaving her chastened and penitent? Their reconciliation could then follow the next day. This would have the further advantage of avoiding the whole "husbandly rape" episode, about which as you know this office has always harbored severe misgivings.*'

Breen to Lewton, 17 January 1939: '*I can only repeat that the spanking scene, as outlined in the latest version of your script, is completely unacceptable to this office. We find it lewd, gratuitous and verging on the sexually perverse. I should add that our research staff can find no such corresponding episode in Miss Mitchell's novel.*

'*Of course, if Mr Selznick wishes to shoot the scene in any case, purely as a dramatic exercise within the context of the production, he is at perfect liberty to do so. And, as ever, this office will be happy to view any footage that you care to submit to it. But I must emphasise that no such scene may be permitted to appear in the film as shown to the public.*'

From which it seems that not only was a spanking scene originally included in the *GWTW* script, but that it may even have been shot – if only for private consumption. So who knows: some day another searcher in those dusty vaults may strike it lucky, and we'll be treated to the delicious spectacle of Clark Gable putting the lovely and eminently spankable Vivien Leigh across his knee for well-deserved discipline. (Judging from accounts of Gable's exasperation with Leigh's on-set behaviour, there's no doubt he'd have made a thorough job of it.) But until then, at least we have the script – and our imaginations . . .

INTERIOR – DINING ROOM – NIGHT

RHETT: I've always admired your spirit, my dear. Never more than now when you're cornered.

SCARLETT draws her robe close about her body and rises, but without haste so as not to reveal her fear. She tightens the robe across her hips and throws her hair back from her face.

SCARLETT [*cuttingly*]: I'm not cornered. You'll never corner me, Rhett Butler – or frighten me! You've lived in dirt so long you can't understand anything else. And you're jealous of something you can't understand. Goodnight.

She turns and makes for the hall.

DARK HALL

Out of the darkness comes RHETT. He seizes her and roughly turns her around to him.

RHETT: It's not that easy, Scarlett. You turned me out while you chased Ashley Wilkes. Well, this is one time you're not turning me out!

He swings her off her feet into his arms and starts up the stairs. She cries out indignantly, but the sounds are muffled against his chest.

SCARLETT'S BEDROOM

*RHETT enters, still carrying the struggling
SCARLETT. He dumps her roughly on the bed, stoops
and kisses her ardently. She recoils and slaps his face –
hard.*

SCARLETT: You drunken fool! Take your hands off
me!

*RHETT staggers slightly, then grins and stoops to kiss
her again. She slaps him even harder, viciously.*

SCARLETT: How dare you! Get out!

RHETT [*still grinning, but now dangerously*]: Oh, I
dare, my dear. I dare that, and more. For a start, I
think you might benefit from a little lesson in
marital obedience.

*He grasps her wrist and pulls her up from the bed, at
the same time sitting down on it himself. In one easy,
practised movement he deposits her face-down across
his lap.*

SCARLETT: Rhett! What are you –? Oh no! No!

*Calm and unhurried, RHETT pushes back his right
shirt-sleeve.*

RHETT: You know, my darling, it's a crying shame
no one did this sooner. It would have done you a
power of good. Still, better late than never, as the
saying goes.

SCARLETT: No, Rhett! Don't! I'll scream!

RHETT: Oh, I expect you will, my pet. And Mammy
will come rushing in, and take one look at what I'm
doing, and say, [*imitating Mammy*] 'Why, Mist'
Rhett, she done bin askin' fer that fer years! Jes'
you give it her good, y'heah me?'

*He smooths her robe over her bottom, then brings his
hand down in a vigorous swat. SCARLETT gasps.*

74

SCARLETT: Ow! Rhett! That hurts!

RHETT: Does it, my dear? I'm delighted to hear it.

He administers several more hearty spanks.
SCARLETT squirms and kicks her legs wildly, but can't get away.

SCARLETT: Ow! No! You brute! Stop it! Oww! I hate you!

RHETT [*pausing*]: Shame on you, young lady – is that the voice of dutiful wifely obedience? I can see this isn't achieving the desired effect. Let's try closer quarters.

He reaches down, grasps the hem of her robe and hauls it up above her waist. The move exposes SCARLETT's shapely bare bottom, already turned a fetching pink from RHETT's attentions.

SCARLETT [*peering apprehensively over her shoulder*]: Oh no! Not that! Not bare! Rhett, I'll never speak to you again!

RHETT: Frankly, my dear, I don't give [*his hand descends with a ringing smack*] a damn!

SCARLETT squeals as the smack stings her defenceless rear. She tries to protect herself with her hand, but RHETT captures it and holds it clear, then proceeds to spank her hard and steadily. She yelps at each stroke, wriggling frantically.

MAMMY enters in the background. CLOSE UP as her look of alarm changes to a huge smile when she sees what's happening.

MAMMY's POV. RHETT, grinning cheerfully, is laying on with a will, each smack deepening the blush on SCARLETT's squirming bottom-cheeks.

SCARLETT: Oooh! Owww! Let me *go*! Ahahahah-OWWW! Oh, Rhett, that's enough! It really – yee-owww! – *hurts*!

RHETT [*continuing to spank without a pause*]: That, my sweet, is the general idea. But it's good to know my efforts are appreciated.

SCARLETT: Owww! Aaah! Help! Oh no more, please!

MAMMY watches with an air of satisfaction. We hear the spanking, and SCARLETT's wails, offscreen.

MAMMY [*quietly*]: Mmm-hmmm!

She slips away unnoticed, giving the scene a final gratified backwards glance.

Meanwhile, the spanking continues, but SCARLETT's indignant protests are giving way to more contrite tones.

SCARLETT: Ow! Oh, Rhett, please, no more! Ow-ow! I'm sorry! I'll be a good wife – oww! – I promise! I won't see Ashley – OWWW! – again! Oh, darling Rhett, I'll do anything – oww-ooh! – only please don't – oww! – spank me any more!

RHETT pauses, caressing SCARLETT's bright-red bottom.

RHETT: Well, Mrs Butler, that's better. You know, I think you may have learnt your lesson. [*He grins wickedly.*] You're certainly living up to your name, my dear. This is the most scarlet bottom I've ever seen!

SCARLETT wriggles round on his lap. Her eyes are full of tears, and she pouts reproachfully at him.

SCARLETT: Oh Rhett, that was cruel! How *could* you?

RHETT: Oh, very easily, my darling. And, if necessary, I could just as easily do it again.

SCARLETT [*very softly*]: Brute!

Her arm goes around his neck. She pulls his face down to hers and their lips meet in a passionate kiss.

76

SLOWLY FADE OUT

FADE IN:

INTERIOR – SCARLETT'S BEDROOM – NEXT MORNING

SCARLETT in bed. She wakes, stretching luxuriantly, then grimaces and reaches round behind her to rub what is still evidently a slightly tender area. A secret, reminiscent smile of pleasure creeps over her face . . .

7

Academic Discipline

It was a perfect June afternoon in Oxford. The sun, for once, was shining. From the Chapel Quad came the austere click of croquet balls, interspersed with occasional muttered donnish imprecations. Among the college's ancient stone turrets and spires, pigeons strutted self-importantly or pursued their absurd mating rituals; closer to ground level, undergraduates did likewise. A faint but unmistakable herbal aroma drifted down from the rooms of the Senior Reader in Theology. Altogether, an idyllic scene. Yet as he gazed out through the mullioned panes, Dr Abel Kendrick, Junior Lecturer in Medieval History at Gloucester College, was frowning. It was ten past three, and Louise Gray was late for her tutorial. Again.

As he watched, Abel saw her come dashing wildly through the college gateway and across the quad towards his staircase, books crammed anyhow under her arm, her tousled chestnut hair flying. For all her haste she ran with a lithe unconscious grace, her breasts bouncing merrily beneath her Glastonbury '04 T-shirt. Repressing an impulse to smile, Abel retreated to his leather armchair and composed his face into an expression of severe reproof as her hurried knock sounded on the stout oaken door.

'In,' he commanded sternly.

Louise irrupted breathlessly into the room in a flurry of excuses and apologies. Abel hushed her with a gesture and pointed to an adjacent chair. She turned to deposit her untidy mass of books on the desk, offering him a fleeting view of tight-fitting and pleasingly upholstered faded-blue denim, then sank into the chair, sitting respectably upright with her knees together.

'Dr Kendrick,' she began, hesitantly.

This was something serious – more serious than ten minutes' lateness. Usually she called him 'Abel' and curled coquettishly up in her chair like a cat, her long legs coiled beneath her. Abel raised one eyebrow and waited.

'I'm – I'm afraid I haven't finished my essay. Not quite.'

'Ah,' said Abel. He let the 'Ah' hang in the air between them for a moment like a small thundercloud, then continued, 'In that case, read me what you've written so far.'

'Well, there's – that is, it's not really . . .'

Abel smiled grimly. 'You haven't started it yet, have you?'

Louise blushed, gazing at the carpet. 'No,' she said in a small voice. It was absurd, she told herself firmly, to blush like this. But somehow Abel Kendrick had that effect on her.

Abel sighed, a little theatrically. (Academia, he liked to remind his students, was essentially a branch of showbiz.) 'Louise, this isn't good enough. You didn't present an essay last week, either. In fact, this is the third you've missed this term. I used to think you were one of my best first-year students. Your essays were excellent and on time. They were well researched, and you have a quick original mind. You seemed to be in line for a brilliant First. But this term – well?'

Louise looked wretched, shifting unhappily in her chair. 'I don't know, Abel. I am trying, honestly. I was working on this all yesterday, really hard.'

'*Were* you now?' A vivid image leapt into Abel's mind – a memory barely 24 hours old.

The previous day, after lunch in college, he had chosen to walk to his flat in Banbury Road the longer way round: through the flowery, long-grassed meadows beside the Cherwell, a small tributary of the Thames much favoured for punting in the summer months. It was a glorious afternoon, and the gentle Oxfordshire countryside was at its best. As he paused to drink in the scents and sounds of the riverbank he heard, not far away, a melodious and oddly familiar female laugh, warm and sensuous.

Slightly ashamed at his own curiosity, Abel left the path and quietly parted the bushes that fringed the river. Moored immediately below him in a narrow secluded backwater was a punt with two people in it. The one lying on his back was male. Abel recognised him as Jake Manning, a second-year law student so low on intelligence that even the other law students noticed; though rumour had it he made up in other attributes for what he lacked in brains.

Straddling Jake was a young woman, naked to the waist. She had her back to Abel, but the luxuriant chestnut hair and the sexy laugh were unmistakable. As he watched, Louise Gray lifted her hips to allow her companion to slide down her jeans, and her panties with them, revealing a delectably rounded bare bottom. At the sight of it, Abel felt himself gripped by a pang of mingled lust and jealousy.

With a gasp of pleasure, Louise lowered herself on to Jake's rampant penis and began to writhe her hips lasciviously. He grunted, eyes closed in ecstasy, while his broad hands reached round to knead and squeeze her superb rear end. Abel, furious at himself, slipped quietly away.

Now, gazing at the lovely girl's convincing display of penitence, he smiled wryly. 'Were you, indeed?' he repeated. 'Well, of course it's up to you how you do your research. But I wouldn't have thought you'd learn much about – what was it? – "The Role of Abelard and the Scholastics in the French Medieval Church" in a punt on the Cherwell.'

She gasped, gazing at him wide-eyed. 'Nor,' he pursued remorselessly, 'does Jake Manning seem the most likely source of enlightenment. At least, not on your essay subject.'

The slow hot blush suffused Louise's face and neck. Oh, *God*, she thought, what a damn stupid thing that was to do. What *was* I thinking of? 'You saw us when we . . .?' Her voice tailed off.

'You weren't exactly being discreet about it. Don't get me wrong: open-air sex, especially in punts, is a fine old Oxford tradition, and I'm in no position to be censorious even if I wanted to. But I can't help wondering if what I saw yesterday has any connection with the decline in your work this term. Still, that's beside the point. Whether because of Jake Manning or not, your work's falling well below standard, and at this rate I'll have to give you a very poor end-of-year report. You know that, don't you?'

His tone was severe, but more reproachful than angry. It caused Louise an unaccustomed fluttering in her stomach. Of all her tutors, Abel Kendrick was the one she most liked and respected – and, she had to admit, secretly fancied. And now she had let him down. She saw the disappointment in his eyes. He deserved better of her; and she was beginning to realise what she deserved of him. If, that is, she had the nerve to suggest it.

His next remark gave her the opening she needed. 'The term's not over yet, Louise; you've still time to make good. And you know I'm ready to help you in any way I can. Extra tutorials or whatever. Any ideas as to what might work for you?'

Did she dare? She shot him a sidelong look. 'Well . . . you know what Peter Abelard would have done.'

Abel Kendrick's dark eyebrows arched up. 'Just what are you suggesting, Louise?'

She plunged on recklessly. 'Well, Héloise was Abelard's best pupil, wasn't she? Brighter than all the rest. But, when she was lazy, he didn't hesitate to – to chastise her.'

Abel laughed. 'True, so he did. But you're overlooking a couple of things. First, what was quite OK in twelfth-century Paris would get me sacked, and probably jailed, these days. Then, as you've obviously read Abelard's letters, you know those beatings were just a pretext. "Sometimes I went so far as to strike her,"' he quoted, '"not in anger but in love, not from hate but from affection, and the blows were sweeter than any balm. Under pretext of discipline, we abandoned ourselves entirely to love." Is that what you're angling for, Louise – an erotic spanking? If so, I'm sure Jake would be happy to oblige.'

He spoke flippantly, but he was covertly aware of a stirring in his loins. The idea of putting this lovely errant girl across his knee was irresistibly tempting. It was precisely what she deserved – for indolence, for lying to him and, above all, for letting herself down. And she certainly had the ideal physique for it: that bottom so enticingly bared in the punt yesterday had revealed itself as full, flawless and beautifully spankable. Oh, the motivation was there, all right – on both sides. But he would have to play this one very carefully.

Louise grimaced. 'Oh, I'm sure you're right. I'd have no trouble getting Jake to spank me. But he won't, because he's got no right to – no authority over me. But you have, Abel. You're my tutor, which means you're *in loco parentis*. It says so in the college statutes. And I know damn well what my dad would do, if he knew I was fooling around in punts instead of getting on with my work.'

'Namely?'

'Namely – put me across his knee and tan the living daylights out of me.' Inwardly, Louise gasped at her own audacity. The idea of Dr Richard Gray, that most mild and tolerant of men, whaling away at his eighteen-year-old daughter's bottom like some irate Victorian paterfamilias was so outlandish as to be farcical. Luckily Abel was most unlikely to meet him, since he was away on a two-year sabbatical in Auckland.

'Evidently a man of old-fashioned principles,' Abel observed. 'And I'm not saying you wouldn't deserve it. But I think you'll find, whatever the college founders may have intended, that these days the phrase *in loco parentis* scarcely covers physical chastisement. Especially not of a female undergraduate by a male tutor. Assault, gross indecency, sexual harassment and several other unpleasant terms are much more likely descriptions.'

'Only if I complain to someone,' Louise countered. 'And I shan't. You know I shan't. I mean, why should I? It's what I need to help me work, I'm sure of it. You *did* say you'd help me in any way you could. Well, this is the help I need. *Please*, Abel.'

She gazed at him imploringly, her dark-brown eyes full of entreaty. As if uneasy under the intensity of her regard, Abel got up and stared thoughtfully out of the window. Finally, he turned and looked at her.

'All right,' he said, 'I'll do what you want, though I strongly suspect I'm being several kinds of fool. But you needn't look so smug, young lady. There are conditions.

'First, if I find you've told anybody – *anybody* at all – about this, I'll immediately resign as your tutor on grounds of overload, and have you reassigned to Professor Mulvey.'

He permitted himself a brief grin at her expression of dismay. Angus Mulvey was notorious for giving the most stultifyingly dull and intellectually vapid lectures in the entire History Faculty. According to scurrilous rumour, he only retained tenure through the personal intercession of the Vice-Chancellor, following a brief but ecstatic episode of reciprocal sodomy during the 1997 History Summer School in Izmir.

'Then, whatever Héloise and Abelard may have got up to, all I'm going to do with you is spank you. Just that, and nothing else. Understood?'

Louise nodded. 'That's OK. I wouldn't want to get on the wrong side of Mary.'

Abel raised an eyebrow.

'Oh come on, Abel. Everyone knows you two are an item.'

This was true. Indeed, there had been prurient whispers about Abel and Mary Linklater, the most brilliant of his students, even before she graduated two years earlier. She was now a probationary lecturer, having stayed on to complete her PhD, and as such the morality of her exact relationship with her former tutor was of less concern to the college authorities. Still, Abel was under the impression they'd been reasonably discreet. Evidently not, he acknowledged with a wry smile.

'OK, but it's not only that. You're still an undergraduate – *in statu pupillari*, since you have a taste for clerical dog-latin. As such, I'm supposed to protect you from moral turpitude, not lead you into it. In two years' time, when you've graduated – well, that'll be another matter. But, for the time being, I'll be sailing quite close enough to the wind by spanking you.'

'One final thing,' he added, fixing her with his gaze. 'This is intended as discipline, remember, not fun. If all I do is give you the kind of playful spanking I suspect you enjoy, you'll have no incentive to work harder. Rather the reverse, in fact. So I'm warning you now, Louise: what you're asking for is a real discipline spanking – long and hard and painful. Are you sure you can take it? If not, now's your chance to back out.'

Under his dark-eyed stare, Louise felt a thrill of anticipation tingle her rear end. Just what had she let herself in for? Abel always meant what he said: if he told her this spanking was going to hurt, then hurt it would. The memory of watching him playing tennis flashed before her mind's eye. He wasn't the most skilled of players, but his forearm smash was ferocious. At the thought of those sinewy arms administering the same kind of punishment to her soft bottom that he'd been giving the tennis ball, she was seized with a shiver of mingled excitement and terror.

He was right, though. If this treatment was going to be truly effective and give her the vital incentive to work at her best, a really severe spanking was what she badly needed. Besides, how could she back out now? She'd never be able to face him again.

'All right,' she said in a small voice, her gaze fixed on the carpet, 'I agree.' She felt her bottom flinch as she spoke.

'So be it,' Abel said, standing up. 'Then to start with I'd better sport my oak.' He went and closed the heavy oaken outer door to his rooms that signalled a desire for privacy and also provided excellent sound-proofing; then he shut and locked the inner door. 'Oh, and close those windows, would you? We don't want your squeals echoing around the quad.'

'I shan't squeal,' Louise protested even as she obeyed.

'Don't be so sure, young lady,' he retorted, opening a desk drawer and rummaging inside. 'Wait until you feel this.'

Louise couldn't repress a gasp of dismay. Abel was holding by its handle an old-fashioned clothesbrush of glossy dark-brown wood, shaped in a long oval. He grinned wickedly at her expression of alarm. 'Fine specimen, isn't it? Edwardian, probably. The wood matches your hair rather nicely. But I think it'll match your bottom even better.'

'But – I thought you were going to use your hand!'

'Oh, I am,' Abel said mildly, 'to begin with.' Taking her by the wrist, he led her over to the upright chair she'd recently vacated and sat down on it. 'This –' he deposited the brush on the desk behind him '– is for Act Two.'

As if in a dream, Louise felt him unbuckle her belt, unzip her jeans and slide them down to her knees. Then, gently but firmly, he drew her down over his lap. Her stomach fluttered as he settled her across his thighs, her head to the left with her hair brushing the carpet, her long legs stretched out straight and her bottom curved invitingly uppermost, ready to his hand.

Abel gazed with delight at the sweet prospect before him. A triangle of pink nylon panties, discreetly fringed with lace, covered scarcely half the expanse of Louise's shapely rump. Gently, he pushed her T-shirt up past her waist, whose slimness accentuated the swell of her hips, then stroked the luscious mounds. They felt cool, smooth and alluringly soft, trembling at his touch. He was conscious of his erection stiffening in appreciation. This girl would be sheer joy to spank. Was Héloïse's bottom anything like as lovely? he wondered. If so, no wonder Abelard was tempted.

'Very pretty,' he observed, 'and your choice of underwear is charming. But I think we'll have these clear of the target area, all the same.' Hooking a finger in the waistband of the skimpy briefs, he drew them slowly down over her ripe rearward curves.

Louise shuddered involuntarily as she felt herself denuded of her most intimate garment. The air was cool on her bare and vulnerable bottom, and Abel's left arm held her firmly in position. She was wholly under his control; the thought was scary but strangely comforting, the realisation of her long-cherished fantasy of a punishment deserved and desired, but feared. Peering over her shoulder, she glimpsed his grin of determination and delight at the task in hand, and, despite herself, a low moan of apprehension escaped her lips.

'Right, young lady,' said Abel, raising his open hand, 'this is what you asked for, so this is what you're going to get. And don't say I didn't warn you if it hurts like hell.'

Taking good aim, he brought his flattened palm down vigorously on the plumpest part of Louise's left bottom-cheek. She gave a sharp intake of breath as its impact stung her tender flesh, and a matching spank, no less hard, connected with her right cheek. Abel paused and watched, enchanted, as twin hand-shapes, pink and distinct, sprang out on the cool white mounds.

Having marked out his territory, he pulled back and for the next few minutes spanked her more lightly, just hard enough to sting, covering the whole adorable target area and relishing the way her soft young bottom-flesh jounced and wobbled beneath his punishing palm. After only a dozen or so smacks, a delicate pink blush mantled the lovely cheeks, gradually deepening to rose-red with each new spank. As the heat built up in her smacked rear end, Louise began to squirm slightly, emitting little mews and whimpers, more to encourage him than from any real discomfort. It was thrilling to lie across Abel's lap, subjected to his will and feeling his hand swatting down on her bare bottom. But at the same time there was a sense of disappointment. This wasn't hurting anything like as much as she'd hoped – and dreaded.

Abel, though, knew just what he was doing. After a few minutes he paused again and stroked the glowing curves, admiring the results of his handiwork. Her bottom felt warm to the touch, and looked even sexier now that it was blushing so prettily.

'OK, Louise,' he said, 'that was just by way of a warm-up, to get this lovely bottom into perfect spanking condition. Now your real punishment begins.' Taking a firmer grip on her midriff, he began to spank her with the full force of his powerful right arm.

Louise gasped in surprise. She'd never realised how sharply a hard male hand could sting a soft bare female bottom – especially when that bottom had been rendered extra sensitive and tender by a shrewdly administered warm-up. Her fantasy had collided head-on (or should that be rear-on?) with reality, and she wasn't so sure she liked the results. 'Oww!' she protested, wriggling on his lap. 'Abel, that really *hurts*! Please, not so hard!'

'Of course it hurts, silly girl,' he retorted heartlessly, spanking her with gusto. 'It's *meant* to. This is discipline, remember? To teach you to finish your essay each week as you're supposed to, and not to show up late for my tutorials.' Turning his attention to the soft undercurves of her bottom, he smacked them with wristy sideways swats that made her squirm and yip. 'From now on, any time you feel tempted to skive off in a punt instead of doing the work you've been set, remember how humiliating it is to be put over my knee and spanked on your bare bottom like a naughty child. Remember how hot and red and sore your bottom is getting – and, believe me, it's going to be a lot redder and sorer before I'm through. And remember that any further indolence, young lady, will put you back across my knee to be spanked twice as hard for twice as long. Understood?' he demanded, with an extra-hard swat.

'Owww! Yes, Abel! I'm sorry! I'm *really* sorry! Oh, stop, please!'

But Abel was in no mood to stop. Quite apart from anything else, he was enjoying himself far too much. Louise was proving even more deliciously spankable than he'd anticipated; he rejoiced in her yelps and wriggles, and in the soft yieldingness of her sweet quivering flesh-cushions, their whole expanse now suffused with a rich sunset glow.

So, for several more minutes, he hand-spanked her beautiful bottom to his heart's content – now spanking slowly and deliberately, pausing after each stroke to let the sting sink in; now applying a fast hard volley of spanks, twenty or so in quick succession to the same spot, making her yip and writhe frantically. And when at last he stopped, it was only to reach round behind him and pick up the clothesbrush.

Louise, twisting round to see what he was doing, gasped in dismay. She'd been so lost in the agony and the ecstasy of the spanking that she'd forgotten all about the brush. 'Oh *no*!' she wailed. 'No, Abel, please don't! I've had enough! My poor bottom's so sore already! *Please* let me off!'

'Not a chance,' came the pitiless response. 'The hand-spanking was for neglecting your essays and being late. This is for something much more serious – selling yourself short, wasting your time with dead-end knuckleheads like Jake Manning.' He stroked the back of the brush across her bottom; it felt cool on her blazing cheeks. 'You deserve better that that, Louise; and you deserve a damn good hiding with this brush to help you realise it. But you've taken your punishment very well so far, so I'll let you off with just fifty strokes. Next time I won't be so lenient.'

Did he say *lenient*? thought Louise, her bottom on fire and her mind in a daze. Well, you asked for it, girl, she told herself ruefully; this'll teach you to play power games with dishy older men. Taking a firm grip on Abel's leg, she awaited the worst.

'Yee-*OWWWW*!' She'd said she wouldn't squeal, but squeal she did. The biting kiss of the clothesbrush stung fire across her already well-spanked bottom, its broad oval length catching both cheeks at once. And she continued to squeal, her dark tousled hair tossing and her legs kicking madly, as the hard wood cracked down again and again on her anguished bottom-cheeks, turning them from scarlet to a rich deep crimson, until the heat and exquisite hurt of it took her and lifted her to some place she had never been before. When the spanking finally stopped she scarcely seemed to notice, but lay limp as a rag-doll over Abel's knee, gasping and whimpering, entirely passive.

Abel contemplated the slim lovely girl lying prone across his lap, every inch of her soundly spanked rear blushing a hot cherry-red. Gently, he stroked the twin trembling masses of fiery flesh. 'OK, Louise,' he murmured, 'it's all over. You've had the spanking you were asking for. Up you get.' He helped her up off his lap and hugged her, and she clung to him, sobbing and shuddering on his shoulder. When at length she disengaged herself, her brown eyes were still wet with tears, but she gave him a tremulous smile as she gingerly rubbed her flaming curves. 'Bloody hell,' she complained, 'you spank horribly hard, Abel. I bet Abelard never spanked Héloïse as hard as that!'

'On the contrary, I bet he did. And she'd probably have been the first to complain if he hadn't.'

Louise gave a rueful grin as she carefully eased her panties back into place. 'Mm, you may be right. But at least she didn't have to get jeans on again afterwards. Oooh, owww, help! I think my bottom's too swollen to get into them!'

There was a spring in Abel's step as he strolled home to North Oxford that afternoon. Spanking Louise had proved a deliciously stimulating experience – for both participants, he suspected. In fact, though her work would no doubt show an immediate improvement, he foresaw that she would still feel the need of further disciplinary incentives from time to time. It was an enchanting likelihood.

He let himself into his apartment. The door on to the patio was open, and a tall slim honey-blonde girl wearing well-filled white shorts was leaning over the parapet with her back to him. After approaching quietly, he delivered a resounding smack to the nearside of the proffered rump.

'Owww!' exclaimed Mary Linklater, swinging round and clapping a hand to her injured rear. 'God, you made me jump, you rotten – mmm!' Further invective was cut off as Abel pulled her to him and kissed her thoroughly.

'Now how could I resist such a tempting target?' he demanded, his hands sliding down to cup and squeeze the lush globes of the target in question.

'When did you ever – mine or any other girl's?' enquired Mary sardonically as, after extricating herself, she headed in to retrieve a bottle of white wine from the fridge.

'Well, you know what Oscar said,' he teased. 'I can resist anything except temptation.'

'Talking of which,' said Mary as they settled back on the patio with their drinks, 'you're looking rather pleased with yourself. Didn't you have a tutorial with Louise Gray this afternoon?'

Abel nodded.

'And didn't you say she'd been falling behind with her work?'

Abel nodded again, unable to repress a sly grin.

Mary's blue eyes widened. 'You so-and-so! You set her the Abelard essay, didn't you?'

Abel's grin grew broader.

'And she read the letters, and came and all but begged you on bended knee to spank her? That damn trick works for you every time, doesn't it?'

'Not *every* time, alas. But often enough to be worth trying. And I'm sure you remember, my love –' he favoured her with his most charming smile '– just who inspired the idea when she discovered Abelard's letters on her own account – and then came and offered up her lovely bare bottom for chastisement?'

91

'Abel Kendrick!' Mary exclaimed in mock outrage. 'Has anyone ever told you you're a kinky, sadistic, underhand scheming lecher?'

'And has anyone ever told *you*, young lady,' Abel retorted, reaching out to pull her across his knee in one practised movement, 'just what happens to impertinent female students who indulge in wanton abuse of their poor long-suffering tutors?'

'No! Don't you *dare!*' Mary yelped, struggling indignantly.

Disregarding her protests, Abel took a firm grip on her shapely torso and tugged her shorts down to half-mast – revealing, as he'd guessed, that she wasn't wearing panties.

'*No*, Abel! Not on the bare! Not out here! What if someone sees us?'

'If they do, my sweet,' said Abel, happily contemplating the prospect of spanking a second soft bare and beautifully rounded girlish bottom in the space of one afternoon, 'I'm sure they'll be gratified that standards of academic discipline haven't slipped since the days of Peter Abelard.'

8

Shrewd Treatment

'Jemma!' Helena Mason's voice cut through the hub-
bub of the crowded greenroom. 'Jemma, where the hell
is that sodding brooch? You know I need it for Act
Five!'

Jemma, Helena's dresser, looked up in surprise – as
did several other members of the National Shakespeare
Company. 'Sorry, Helena, I haven't seen it. Isn't it on
your dressing table?'

'Of course it bloody isn't – d'you think I haven't
looked there?' Furious, Helena rammed her hands into
the pockets of her dressing robe. 'Goddammit, Jemma,
can't you – oh.' Her hand emerged again from the
right-hand pocket, holding a costume brooch. 'Oh shit.
I must have . . . Jemma, I'm really sorry.'

In the awkward silence that followed, Helena realised
attention was focused not on her, but on someone
behind her. She turned. In the doorway stood a stocky
man in his forties with a neat brown beard: Stephen
Berman, the play's director.

'I'd like a word with you, Helena, if you don't mind
– after the show.' Stephen's voice was quiet, as always,
but the anger in his eyes was unmistakable.

'Sure, OK, Stephen,' muttered Helena, shamefaced.
'Jemma, I'm really – I – oh, hell.' Brushing past
Stephen, she fled down the corridor. Behind her a buzz

of voices arose, shocked and delighted at this new source of gossip.

That was the trouble with acting, Helena reflected, safely back in the refuge of her dressing room. Roles could take you over. The more you set yourself to get into the character, the more the character could get into you. Especially, she had to admit, if there was a little of that particular character in you already.

Not that she was really prone to throwing tantrums – not compared to some actresses she could name, anyway – but, yes, it had been known to happen. And just recently it seemed to have been happening quite a lot. Could it just be because she was playing Kate in *The Taming of the Shrew*?

Whatever the cause, five weeks into the play's six-week West End run the short-fused, prize-bitch side of Helena did seem to be getting out of control. This evening had been the worst so far. All in all, it would be a relief when the run finished, and she could move on to *Twelfth Night*. Olivia was a much more agreeable role – not a weak woman by any means, but far better-natured than Kate.

Meanwhile, though, there was the last act of the *Shrew* to get through. Helena tried to put herself into a suitably submissive frame of mind for the final contrition scene:

Such duty as the subject owes the prince
E'en such a woman oweth to her husband:
And when she is froward, peevish, sullen, sour,
And not obedient to his honest will,
What is she but a foul contending rebel . . .?

If only, she thought, Mike wasn't quite such a nice guy. Oh, he looked well as Petruchio, and swaggered convincingly, but there was no fire behind those warm brown eyes. In their fight scenes he considerately pulled

94

all his punches, which was more than Helena always did. She'd landed him a good clout or two, she knew, hoping to provoke some kind of response – hell, if the *Shrew* wasn't about sexual attraction expressed through sheer physical antagonism, what was it about? – but Mike was too much the gentleman to retaliate in kind. No wallops in return – not even so much as an angry glance.

Which reminded her, there was something else to be got through this evening: her little talk with Stephen. He was a good director, imaginative, open, supportive and utterly professional, expecting no less from all his team. Normally the soul of patience, unprofessional behaviour was the one thing that angered him – and Helena's outburst, she was uneasily aware, had been anything but professional.

As if hoping to atone, she put all she had into her performance and was rewarded by rapturous applause at the final curtain.

Afterwards, some of the cast drifted into her dressing room to congratulate her – but diffidently, as if knowing she was in disgrace. And, in due course, when Stephen arrived, they quietly slipped out without needing to be told. Jemma unobtrusively vanished too, and Stephen closed the door and – Helena noted, with a twinge of what might be alarm or excitement – locked it.

'Well?' he demanded, standing over her. 'What have you to say for yourself?'

Helena had removed her make-up and wig and, sitting at the dressing table in her robe, was brushing her short auburn page-boy cut. She had planned to apologise, but at the sight of Stephen's stern expression some imp of perversity possessed her. She smiled provocatively at him in the mirror. 'What *should* I have to say, Stephen? Didn't I give a good performance?'

'On stage, yes. But during the interval – what about *that* performance?'

'OK, I went a bit OTT. But I told Jemma I was sorry.'

'Oh, and that makes everything all right? Helena, your behaviour was utterly unprofessional —' oh, that dreaded word, thought Helena; now I'm for it '— and you know it. And it's not the first time. You've been behaving like a spoilt bitch for weeks, and I've had about enough of it.'

'Oh, you have, have you? Well, I crave your pardon, my liege!' Helena slipped off her stool and knelt at Stephen's feet in mock supplication, launching into a parody of the *Shrew* speech. 'My director is my lord, my life, my keeper . . .' What on earth are you playing at, girl? she asked herself. Are you *really* looking for trouble? But the provocative impulse seemed beyond her control. 'My head, my sovereign; one that cares for me . . .'

Stephen's dark eyes blazed with fury, but he still spoke quietly. 'Right, young lady, you've asked for it. In fact, you've been asking for it for some time.' He sat down on the stool she'd just vacated. 'Stand up, please.'

Given what she suspected Stephen was about to do, Helena found his 'please' irresistibly amusing. She stood up, grinning. 'Well, of course, since you ask me so nicely . . .'

Stephen smiled grimly. 'You find it funny, do you? OK, my girl, let's see how much *this* amuses you.' Seizing her by the wrist, he pulled her down across his knee. 'You like playing the Shrew, it seems. Well, let's see how you enjoy my performance as Petruchio!'

Rather to her own surprise, Helena scarcely resisted — partly because she felt a good spanking was just what she deserved. But also it made sense in dramatic terms: Stephen was providing exactly the sort of response she'd been trying to elicit on-stage from Mike. And then, of course, Stephen *was* quite fanciable, and the thought of being spanked by him, she had to admit, was very exciting. Helena had now and then had her bottom smacked by a boyfriend, and had found it quite a turn-on.

Stephen, too, was aware of a distinct current of sexual excitement underlying his anger. His chief impulse had simply been to punish Helena as she deserved, but now that it was about to happen ... She was a very fetching young woman, of course, with just the sort of looks he liked: a wide sexy mouth, cheeky grin, long legs, small firm breasts and a slim waist that elegantly set off the lush swell of her hips and buttocks. More than once, during her recent displays of temper, he'd felt tempted to smack that sweet shapely bottom. And now as she lay submissively across his lap – almost too submissively, in fact, a bit of spirited resistance would have added spice – the thin robe outlining her ripe rearward contours, he could feel a huge erection straining eagerly at his trousers, and knew that Helena could feel it too, pressing against her belly.

He flipped aside the robe. Under it, as he had suspected, Helena was naked, and there was revealed to his gaze a beautifully rounded bare bottom, sweetly shaped for spanking. He rested his hand on the nearest plump globe, squeezing it gently and making the tender flesh tremble beneath his hand. It felt deliciously cool and soft. '"Who knows not where a wasp doth wear her sting? In her tail,"' he quoted Petruchio. 'You have a very pretty tail, my sweet Kate. And, believe me, it's going to have quite a sting in it before I've finished.'

Helena wriggled apprehensively. She knew she had a sexy bottom, and to have Stephen admiring, and indeed feeling, its naked charms was quite stimulating, especially since he was obviously getting turned on by it. But the allurements of her rear end, she suspected, wouldn't distract him from subjecting it to severely punitive treatment – rather the reverse, if anything. Stephen might be turned on, but he was still very angry and in no mood, she guessed, to let her off lightly.

She wasn't left long in doubt, since her glorious bottom offered an irresistible temptation to Stephen's palm. He pushed the robe well clear of the target area, exposing her slim back almost up to the shoulder-blades. 'Right, young lady,' he said, raising his hand, 'tantrums I don't tolerate in my productions. Nor spoilt brats. And if you act like one – then *this* is what you get!'

'Owwww!' Helena gasped in surprise as Stephen's hard hand connected stingingly with the curve of her right cheek. Smack! The left cheek this time, followed by four more smacks that alternated right and left in rapid succession. 'Hey! That *hurts*!' yelped Helena. 'Bloody hell! Stop it!' She was a good actress, but she wasn't acting now – and neither was Stephen. These spanks were for real; by comparison, the smacks her boyfriends had given her were mere love-pats. After only half-a-dozen strokes, her bottom was already smarting furiously, and Stephen, she could tell, had scarcely even started.

She was right there. Quite apart from the fact that Helena richly deserved a good hiding, Stephen found he was enjoying the experience even more than he'd expected. It was a while since he'd administered a real punishment spanking, and he'd forgotten what an intoxicating mixture of power and tenderness, cruelty and erotic delight it could be. Especially when the girl in question was as delectably spankable as Helena. Hers was a bottom that just begged to be spanked, and Stephen intended to do it full justice. Already a delicate pink blush was suffusing the lovely cheeks, and he relished the prospect of reddening them far more vividly in the next few minutes.

So, after the first half-dozen smacks he slowed down, taking his time and spanking Helena steadily and hard, covering every inch of the luscious target area from flank to flank and from the dimpled upland swell down to the plump undercurve where bottom met thigh. Helena gasped and wriggled at each spank, her bottom gyrating and her long legs kicking wildly, though she still made no real attempt to escape, or even to put a protective hand over her burning cheeks. The spanking was stinging far worse than any she'd undergone before, yet somehow she didn't really want it to stop. Apart from anything else, the increasing moistness between her legs was transmitting a signal she couldn't ignore.

Even so she continued to protest, if only for form's sake, though the note of indignation appropriate to the Shrew soon gave way to submissive pleas much more typical of the natural Helena.

'Owwww! Oh please, Stephen, I'm sorry! Oh no more – please!'

'Sorry, are you?' responded Stephen calmly, continuing to spank her with unabated vigour. 'I'm sure you are, young lady. But you'll be a lot sorrier before I've finished. This is a very pretty bottom, but it's been begging for a good sound spanking for a long time. So that, my girl, is just what it's going to get, to teach you not to be –' he slowed down, matching an extra-hard spank to each word '– such – a – spoilt – little – *brat*!!'

'Ooooh-*owww*!' yelped Helena, wriggling desperately and trying to evade the stinging smacks that were burning her increasingly tender rear. 'No more tantrums, I promise! Not ever! Oh stop, please!'

But it was to no avail. Quite apart from anything else, Stephen was enjoying himself far too much to lay off yet. If ever a girl was made to be spanked, thoroughly and often, it was this sweet, stubborn, temperamental young actress.

In any case, it was evident that, despite her pleas, Helena was getting increasingly turned on by her punishment. Her squirmings across Stephen's lap were taking on a voluptuous quality; her bottom seemed to be arching itself, almost of its own volition, to meet his hand, and the warm musky aroma that greeted his nostrils told its own story.

So, for a good fifteen minutes, his hand rose and fell, steadily smacking Helena's defenceless rear. Occasionally he paused to admire the blush mantling her cheeks as it deepened from warm pink to rosy red to a rich scarlet glow.

Was ever, even in Shakespeare's day, a shrew more soundly spanked? Each smack rang round the tiny dressing room like a pistol shot. The sound could surely – Helena realised with horror – be heard up and down the corridor, leaving her colleagues in no doubt what form her punishment was taking. 'Ooooh!' she wailed, imagining the giggles and smirks, the snide comments and solicitously proffered cushions she would have to endure the next day. Although at this rate, she reflected ruefully, the cushions might – owwww! – well prove necessary.

When at last he stopped, Stephen's palm was stinging vividly; how much more so, he mused, the far softer flesh on the receiving end. A sunset blush now adorned every inch of Helena's quivering bottom, contrasting exquisitely with the whiteness of her back and thighs. 'OK, my pretty Shrew,' he said, 'I think you've been tamed enough – for now.' After giving her roseate curves a farewell pat, he stood her up on her feet.

'Ooooh!' Reaching behind her, Helena gingerly massaged the blazing mounds of her tender rear. They felt sizzling hot and swollen to about twice their usual size. 'My poor bottom! Stephen, you bastard, how *could* you? OK, I deserved a spanking, but did you have to do it so bloody hard?' She twisted round, trying to catch a glimpse of her rearward contours in the mirror. 'Oh my God, it's red as a tomato!'

How appealing she looked, Stephen thought, with tears in her hazel eyes and her face flushed (though

100

nowhere near as red as her other cheeks). She pouted at him reproachfully, but there was a sparkle in her eyes that belied her feigned resentment. Her robe had fallen open, giving him a full-frontal view of her charms, but Helena didn't appear to notice, seemingly far more preoccupied with rubbing her stinging rump. The action made her breasts jiggle charmingly. Stephen reached out and stroked first the left one, then the right. The small brown nipples stood proud beneath his fingers, perking up hard as he caressed them. Still stroking with one hand, he allowed the other to stray down over Helena's gently rounded belly and between her legs. Her cleft was hot and sopping wet, and at the touch of his fingers she moaned softly and moved closer to him.

Dropping to his knees, Stephen buried his face in the auburn curls of her pubic hair, tonguing her swollen clitoris, while his hands reached round to stroke and squeeze the hot tender masses of her glowing bottom. Writhing and moaning, Helena caressed his head before yielding to a shuddering series of climaxes that finally left her quivering beside him on the floor, her eyes closed in ecstasy while her hand reached down to his groin to liberate his throbbing erection.

Later – quite a lot later – they lay naked together on a prop fur rug Stephen had found in a cupboard. Helena lay face-down, her head pillowed on Stephen's shoulder, while he gently stroked the rosy curves of her well-spanked bottom. 'Shakespeare knew his stuff, all right,' he murmured in her ear. 'Taming does shrews a lot of good. I think I must tame you some more, my sweet Kate.'

'Sadistic bastard!' Helena responded, pinching his thigh, then yelped as he retaliated with a crisp smack on her still smarting rear. 'Owww! Beast! Chauvinist pig! I ought to report you to Equity.'

'You do that. And of course you'll show them this pretty red bottom, won't you? And tell them how randy it made you to have it spanked? We could even put on a repeat performance, just for the panel. I bet they'd enjoy that. They'd probably sell tickets.'

'Brute!' said Helena, but she snuggled closer. 'Oh, all right, yes, it did make me horny. But next time, don't spank me *quite* so hard, OK?'

'That, my favourite actress,' said Stephen with a wicked grin, caressing the soft radiant mounds of her bottom as he luxuriated in the thought of many such erotically punitive sessions yet to come, 'will depend entirely on how you act.'

Snow White and Rose Red or, The Three Lessons

Once upon a time there was a beautiful princess. She was tall and slim and dark, with hair like ebony and skin like ivory. She was the only child of her father the King, and had many suitors. Some came in hope they might marry her and inherit the kingdom, but many more came drawn by her great beauty. Some were handsome, some were rich, some were brave and some were clever. And a few were all these things. But she favoured none of them. She was lovely but cold, and no man had ever warmed her. For this reason she was called Princess Snow White.

The King was in despair. He had no son, and Snow White was the child of his old age. His wife had died in childbirth and the King, heartbroken, had never married again. Now he was aged and white-haired, and on the frontiers the neighbour states waited and watched his kingdom with greedy eyes. If only I had an heir, he would lament silently in the long dead hours of the night. If only my beloved daughter would marry, and secure the succession. If only she could meet a man who could warm her.

'Does none of them please you?' the old King begged his daughter. 'You are but eighteen, my child. We old folk may have cold blood. But at your age, my darling, the blood should run hot in your veins. Does none of these fine young men warm your interest?'

'None of them, father,' replied Snow White with cool disdain, gazing at her pale beauty in the mirror. I am so lovely, she thought; what man could be worthy of me?

'The Prince Magnifico, now,' suggested her father, 'a fine young man, surely, strong and valiant?'

'Valiant indeed, father,' said Snow White. 'But very stupid.'

'Then what of Count Lodovico, my dear? Witty and cultured, is he not?'

'Very witty,' said Snow White coolly. 'And he squints.'

'The Archduke Bernhard, then? A tall handsome fellow, much admired.'

'Tall, handsome and penniless,' said the Princess, yawning. 'He cares for my fortune, not for me.'

The King sighed. 'Earl Pomposo is vastly rich, my dear. Richer than I, indeed.'

'Rich he is,' retorted Snow White. 'And a notorious coward. What woman could marry a poltroon and keep her pride?'

'I despair,' groaned the King. 'Is there not one among so many who is brave and clever, handsome and rich? Young Duke Sveynbart, now?'

'Indeed he is,' said the Princess. 'You might add that he stinks of garlic.'

'Oh, daughter,' cried the King, 'think of our poor subjects. What will become of them if I die with no male heir? The ravening wolves who prowl my frontiers will devour them. And you, my darling child, they will force into whatever loveless alliance suits their purpose. Is there no man alive who can warm you? If only your sweet mother were here to counsel me!'

Snow White was not malicious, simply cold and spoilt, and in her cool way she loved her father. She softened a little. 'Poor father,' she said, 'I would marry to please you if I could. But I must marry a man who can warm me – and no man has yet been able to do that.'

That night the old King had a dream. His beloved wife, as beautiful as her daughter but warmer far even in death, came and stood by his bedside. 'What ails you, sweet husband?' she asked gently.

'Oh, my darling,' murmured the King, 'why did you die and leave me? How may I save my kingdom? Where can I find a man who will warm our daughter and make her blood flow hot in her veins? Help me, my love, or we perish.'

And, in his dream, the lonely old King's dead wife lay down beside him, and took him in her arms and comforted him. And very quietly she gave him her advice.

Next day the King summoned his heralds for a proclamation. 'I am old,' he said, 'and weary. To be King is a task for a young man. I would fain resign the throne, and live out my last few years in peace. If any man, be he noble, merchant or peasant, can warm my daughter, the Princess Snow White, and make her love him, he shall marry her and become King. Their marriage, and the coronation, shall take place the very same day.'

When this was proclaimed, there was great excitement throughout the land. From city and town, village and hamlet, young men flocked to the capital, each one certain that his charms were irresistible, and that he alone could warm the Princess's ardour. One by one they came before her, and their eagerness was chilled in the cool green glance of her eyes. And one by one they fell silent, and turned away in despair.

As the last suitor despondently left the palace, he met a young man at the foot of the steps. 'Best to hurry,' said the suitor. 'The palace gates will close soon.'

'What are the palace gates to me?' asked the young man. 'I have sold all my goats' cheese, and am on my way home.'

'Have you not heard the King's proclamation?' asked the other.

'What do I care for kings or proclamations?' said the young man. 'I have my hut and my goats. They are enough for me.'

So the suitor told him of the proclamation, and how no man could be found to warm the Princess.

'Oh, is that all?' said the young man. 'It sounds easy enough. Still, if no one else can do it, I may as well offer my help.'

So he marched into the palace and came before the King.

'Who are you?' demanded the King.

'My name is Garth,' replied the young man. 'I am twenty years old. I am a goatherd and I live in a hut by the forest. I came to the city to sell my goats' cheese, and they told me no man could warm your daughter. So I have come to offer my help.'

'You believe you can do it?' asked the King, amazed.

'Of course,' said Garth. 'It is no great feat.' And he looked at the Princess. She gazed back with her cold green eyes in her pale face, as though he were an insect.

'Do you still think you can do it?' said the King.

'Certainly,' said Garth. 'But it must be on my conditions.'

'Who are you to speak of conditions to me?' roared the King.

'No one in particular,' said Garth. 'But I thought you wanted help.'

'Very well, then,' said the King. 'Name your conditions.'

'I can do nothing with her here, in this cold marble palace,' said Garth. 'She must come and live in my hut for a week.'

'What?' exclaimed the King. 'You think I will let my beautiful virgin daughter, a Royal Princess, live alone for a week with you, you clod-hopper?'

'Her virginity will not be harmed,' said Garth. 'You have my word on that.'

'The word of a goatherd?' cried the King.

'It is as good as the word of a King,' said Garth. 'Better, probably.'

At this the Princess, who had listened in disbelief, broke her silence. 'And what about *my* opinion?' she enquired icily. 'Had anyone thought to ask *me* if I would live in some smelly goatherd's hut for a week?'

'My hut is not smelly,' said Garth, 'and nor am I. It is clean and warm and far more comfortable than this palace. There is good food, and soft beds, and my goats are friendly. My mother is dead these three years, but you may use her bedchamber and have privacy.'

Snow White stared at him contemptuously. 'I am honoured by your offer,' she said, 'but I regret I must decline.'

'Oh well,' said Garth, 'of course, if you are afraid . . .' And he turned to go.

'I am afraid of nothing!' cried the Princess, a sudden brief colour appearing in her cheeks.

'Then come,' said Garth.

'Very well,' said Snow White. 'I shall.'

'My dear,' said the King, 'are you sure? You must take your waiting women to care for you, and I will furnish a bodyguard.'

'No waiting women,' said Snow White haughtily, 'and no bodyguard. Or we shall have this yokel saying that I, Princess Snow White, am afraid of him. He would not dare touch me.'

'But my dear –' began the King.

'No more,' snapped Snow White. 'My mind is made up. Let none from the Court accompany me. Return to your hut, peasant, and prepare it to receive a Royal

Princess. Tomorrow you may come and escort me thither.'

'Very well,' said Garth quietly, and he left.

The next day Garth returned to the palace with a horse-drawn cart. The Princess climbed into it, suppressing a shudder, and he drove her to his hut on the edge of the forest. On their way he spoke to her in friendly fashion, but she stared ahead and made no reply.

The hut stood in a sunny clearing just inside the forest. Around it a herd of goats cropped the grass. When they saw Garth they stopped eating and came over to greet him. As he handed Snow White down from the cart, they sniffed curiously at her.

'Go away, horrid creatures,' she cried and struck out, hitting one of them on the nose. It snorted and ran off, shaking its head.

'Do not hit my goats, Princess,' said Garth softly. 'They mean you no harm.'

'I shall hit them if I wish,' said she. 'Why should I not?'

'Because I ask it,' he replied. 'And because, if you do, you may have cause to regret it.'

'Do you dare threaten me, rustic oaf?' cried Snow White angrily.

'I threaten nobody,' said he. 'But I give you fair warning.'

Snow White tossed her pretty head scornfully and marched into the hut. It was indeed warm and clean and comfortable, with the agreeable smell of fresh bread baking in the oven. There was a table, a chair or two, and an old oaken chest. In one corner a door led to a bedchamber. In another corner was a single bed. When Garth came in after tending the horse, the Princess was standing impatiently in the middle of the hut.

'Help me to a chair, churl,' she ordered.

'Help yourself to one,' said Garth amiably, and went to the oven.

The Princess gasped, but sat down. 'I am hungry,' she announced.

'Good,' said Garth. 'The bread is new-baked and ready. I hope you like goats' cheese?'

'Bring me some and I shall tell you,' said Snow White, making a mighty effort to condescend.

'It is here on the table,' said Garth. 'Come and try it.'

'Certainly not,' said Snow White. 'I am a princess, I do not fetch my own food. You must serve me.'

'Must I?' said Garth. 'Well then, you may get rather hungry.' And he sat down at the table and began to eat with a good appetite. His favourite nanny goat wandered in and nuzzled him affectionately.

Snow White stared in amazement. 'Do as I say, peasant,' she ordered, 'or I shall have you punished.'

'Will you?' said Garth, quite unabashed. 'By whom, pray? There is no one here but you and me. If you want to punish me you must do it yourself.'

'Very well, I shall,' said the Princess. She got up, walked over to where Garth sat and slapped him hard across the face.

He blinked, but kept his temper. 'That, too, I would advise you not to do again,' he said quietly.

'I shall do as I wish,' stated Snow White. 'I care little for a yokel's threats. Now do my bidding and serve me food.'

As Garth was about to reply, the goat nuzzled Snow White's legs. She cried out in fury and kicked it. The animal bleated in pain and ran off.

To her astonishment, the Princess felt her wrist grasped from behind. She swung round. In Garth's eyes she saw something she had seen in no man's eyes before. It was anger.

Alarmed, she made to slap him again with her free hand. But before it struck his cheek that hand too was gripped, as firmly as the other.

'I gave you fair warning, Snow White,' said Garth quietly. 'I told you not to hit my goats or me. But you

109

think you can hit anyone you like. Well, you cannot – for all you may be a princess, and my liege lady. This, my girl, is the first lesson you must learn.'

Holding both her wrists in his strong grip, he drew her towards him. 'You gave your word!' cried Snow White. 'Is this how you keep it?'

'I gave my word I would not harm your virginity,' replied Garth. 'Nor shall I. I made no other promise.'

He reached to the table and picked up a flat implement shaped like a small paddle. It was a thin slat of wood some twelve inches long with rounded corners, a handspan across at its broader end.

'Do you know what this is, Princess?' he asked.

'Why should I?'

'No reason at all. But I shall tell you. It is a magic wand.'

'There is no such thing,' scoffed Snow White. 'These are tales for children.'

'Maybe so. Nonetheless, this wand can work certain kinds of simple magic. Its true name is a spatula, and I use it for making cheese. But it has other uses – as you, my lady, shall soon find out.'

The next thing the Princess knew, the floor was six inches from her nose, and she was face-down across Garth's lap. 'Let me go at once!' she cried in rage. 'What do you think you're doing, you wretch?'

Now, strange as it may seem, she really had no idea what was to happen to her. She had never known a mother, and her father had spoilt her from birth. None in the Palace dared reprimand her, though once or twice her nurse's palm had itched to give the young madam what she was asking for. But the old woman had prudently stayed her hand, and never in her eighteen years had anyone lifted a finger to Princess Snow White.

Still, she had heard and read of spankings being given to naughty children. And now she realised with horror that the unspeakable indignity of a smacked bottom was about to happen to her, a Royal Princess.

'How dare you!' she shrieked. 'Let me go, you churl! This is *lèse majesté*! Release me at once! I shall summon help!'

'Summon away,' retorted Garth, as he rucked her dress up above her waist. 'There's nobody within five miles but me and my goats. So yell all you want; you'll have your bottom well and truly tanned all the same. What you do about it after that is up to you. But at least I'll have given you what you richly deserve, and I wager that's more than any other man has dared.'

'Help!' cried Snow White, struggling wildly. 'Let me go, you wretched peasant! You shall die for this!'

'Maybe I shall,' said Garth equably, 'and maybe I shan't. But one thing is certain beyond all maybes, my girl. Princess or no, you're in for the finest spanking of your young life.'

Ignoring her struggles and outraged shrieks, he gazed on the charming prospect before him. The Princess was tall and slim, but also shapely, and her bottom proved to be pleasingly curved. Nothing now protected its ripe contours but white silken drawers. Few people wore underwear in those days, and Garth had never seen such a garment. He paused and stroked its softness. But the tender flesh beneath felt softer still, and with one swift movement he peeled down the sheer fabric to reveal as alluring a bottom as one could wish to see. Full and white and flawless, it swelled delectably upwards, inviting prompt attention.

'You have a very pretty bottom, Princess,' he told her, fondling the cool smooth flesh. 'Yet it has one great flaw. It is far too white for my taste. I would fain see it red – red as a rose, red as a sunset, red as a ripe apple. And soon it will be so.

'For such, my lady, is the magic that this wand of mine shall work. At present, as these pale cool cheeks

111

attest, you are the Princess Snow White, cold and haughty. But when my wand has worked its magic then behold! you shall be transformed into Princess Rose Red, she of the blushing cheeks.

'You may say that such magic will not last, that soon you will become Princess Snow White once more. And I cannot gainsay you. But though my magic prove short-lived, there is no shortage of it. Whenever it is needed it will be ready to change you again from Snow White to Rose Red – as often as may be required.

'And now, Princess,' said Garth, raising his spatula, 'let the spell begin!' So saying, he brought the flat wooden blade down hard on Snow White's right bottom-cheek, making her cry out as much from surprise as from pain. Never before, in all her eighteen years, had she felt such a burning smart. It was as though a hot iron had seared her flesh. A bright-pink patch sprang out on the flawless whiteness of her cheek. Garth regarded it with pleasure, then with equal vigour imprinted its twin on her other cheek.

Smack! Smack! Smack! Smack! Again and again, the spatula's merciless blade stung the soft flesh of Snow White's squirming bottom. She shrieked and struggled with wild indignation, kicking her long legs and threatening all manner of retribution.

After a dozen spanks had imprinted their signature on the snowy mounds, Garth paused to admire his handi-work. A warm pink blush now suffused every inch of Snow White's rearward curves, enhancing their ripe beauty.

The Princess, thinking her punishment was over, tried to rise, but Garth's strong right arm still held her pinioned over his knee. 'Oh no, my sweet,' he said, gently stroking the blade of the spatula across her stinging cheeks, 'we're not finished yet. Not by a long way.

'You have three lessons to learn, young lady, and the first of them is that simply being born your father's

112

daughter does not allow you to maltreat any creature you like with impunity. Such is your first lesson, my girl, and I hope this spanking will help you remember it. So you may threaten all you wish, my lady, but to no avail. Until I choose to stop, you will find yourself being soundly spanked on your bare bottom, and there's nothing you can do to prevent it.'

So saying, Garth tightened his grip on the Princess and resumed her punishment. If truth be told, she was not the first young woman he had treated thus. But she was the prettiest – and by far the most deserving of chastisement. So for ten minutes or more he spanked her to his heart's content.

At first the Princess screamed and threatened, then she wailed and pleaded, and at last she wept and promised to be good, if only he would please, please stop spanking her poor sore burning bottom. But, no matter what she said or did, the spatula mercilessly rose and fell, working its magic to transform her lovely bottom-cheeks from snow white to rose red.

And, while Garth spanked her, he talked to her. Not angrily, but in warm gentle tones, telling her how richly she deserved to be spanked, and how pretty her bottom looked as it blushed and quivered beneath his stinging spanks.

'You're not really a bad girl, Snow White,' he said, never ceasing to smack her roundly. 'But you are selfish and thoughtless and you've been badly spoilt. So spoilt, indeed, that I think you need to be well spanked for many years to come. And whoever has the spanking of you, my sweet, will be a very lucky man.'

And when at last he released her, she fled gasping and sobbing to the refuge of his mother's bedchamber and lay there face-down on the bed, nursing the fiery throbbing masses of her bottom and shedding hot tears of pain and fury. How dare he? How *dare* he? The brute! The peasant! That she, the Princess Snow White, whom no man addressed save with respect, whom few dared touch even with their fingertips – that a countrified boor, a *goatherd* indeed, should dare to – to – to *spank* her, to thrash her bare bottom with a kitchen implement! It was outrageous! It was treasonable! She, the first lady of the land, had been – the humiliation of it! – *spanked* by a goatherd! He would die. She would have him thrown in the deepest dungeon, flogged, tortured, executed! The very next day she would summon the royal guard and this cloddish yokel, who knew no other way to woo a woman than to beat her, should die. Slowly and painfully, while she gloated over his agonies . . .

Hugging this comforting thought to her, Princess Snow White sobbed herself to sleep. Some hours later she woke with a start. It was deep night, but rays of moonlight filtered into the room. She lay there, forgetting for a moment where she was. Then an unaccustomed smarting in her nether regions brought it all back to her. She was in the goatherd's hut – and he had *spanked* her!

Yet the feeling of outrage had left her. Her bottom no longer hurt so much. The pain had turned to a tingling warmth, and the Princess was aware of a new sensation: the heat of her young blood coursing in her veins. As if flowing from her spanked rear end, the aroused blood spread its heat, and Snow White, still half-asleep, found her fingers straying to a place not far from her bottom where the warmth needed urgent attention.

Her secret cleft was hot and wet to her touch. As her fingers attended to her needs, an image swam unbidden into her mind: the face of Garth the goatherd, now sleeping but a few feet away. His face as she had seen it, angry and determined, just before he had put her across his knee – and treated her so shamefully.

But perhaps she had to some extent deserved it? The thought surprised her. For the first time in her life the

Princess tried to imagine herself in someone else's shoes. Selfish and spoilt, Garth had called her, even as he smacked her bottom. She saw herself, an absurd figure in that simple hut, putting on airs, demanding attention, slapping his face. Might a spanking not have seemed the apt response to such behaviour?

Snow White moaned quietly, and as her pleasure mounted she relived her punishment. She became two people at once: Snow White, haughty and provocative, and Garth, angry and provoked. She shared his delight as he reddened her bottom with ringing smacks; she felt those smacks, painful yet strangely exciting, sting her defenceless flesh. She was spanker and spanked, Garth and Snow White – and her pleasure swelled, and burst, and flowed through her like the juice of a sun-ripened fruit.

With her cheeks flushed and a smile on her face, Princess Snow White sank into a long dreamless sleep.

When the Princess woke, it was daylight. From outside came the voice of Garth talking to his goats, his tone friendly and cheerful. She found it hard to hate him. For a peasant, he was not bad looking. True, he had spanked her mercilessly; but there were worse things, she mused, than having one's bottom smacked. She must simply be sure not to deserve it again. That shouldn't be too difficult.

So that morning Snow White set out with every intention of improving her behaviour. Garth greeted her cheerily and offered her breakfast. The Princess smiled prettily – she could be charming when she chose – and condescended to fetch her food to table with her own fair hands. And when she lowered herself a trifle gingerly on to her chair Garth smiled quietly but made no comment.

The morning passed pleasantly, until Snow White was unwise enough to say that she forgave Garth, if he promised never to do such a thing again.

115

'Do you now?' said Garth. 'Forgive me for what, pray?'

'Why, for using me so shamefully, of course!' snapped the Princess. 'For daring to spank my – my person!'

'Your person, my girl, sorely needed spanking,' retorted Garth. 'Someone should have done it long ago. As for not doing it again – on the contrary, be sure I shall put you back across my knee and spank you as hard, or harder, whenever you need it.'

Snow White rose with all the hauteur at her command. 'In that case, fellow, I quit your wretched hut this minute! Take me back to the palace at once!'

'You may go whenever you like,' answered Garth, unmoved. 'But, if you do, you go on your own two feet. I have better things to do than waste time driving you back to the city.'

Snow White stamped in fury, quite forgetting where she was. 'How dare you!' she cried. 'Insolent churl! Do my bidding this instant!'

Garth smiled – a slow lazy smile – and with a sinking feeling in her stomach Snow White realised she knew what that smile meant. 'Royal commands are not welcome in this house, young lady,' he said quietly. 'I told you there were three lessons you must learn. The first was that you cannot mistreat any creature you choose. That I hope you have learned well – with the help of my magic wand.

'Now we come to the second lesson – that you cannot impose your commands, royal or no, on whomever you wish. I'd hoped you might realise it for yourself. But I fear the effect of my wand is wearing off. It must work its magic on you again, it seems.'

'No, please! I'm sorry! I won't do it again!' cried the Princess, backing away.

'Too late, my girl,' responded Garth, picking up the spatula and advancing on her. 'I'm sure you are sorry.

116

But, believe me, your Royal Highness, you'll soon be even sorrier.'

And indeed she was. A moment later Princess Snow White found herself once again across Garth's knee, held fast while his strong right arm wielded the spatula in a fusillade of spanks upon her squirming rear.

This, her second spanking, hurt even worse than the first. For as Garth explained, even as he bared her bottom, 'Yesterday I spanked you only lightly. For I guessed you had never been spanked before, and thought you might learn your lesson from just a single spanking.

'But it seems you haven't, even though I'm sure these lovely cheeks are still tender from yesterday's spanks. Well, young lady, since you need a further lesson, I shall make sure it's a good one.'

So on that fine summer day the grazing goats listened in mild wonder to the rhythmic succession of ringing smacks that echoed round the little glade, accompanied by the gasps and wails of an increasingly penitent young lady. Inexorably, the spatula rose and fell, and once again the Princess's snow-white mounds turned pink, then rosy-red, then glowing scarlet beneath its stinging kisses.

In vain did Snow White weep and plead and promise better behaviour. Not until some fivescore resounding spanks had been meted out to each quivering bottom-cheek did Garth release her, taking her in his arms and wiping away her hot tears.

How amazed the courtiers would have been could they have seen their ice-princess now! Her lovely face was flushed – though far less red than her other cheeks – her green eyes were full of tears and she clung to Garth, sobbing piteously.

'Oh please, please,' she begged, 'I'm sorry, I'm so sorry. Oh my poor bottom, it hurts so much! Please, if I promise to be good, say you'll never spank me like that again!'

Garth hugged her, stroking her hair. 'All right,' he murmured. 'I promise. I won't spank you like that again.' He grinned wickedly. 'Today.'

Laughing at her wail of fury, he lifted her gently off his lap and laid her face-down on the bed. 'Wait there a moment, my sweet,' he said. 'I have something to make you feel better.'

A moment later he returned with a small wooden pail. Snow White lay where he had left her, the full expanse of her freshly spanked bottom still bared. Its crimson blush contrasted deliciously with the whiteness of her waist and thighs. Garth leant down and planted a soft kiss on each glowing mound. She wriggled at the touch of his lips, a moan of pleasure sounding deep in her throat.

Reaching into the pail, Garth scooped out a handful of fresh cream and slapped a cool dollop on the fiery curves.

'Ooooh!' cried Snow White. 'Aaaah! Oh, that feels so good!'

Garth began gently to massage the cream into her spanked mounds. Snow White squirmed luxuriously, the noise in her throat turning to a sensual purr as the cream soothed her burning flesh.

Garth smoothed the cream down between the rosy buttocks, letting his fingertips stroke lightly over the dark pucker of her anus. Snow White writhed in ecstasy. Reaching round, she grasped Garth's hand and tried to draw it down between her legs. Once again the glow of her spanked bottom was transmitting itself elsewhere, and she longed to feel his fingers, all slick and creamy, caressing her most intimate parts.

'No, my sweet,' said Garth, gently withdrawing his hand. 'Not there. Not now. Soon, maybe. But not until I'm released from my promise.'

'But I *want* you to!' wailed Snow White.

'No doubt. But I can't. Now be obedient, sweet girl.'

118

'Don't want to be obedient!' exclaimed the Princess like a petulant five-year-old.

'I think you had better be,' said Garth, a note of warning in his voice. 'Remember – you have three lessons to learn.'

'But you promised you wouldn't spank me any more today!' whimpered Snow White.

'Nor shall I. But tomorrow is another day.'

As indeed it was – and a beautiful day, too. High summer, the birds singing merrily, the forest in its full green garb. They breakfasted happily together. She fetched and carried for herself and issued no commands. You would have thought her a changed girl.

'How would you like a ride in the forest?' asked Garth. 'We can take food with us.'

'I would love to!' cried Snow White excitedly. She might never have been on a picnic in her life. And nor had she, unless an expedition including flunkies bearing trestle tables, tureens of soup, stuffed guinea-fowl, sedan chairs for the ladies, and so forth, can seriously be called a picnic.

'Good,' said Garth. 'I'll go and harness Jenny. You clear away the breakfast things and wash them.'

Now you may think the Princess slow on the uptake. Surely she would have learnt by now? But she had lived in a palace all her life, giving commands and doing just as she wished. The habits of a lifetime are hard to break in three days.

So, as soon as Garth had left, Snow White pushed the plates aside and gave them no further mind, lost instead in thoughts of how gentle and caring Garth had been after her last spanking. Then she strolled outside to enjoy the sunshine and watch him harness Jenny to the cart.

Having done so, he went back into the hut for the food. A moment later he called, 'Snow White – here a moment, please.'

When she entered the hut he was standing by the table. He spoke quietly, as ever, but there was an edge to his voice. 'Were you not to wash the dishes?'

'Oh yes,' responded Snow White carelessly, 'it slipped my mind. Does it matter? The servants can –' She stopped, realising what she was saying.

Garth smiled grimly. 'No, Princess, the servants cannot. There are no servants here, just you and me. If we divide the work between us, it goes on easily. If one of us shirks, it becomes hard.'

'But I would have done it later!' cried Snow White. She recognised the look in Garth's eye, and her bottom tingled in anticipation.

'Maybe you would, my girl. And maybe you would have left it for me. But what is beyond maybe is that you must now learn your third lesson – the lesson of obedience.'

'But that's not fair!' protested Snow White. 'I get spanked if I command! But *you* command, and now you will spank me for not obeying!'

'True. But the difference is that this is a task you undertook to do, and no very onerous one at that. And in my kingdom, young lady, undertakings are to be honoured.'

Snow White pouted. 'So instead of giving me a ride in the forest, you will give me another spanking. It is too cruel.'

'No,' said Garth with a strange smile. 'I am not going to give you a spanking.'

'What?' An observer might have detected the least note of disappointment in the Princess's voice.

'No. You see, till now I have indeed *given* you spankings. You have been held down over my knee and smacked whether you would or no. But today's lesson is obedience. So I want you to accept a spanking – of your own accord.'

Snow White's eyes widened. 'Accept?'

'Just so. I shall not hold you down, or force you. I want you to bend over this table and *ask* me to spank you for disobedience. Will you do that?'

'And if I do not?'

'Then I shall put you in the cart and drive you back to the palace, and you need never see me again.'

Snow White was silent. Finally she sighed and said, 'Very well, Garth, since you wish it. But please, let this spanking be less severe. My poor bottom is still sore from yesterday.'

'That will be up to you,' answered Garth, 'according to how well you obey.' He picked up the spatula. 'Bend over the table, please. Good girl. Raise your skirts right up. Good. Now lower your drawers.'

Reluctantly the Princess obeyed, feeling cool air on her rump as the silken fabric slid down, leaving her cheeks bare and vulnerable.

'Good,' said Garth again. 'Now ask me to spank you on your bare bottom for being disobedient. Say, "Dear Garth".'

The words seemed to stick in Snow White's throat, but she forced herself to utter them. 'Dear Garth – please spank me on my – my bare bottom for – for being disobedient.'

'With pleasure, my sweet. Now – you'll receive just two dozen spanks. A dozen on one cheek, then a dozen on the other. But you must stay bent over. If you stand up or put your hands over your bottom, you'll earn six extra strokes.'

Taking good aim, Garth brought the spatula down with full force on the plumpest part of Snow White's right bottom-cheek.

SMAAACK!!

'Yeee-owww!' she squealed, bounding up despite herself and clapping both hands to the injured portion. She was amazed how much harder he could spank standing up, with all the power of his shoulder muscles behind the stroke.

'Down again, please,' said Garth calmly. 'That'll be six extra strokes for standing up, my girl, and six more for covering your bottom.'

'Oh please, no!' wailed the Princess. But she obediently bent over once more, and somehow stayed down while seventeen more resounding spanks left their signature on the same cheek.

Garth paused to admire his handiwork. One half of the girl's lovely bottom was mantled with a scarlet glow. The other side was still white and unmarked.

'Behold the magic of my wand, Princess,' he said, grinning. 'Now you are two Princesses in one. Half your bottom belongs to Princess Rose Red, half to Princess Snow White. An enchanting sight. But, alas, this magic will soon fade. So while the spell lasts let us complete the transformation.'

'Swine!' muttered Snow White tearfully. 'I *hate* you! You're cruel, and horrible, and I wish I'd never met you! Go on – get it over with!'

'Your wish,' said Garth politely, 'is my command.'

SMACK!! SMACK!! SMACK!! The Princess yelped and squealed, hopping from foot to foot, while the spatula swished down eighteen times, raising a matching blush on her other cheek. Then Garth raised her up and hugged her, kissing away her tears.

'You took that very well, my sweet girl,' he murmured. 'Now it's time for our ride. You'd better bring something soft to sit on.'

Meanwhile, the King was growing anxious. His daughter had been away three days and had not sent a word. Had he been foolish to entrust her to this goatherd? He was in awe of his imperious daughter and loath to flout her commands, but he reasoned that, though she had forbidden waiting women and bodyguards, the prohibition might not extend to her old father. So, on the fourth morning he donned shabby clothes, chose a

122

nondescript horse from the stables and set off alone to the forest.

As an afterthought he buckled on an ancient sword. He was old and feeble, and Garth was young and strong. Yet was it not a father's duty to defend his child as best he could?

It took him a while to find the goatherd's hut. When he sighted it, he tethered his horse at a distance and approached quietly on foot. As he drew near he heard the sound of carefree girlish laughter, full of joy and mischief.

'If I didn't know better,' he thought to himself, 'I would say that was my daughter's voice. But she has never laughed like that in her life.'

Creeping up to the hut, he peered in through the window. Garth sat at table facing the window, a loaf and cheese before him. Opposite him sat a tousle-haired girl with a fine figure, wearing simple clothes and laughing merrily. As he watched, she half-turned and he glimpsed her face. The King gasped. The girl's cheek was flushed with pleasure and her eyes sparkled with naughtiness.

'So, you dare spurn my charms, Sir Garth?' she demanded mock-haughtily.

The goatherd grinned. 'My sweet,' he replied, 'I would dearly love to bed you this very minute. But I gave my word. Once the week is up, then if you wish I'll be happy to acquaint you with another wand of mine, and show you what magic I can work with it. But until then I keep my word, no matter how you tease.'

'What if I release you from your promise?' asked the girl.

'You cannot. I gave it to your father, not to you.'

'And if I order you, on Royal Command?'

Garth half-rose, threatening her playfully. 'You know what happens to young ladies who issue Royal Commands in this hut, my girl.'

Quick as a flash the girl grabbed a spatula from the table and tossed it through the window, just missing the King's nose. 'Hah!' she cried. 'Now you can't spank me! Your wand is gone!'

Grinning, Garth made a grab at her. 'Oho, my sweet, I don't need my wand to spank your bottom soundly.' He laughed. 'My hands too have warming magic in them, as you will soon learn.'

'You must catch me first, Sir Bully!' cried the girl. After dodging round the table, she made a dash for the door with Garth in close pursuit.

The King dived hastily behind a woodpile as the pair shot out the door. The girl had a few yards' lead until, with a shriek, she tripped over a tether. In a trice Garth was on her. Chuckling exultantly, he scooped her up, carried her to a nearby tree-stump and sat down, draping her face-down across his lap. She yelped and giggled, beating on his legs with her fists.

The King watched in amazement. Could this be his daughter, the cool conceited Princess Snow White, so remote and forbidding? This carefree laughing girl with tousled hair, rosy cheeks and sparkling eyes? Now she was giggling and squealing as the goatherd flipped up her skirt to reveal long legs, shapely thighs and a rounded and very spankable bare bottom.

'Now, young lady,' said Garth, caressing the soft mounds, 'you'll learn that I can work magic just with my hands. For once again I shall bring a blush to these pretty cheeks, and swiftly transform you from Snow White to Rose Red!' So saying, he proceeded to administer a sound smacking to her squirming rump.

'Oww!' she cried, wriggling as her bottom turned a fetching pink. 'Beast! Stop it! Help! How dare you treat a princess so, sir? Oooh! Owww! I shall have you executed for treasonable assault upon a royal – yee-owww! – bottom!'

'*Will* you now?' said Garth, spanking her lustily. 'Then as well be hanged for a sheep as a lamb! If this must be the last spanking I give you, sweet lady, I'll see to it that your royal bottom is most royally toasted!'

'Oww, no, stop! I command you! *Owww!* I am the Princess Snow White! Unhand my – owww! – bottom this instant! Brute! Help!'

'Not any more you're not, my lady,' retorted Garth, pausing to stroke the radiant cushions beneath his hand, 'for all the world knows that Snow White is cold and pale and disdainful, and has never yet been warmed by any man. You, however, are the Princess Rose Red, as these soft blushing cheeks plainly show, who has been well warmed these past three days, and is even now being warmed again. Aye, and shall be many a time to come, if I have aught to do with it.'

So saying, he happily renewed his assault on the girl's sweet rearward curves, settling in for a good long leisurely spanking. She for her part squealed and kicked and squirmed, yelping with pain and excitement, and pleading most unconvincingly for mercy.

The King crept quietly away, retrieved his horse and rode off, wondering. His sword thumped at his side. He had come resolved to defend his daughter from harm, even at the cost of his own life. Yet had he not seen her pursued and captured, half-denuded and soundly smacked – and made not a move to intervene?

The King shook his white old head. He had always thought himself a good father, dedicated to his daughter's happiness, and leaving no paternal duty unfulfilled. But now it occurred to him that there had, perhaps, been one crucial omission . . .

Three days later, punctual to the hour, Garth returned the Princess to the palace. She stood before the Court in the simple peasant dress she had worn in Garth's hut. There was a smile on her lips, and her eyes that formerly

125

glinted like green ice now sparkled like emeralds. Her long dark hair was tousled and there was a flush of secret pleasure on her cheek.

'I return your daughter the Princess, Sir King,' said Garth politely. 'As I promised you, and as she herself will tell you, she is still as virgin for me as when she left your palace.'

'Ah,' said the King. 'Quite so. But tell me – have you, ah, warmed her as you undertook to do?'

'Perhaps you should ask her that,' suggested Garth.

'Well, my dear daughter,' said the King, somewhat flustered, 'tell us, then. Has this young man found how to warm you?'

The Princess almost laughed. 'Oh yes,' she said, 'indeed he has. He has warmed me lovingly and often. There has not been a day this past week when he has not warmed me. Surely no man could warm me better than Garth has done. As you may tell –' she paused, and flashed Garth a secret smile '– from the roses in my cheeks.'

'Indeed,' said the King, who seemed to be struggling with some private recollection. 'Then – do you love him?'

'Oh yes,' said Snow White, taking Garth's right hand and kissing it gently on the palm.

'And would you marry him?'

A long rich flush of colour flowed into the Princess's cheeks. 'Oh, yes,' she said, 'willingly.'

The cheer that followed could be heard outside in the city streets. And when the cause of it was known, the whole city cheered so loud that, far away on the edge of the forest, Garth's goats raised their heads and gazed in surprise at the distant sound.

A week later, Garth and the Princess were married. To the general surprise, she refused to be married as Princess Snow White. 'A married woman,' she said, 'often changes her name, and so shall I. Henceforth I shall be known as Princess Rose Red. This as tribute,' she added with a pretty blush, 'to the magic worked upon me by the love of my dear Garth.'

For his part Garth declined to be crowned King. 'While you live, sir,' he told his father-in-law, 'there can be but one King, and you are he. In any case, from goatherd to King in a single week is too great a leap for any man. So, if you please, I shall be crowned Prince Garth, and serve as your Regent with my beloved wife. And, if in the fullness of time the rank of King should fall vacant, that will be soon enough for me.'

'But at least,' asked the Court Herald anxiously, 'you will take a coat-of-arms, my Prince?'

'Why yes,' said Garth, 'that I think I may do. Saving your expertise, my friend, I have some suggestions.'

'Oh,' said the Herald as Garth sketched on a parchment. 'I see. It is, if your Royal Highness will excuse my saying so, somewhat irregular. I don't recall ever seeing that particular device on an escutcheon before.'

'Nonetheless,' said Prince Garth, 'that is my wish.'

And so it was that the House of Garth ever afterwards bore this proud armature: Between two goats rampant, on a field *blanc neige*, a spatula *or* over two *fesses rouges*. Motto: *Qui ayme bien, chastie bien* – a precept the descendants of that house observe faithfully to this very day.

10

Emma – The Lost Version

The current vogue for Jane Austen has fuelled specula-
tion about her sexuality. In some quarters it's been
suggested that she was lesbian. The jury's still out on
that one; but recent research by the tireless investigators
of the Camden Institute for Disciplinary Studies has
uncovered startling evidence that Jane may have been
into spanking.

Emma Woodhouse, lovely, self-willed and incurably
meddlesome, is Jane Austen's most charming and
infuriating heroine. More than one reader must have
wished that Mr Knightley, Emma's friend, mentor and
– in the end – bridegroom, had taken the spoilt young
lady across his knee and administered the spanking she
so richly deserved. Now, thanks to Dr Kemp's re-
searches, it's revealed that in the newly unearthed
original version of *Emma*, he did just that. More than
once, too. We're proud to present a world exclusive: the
first-ever publication of excerpts from *Emma – the
Spanking Version*.

*Emma Woodhouse has taken under her wing Harriet
Smith, a young woman of humble origins, and has nipped
in the bud an incipient romance between her and a young
farmer, Robert Martin. Emma believes her protégée
destined for higher social rank than that of a farmer's*

'We think so very differently on this point, Mr Knightley,'
replied Emma, 'that there can be no use in canvassing it.
We shall only be making each other more angry. In any
case, Harriet has refused Robert Martin, and so decidedly, I think, as must prevent any second application. As to
the refusal itself, I will not pretend to say that I might not
have influenced her a little; but I assure you there was
very little for me or for anybody to do. I imagine that,
before she had seen anybody superior, she might tolerate
him. But the case is altered now. She knows now what
gentlemen are; and nothing but a gentleman in education
and manner has any chance with Harriet.'

'Nonsense, arrant nonsense, as ever was talked!' cried
Mr Knightley. 'Robert Martin's manners have sense,
sincerity and good humour to recommend them; and his
mind has more true gentility than Harriet Smith could
understand.'

Emma made no answer, and tried to look cheerfully
unconcerned. She did not repent what she had done; she
still thought herself a better judge of such a point of
female right and refinement than he could be; but yet
she had a sort of habitual respect for his judgement in
general, which made her dislike having it so loudly
against her. Some minutes passed in this unpleasant
silence. Mr Knightley was thinking. At last he expressed
the results of his thoughts in these words: 'Emma, we
are old friends, and I have always availed myself of the
privilege of an old friend to speak frankly to you. At the
risk of offending you, I must now test that privilege to
the utmost.'

His aspect was so serious that Emma could not help
but laugh and disclaim all risk of offence.

He continued: 'Very well, then. Emma, I have known
you from an infant. You have many good qualities

which endear you to me, and to all your friends. But, if you have one great fault, it is that you will have your own way. In your mother you lost the only person able to cope with you. Since you were twelve you have been mistress of the house. In consequence you are – forgive me – a lovely, charming, intelligent but badly spoilt young lady.'

As he spoke, Mr Knightley fixed her with a glance at once more grave and more intimate than any she had known from him. She tried to smile and respond playfully. But at the intensity of his gaze she found herself overcome by confusion, and she remained silent as he proceeded.

'Were your father of a more decided nature, I doubt I should need to say these words. But, in this matter of Harriet Smith, Emma, your passion for match-making, and your disregard of any view but your own, have caused serious mischief. Emma, I say this for your own good and that of all around you. If you do not cease this wilful meddling, I shall feel constrained to treat you as the spoilt young woman you are, and requite you fittingly; namely, by taking you across my knee and giving you a sound spanking. Believe me, Emma, I mean what I say. Good morning to you.'

He rose and walked off abruptly, leaving Emma in a state of anger and mortification. She could scarcely credit that he had spoken to her in such terms. No one had chastised her since she was a child, and it was surely not conceivable that a gentleman like Mr Knightley would even consider such an outrage on her person. Yet she had never known him to speak idly.

Emma's agitation was increased by the fact that, at the moment Mr Knightley had talked of spanking her, she had experienced a palpable thrill in which fear and excitement were strangely mixed. At this memory, to her great vexation, she found herself bursting into tears.

* * *

At a picnic organised by Emma on Box Hill (a Surrey beauty spot), she wilfully insults an old friend, the middle-aged Miss Bates, by a thoughtless joke. This and other incidents sour the occasion, and Emma is relieved when the party breaks up.

Such another scheme, composed of so many ill-assorted people, she hoped never to be betrayed into again. Rather than wait for her carriage, she walked a little aside beyond a thicket, seeking solitude. In a few moments the voices and the bustle had faded behind her, and she conceived herself quite alone. But to her surprise, rounding a bush, she came upon Mr Knightley. It was evident that he had expressly made to intercept her, and his visage boded no agreeable speech.

'Emma,' said he without preamble, 'I cannot see you acting wrong, without a remonstrance. How could you be so unfeeling to Miss Bates? How could you be so insolent in your wit to a woman of her character, age and situation? Emma, I had not thought it possible.'

Emma recollected, blushed and was sorry, but tried to laugh it off. 'Nay, how could I help saying what I did? Nobody could have helped it. It was not so very bad. I dare say she did not understand me.'

'I assure you she did. She felt your full meaning. She has talked of it since. I wish you could have heard how she talked of it – with what candour and generosity.'

'Oh!' cried Emma, still trying to treat the matter lightly. 'I know there is not a better creature in the world. But you must allow that what is good and what is ridiculous are most unfortunately blended in her.'

Mr Knightley's eyes flashed with anger, but he yet spoke quietly. 'They are blended, that I acknowledge. And, were she a woman of fortune, I would leave every harmless absurdity to take its chance. But, Emma, consider how far this is from being the case. She is poor; she has sunk from the comforts she was born to; and if

131

she live to old age must probably sink more. Her situation should secure your compassion. No, Emma, it was badly done, indeed! Nor can I forbear to add that your efforts to pass it off, in this frivolous fashion, as mere matter for amusement sorely compound your offence.'

While talking, they had walked on further, round the slope of the hill, and now found themselves in a secluded dell where the woodsmen had been felling trees. The trunk of one of these, a venerable oak, lay horizontally near by. To Emma's surprise, Mr Knightley took her by the hand and led her towards the fallen tree. Not since she quit childhood had he permitted himself so intimate a gesture with her, and her heart beat faster while she wondered what he could intend.

When they reached the tree he turned to face her, still holding her by the hand. 'Emma,' said he gravely, 'do you recall what I told you some weeks past, when you were instrumental in bringing Harriet Smith to break off with Robert Martin?'

As his meaning sank in upon her, Emma felt herself gripped by a thrill of apprehension. She could only gaze at him, unable to utter a word, as he continued.

'I said then that, should your conduct not improve, I must feel constrained to chastise you in the manner best fitted to the correction of spoilt young women. Your inexcusable behaviour towards Miss Bates convinces me that the time for such treatment is long overdue. Emma, you may never find it in yourself to forgive me for what I am about to do – but I know that, should I fail to do it, I could never forgive myself.'

Before Emma could utter more than an incoherent sound of protest, Mr Knightley sat down on the log, drawing her down until, much to her astonishment, she found herself lying face-downwards across his lap. 'Oh!' she exclaimed. 'Mr Knightley! This is shameful conduct, sir! How dare you subject me to such indignity? Release me at once, I insist!'

But Mr Knightley seemed in no way inclined to release her from her ignominious posture. Rather the contrary, indeed; his left arm, laid firmly along her waist, left her quite unable to escape, and Emma's struggles, though spirited, availed her little.

'This will not be pleasant to you, Emma,' said he, 'though it would be hypocritical were I to claim that it will be wholly unpleasant to me. But, pleasant or no, it is a task long overdue – and, since it has fallen to me to perform it, I mean to do so with all due thoroughness.'

Indeed, the prospect which now met his eyes was one which few gentlemen would have found unpleasing. At 21, Emma was at the peak of her youthful ripeness, and her figure wanted for nothing of girlish charms. The weather being seasonably warm, she wore only a light muslin dress, and in her prone position the fine material moulded itself closely around her curves of her lower torso, revealing them to be well defined and appealingly rounded. Not only, Mr Knightley reflected, was Emma Woodhouse eminently deserving of the chastisement he was about to inflict upon her; she was also ideally shaped by nature to receive it.

Emma, for her part, was now in no doubt that Mr Knightley was resolved to execute his threat. She knew him to be both vigorous and resolute, and was uneasily aware that the thin muslin, her sole covering, would afford scant protection to her tender flesh. She retained but faint recollection of her childhood punishments, and these had in any case been rare and lenient; whereas the spanking that Mr Knightley proposed to administer would, she felt sure, be both prolonged and painful.

Surely, she thought desperately, he might even yet be deflected from his purpose? But he was impervious to her protests; let her try what penitence might do.

'Oh! Please, dear Mr Knightley,' she cried, 'forgive me, I beseech you! I acknowledge my misdeed, and am truly sorry for it; pray spare me this once, and I promise faithfully to amend my ways and not offend you again!'

'I have no doubt that you are sorry, Emma. But, were I now to let you off your punishment, how long would your repentance, or your resolution to reform, be likely to last? No, I fear that steps must be taken to impress this reprimand distinctly upon your memory, and I can assure you that the treatment you are about to receive will leave a most lasting impression – both on your mind and on your person.'

With these words he took a firmer grip on Emma's waist, while lifting his right hand high in the air. At the sight of his upraised arm Emma, peering fearfully over her shoulder, could not suppress a tremor of alarm.

The next moment she gasped in surprise. Mr Knightley's palm, descending with the full force of his arm, smote sharply upon her upturned posterior with a ringing slap. The smart it inflicted was acute; to Emma, wholly unused to such treatment, it was as though a hot iron had seared her flesh. This stroke had fallen upon the rightward of her tender mounds; an instant later a second stroke made itself felt, with equally vivid effect, upon its twin.

Poor Emma! Almost before she had time to cry out in protest against such cruel treatment, this opening salvo was succeeded by a whole volley of smacks, landing with fearsome frequency now right, now left, upon her near-unprotected nether cheeks. Never could she have believed that a mere spanking, administered by no instrument more severe than an open hand, could sting her tender flesh so flagrantly. Already, after barely half a minute, a burning sensation suffused all her rearward parts, and Mr Knightley seemed set on prolonging her correction for many minutes yet.

'Oh, sir,' she cried piteously, 'pray have mercy! Oh, how you pain me! It stings – it burns! Oh! Ah! Spank me no more, dear Mr Knightley, I beseech you! I have been punished in full measure, and shall truly reform, I promise you! Ah! Alas, I can bear no more! Help! Oh help! Will no one come to my aid?'

But no help came. Whether the remainder of their party were now out of earshot, or whether, hearing the distant sounds of Emma's punishment, they deduced what was happening and felt that it was no more than she richly deserved, can only be surmised. At all events, no other came to intervene, and the unfortunate Emma had to rely on Mr Knightley's forbearance to bring her ordeal to an end.

Alas for her, he felt in no hurry to do so. On many occasions the warm affection he bore towards Emma had been tempered by a no less warm sense of exasperation, and more than once it had crossed his mind that physical chastisement of the most traditional kind might provide suitable outlet for both emotions at once. And so it proved. Never had he felt more beguiled by Emma's charms, never had he felt more infuriated by her conceit and thoughtlessness, than now when he held her lovely person prone and wriggling across his lap, roundly smacking her shapely bottom with all the force at his command.

But gradually, as his initial anger abated, his satisfaction grew. From the moment when he had first resolved upon this course of action, Mr Knightley had foreseen that to spank Emma Woodhouse would afford great relief to his feelings; what he had not realised was that it would prove such a deep and intense pleasure. Her frantic squirmings; her gasps and increasingly tearful pleas; above all, the delectable sensation of her soft plump flesh-cushions trembling as he smacked them; all this contributed to a voluptuous delight such as he had rarely before experienced. Nor, somewhat to his surprise, was there the least sense of impropriety. Quite the reverse; to hold Emma thus pinioned across his lap, and to spank her long and hard, felt wholly and undeniably fitting. It was as though this transaction between them were pre-ordained, a natural and salutary stage in their intercourse.

Disinclined to curtail so pleasing and salutary an occupation, he continued to spank her with unabated zest. For five minutes or more his palm rose and fell, and the sound of the smacks inflicted upon Emma's anguished posteriors echoed round the little dell. Well before her ordeal was over, she was reduced to small inarticulate cries of distress; and when at last he desisted from punishing her, and raised her gently from off his knee, she could only cling whimpering to him, her hands clasped to the blazing conflagration he had ignited in her ill-used nether quarters.

'Dear Emma,' he murmured as she sobbed in his arms, her tears dampening the shoulder of his coat, 'I blame myself. Not indeed for having spanked you, for that you richly deserved; but for having delayed so long before doing so. Had you an elder brother, a male cousin, or indeed a father of a more determined cast of mind, no doubt my intervention would not have been required. But since I have always stood to you as both friend and in some degree *in loco parentis*, I ought to have seen my duty sooner. Emma, I should have taken you across my knee and spanked you long since. But, now that I have at last made belated amends, I hope you will profit by your ordeal, and see it as having been truly intended for your improvement.'

She could make no answer. But the glance she cast upon him from beneath her tear-fringed lashes conveyed no anger or resentment, rather a sincere contrition. As he guided her gently out of the dell in the direction of her carriage, she found herself seized by a strange confusion of emotions, and could not trust herself to speak.

As they approached the point at which they might once more be overlooked by any of the party yet remaining, Mr Knightley tactfully withdrew his arm from Emma's shoulder, and side by side they walked in silence to her carriage. With his habitual grave courtesy, as if nothing untoward had passed between them, he handed her in, and before she could speak the horses were in motion.

The journey home was a torment to her. Never had she felt so agitated, mortified, grieved at any occasion in her life. The circumstances of her chastisement, in all its shame, were vividly before her eyes. Even had the incident not been so fresh in her memory, each jolt of the carriage served to remind her, in the most tangible form, of the assault that had so recently been inflicted upon her tender posteriors.

Yet still more shameful than the treatment she had endured was the awareness, not to be gainsaid, that she had not found it altogether distasteful. It had hurt a great deal; it had been utterly humiliating; yet Emma could not conceal from herself that, in the innermost part of her being, she had derived excitement – pleasure, even – from such masterful behaviour on the part of a man she respected and admired. What he had done was beyond all question inexcusable; nonetheless Emma found herself wondering whether, given sufficient provocation, he might not feel called upon to do it again?

Gripped by these strange and contradictory sensations, she could not prevent herself from weeping. Happily, Harriet, her only companion in the carriage, seemed out of spirits herself and very willing to be silent; and Emma felt the tears running down her cheeks almost all the way home.

But all ends happily.

Barely a month after the marriage of Harriet Smith to Robert Martin, the services of the Rev Mr Elton were once more called upon, this time to join the hands of Mr George Knightley and Miss Emma Woodhouse. The wedding was very much like other weddings; but the wedding night was, at any rate in its preliminaries, a little out of the ordinary.

Once all the guests were gone, Emma Knightley – as we must now call her – awaited her newly wedded husband in the quiet of the bridal chamber, a warm dark place lit only by a pair of candles and the flickering of a well-banked fire. There where she stood, a picture of bridal loveliness clad in a fine linen nightgown trimmed with pale-blue ribbons, he came to her, took her in his arms and kissed her.

'Dear Emma,' he murmured in her ear, 'do you remember that day of the picnic on Box Hill, when for your impertinence to poor Miss Bates I turned you across my knee and spanked you soundly?'

'Cruel! How could I forget it? My poor bottom was stinging hot for the rest of the day!'

'Even as you deserved, my love. But let me confess a secret – it was then that I resolved to make you my wife.'

'What! For my impertinence?'

'No – for the great pleasure I derived from spanking you. Though perhaps for your impertinence too. For I knew well, my sweet Emma, that you were incorrigible, and therefore as my wife would give me frequent cause to smack your sweet bottom – a duty which, I must confess, I should find it small hardship to discharge.'

Half-laughing, half-outraged, Emma began to protest in lively fashion.

But he stifled her outburst with a kiss, and proceeded: 'In earnest of this, I made a vow: that my first act on our wedding night, once we found ourselves alone together, would be to put you once more over my knee and administer a loving husbandly chastisement. And this, my sweet girl, I now propose to do.'

'But that is most unjust,' cried Emma, 'for I have done nothing to deserve it! My behaviour today has been beyond reproach!'

'True, so it has. But think of it as a token punishment for all those many past occasions when you so richly deserved to be spanked – and were not. A heavy debt, my Emma! Indeed, were I to spank you every day for a year, I think you would scarce receive your just deserts. So reckon yourself fortunate, my love, that you may discharge so great an account in a single payment.'

'Cruel tyrant!' exclaimed Emma. 'Alas! I have yoked myself to a monster!' But there was a sparkle in her eye that belied her words, and she made little resistance as Mr Knightley, taking her by the hand, led her towards the bed. There he kissed her warmly on the lips and then, having sat down, placed her once more over his lap in the posture generally agreed most suitable for the administration of domestic discipline.

Once again he was able to observe how enticingly a fine fabric could shape itself around the contours of Emma's lovely form. But now, in the privacy of the marriage chamber, he need no longer let even this flimsy barrier impede his pleasure. With a sensation of inexpressible delight, he took the hem of her nightgown and slowly turned it up, until all his bride's rearward charms, up to her waist, were revealed to his enraptured gaze.

In the warm glow of the candle flames, the beauteous globes of Emma's hinder parts were displayed to particular advantage. Mr Knightley beheld them with unalloyed rapture and, emboldened by his newfound uxorious state, ventured to caress the tender flesh-cushions.

'Dearest Emma,' said he, 'truly you were formed for this. For not only, sweet girl, does your saucy and wilful nature render you most deserving of frequent chastisement, but these lovely orbs, so soft and rounded, were positively made to be spanked. Such posterior charms should be done full justice; and I am determined they shall receive it, abundantly and often.'

At this, he raised his hand and, pausing only for a brief moment of joyful anticipation, brought it down hard on the plumpest part of his bride's defenceless curves. Emma gasped and squirmed at the sting of it, only to gasp again as another stroke smote her quivering flesh, followed by another and another. Each smack resounded in the bedchamber like a pistol shot, mingled with Emma's gasps and squeals. Even a light layer of muslin, she now understood, could make a signal difference. The punishment Mr Knightley had inflicted upon her in the dell at Box Hill had hurt a great deal; but a spanking applied to her bared bottom stung yet more vividly.

After only a dozen strokes, a warm blush suffused the fair cheeks of Emma's naked rump, much enhancing their beauty. Mr Knightley paused to admire it, then resumed his attentions, spanking his sweet young bride hard and lovingly. Already it was evident that this was to be no token chastisement, given in play; Mr Knightley intended that Emma should suffer her wedding-night spanking in full earnest.

'Oh, my dear Mr Knightley,' cried she, 'how you hurt me! Ah! Oh! How can you use me so? Oh please, dear husband, spank me no more, I beg of you! Truly I repent; I shall never more be saucy or wilful, that I vow! Oh! Ah! Oh take pity, please, no more!'

But in vain did she protest and plead for mercy. Still her remorseless punisher's arm rose and fell; still her trembling mounds bounced and blushed beneath his hearty slaps. And while he spanked her Mr Knightley talked to her, not angrily but gently and with affection. 'I start as I mean to go on, dearest Emma,' said he even as he smacked her with relish. 'Think this of as but a token of events to come. For you may count on it, my love, that during the course of our married life you will frequently find yourself turned across my knee like this, to have your bare bottom soundly spanked. Often it will be because you have deserved it, sweet wilful girl; but at other times it may be simply for the pleasure of the game.'

So saying, he proceeded to unleash upon Emma's quivering flesh such a fusillade of stinging strokes that she squealed in dismay, kicking up her legs and imploring him to spare her further punishment. Yet he showed no inclination to desist, but continued to spank her unmercifully, deepening with each smack the carmine blush that now adorned the full expanse of her lovely naked posteriors; a blush that presented an exquisite contrast with the whiteness of her waist and thighs.

Yet, for all her pleas, deep within her Emma felt delight in submitting thus to her husband's ardent mastery. For to lie across the thighs of a man in whose excellence and judgement she had perfect confidence; to feel her soft bare hinder parts tingled and enflamed by the loving punishment of a man of Mr Knightley's proven sensibility; this to her was true joy, and furthermore a source of deep and secret pleasure.

So, when at last, having administered to her a spanking even more thoroughgoing than the first, Mr Knightley ceased chastising his beloved Emma and raised her up into his arms, she embraced him in no sprit of resentment. True, she pouted at him reproachfully, with tears in her eyes, and murmured 'Cruel!' and 'Heartless monster!' in his ear; true, she rubbed ruefully at the becrimsoned mounds of her suffering backside. But she knew that what seemed cruelty on his part was in truth love and cherishing, a tribute to her intimate charms; and the warmth engendered by the correction she had undergone readily transmitted itself into the ardour of her embrace.

Of the exchanges that followed hard upon this first chastisement of Emma's married life, we need say little. But it may perhaps be pertinent to add that, in this matter as in all, Mr Knightley was as good as his word, and Emma's wedding-night spanking was far from the last she would receive at her husband's loving hands. Quite the contrary; in the years to come Mr Knightley would find frequent occasion to place his sweet Emma across his knee, bare her bottom and induce a roseate hue into her lovely cheeks; and when no occasion offered, it was not unknown for him to devise one. Such disciplines did nothing to weaken the affectionate bond between them. Rather they strengthened it, and enhanced the lively regard each felt for the other, so that the wishes and hopes of their friends were fully answered in the perfect happiness of their union.

11

Bikini Line

'But I *want* to!'

Julie glared indignantly at Daniel. Her full lower lip stuck out petulantly, and a hint of angry tears moistened her blue eyes. She even stamped her foot, though the thick pile of the hotel carpet rather ruined the effect. You couldn't have called it a first-class stamp.

Dan suppressed an impulse to grin. Instead, he sighed quietly. Julie was nineteen, nearly twenty, a grown woman. But right now, he had to admit, the petite blonde looked like nothing so much as a spoilt little girl throwing a temper tantrum.

Dan and Julie had been married only a few months, and he adored his pretty young wife. And he had definite views on marriage. A husband and wife, he believed, should be partners, setting forth as loving equals into the great adventure of married life. True, Julie was younger than him by a year or two, but what of that?

These days, of course, such ideas are nothing new. But this was England in 1960, when husbands were meant to 'wear the trousers', women were expected to 'know their place', and brides at the altar promised to love, honour – and obey. Dan McIntyre, though, prided himself on having modern ideas. There was a young queen on the throne, and in this New Elizabethan Age a lot of things were changing, in his view mostly for the better. Especially in relations between men and women.

Still, he had to admit there were times when he found it hard to treat Julie as a rational adult. And this was one of them. Besides, she did look extremely sexy, posing there in the ultra-brief sky-blue bikini that showed off all the delectable curves of her nubile young figure. Dan was sorely tempted to grab her there and then and make passionate love to her. But then it would be impossible to refuse her anything. No, he had to be firm – and not in the way a certain part of him was getting firm, either.

So he set his jaw and repeated quietly, 'Sorry, darling, but no. You can't wear that costume here.'

'Why *not*?' wailed Julie. 'It's the latest fashion!'

'I'm sure it is, sweetheart. But this isn't the south of France, nor even Brighton. It's Bournemouth – and you know how prim and proper they are here. You wear that bikini on the beach, you'll cause a riot. Respectable old ladies will have heart attacks.'

'Don't care!' sulked Julie mutinously.

'Well, I do. This is our first real holiday together, darling, and I don't want it spoilt by people pointing and sniggering. It's a lovely bikini, my sweet, and you look terrific in it. But you've got to admit it *is* scandalously brief. Look, it leaves nearly all your bottom bare!'

'You said I had a delicious bottom,' pouted his young wife.

'You do, my angel. But I'd rather you didn't display it to half the South Coast. No, sorry, darling, but my mind's made up. You can't wear that bikini on the beach here, and that's final.'

'It's not *fair*!' wailed Julie. 'I hate you!' Bursting into tears, she stalked into the bathroom and slammed the door.

Dan sighed again. When Julie was in a good mood, she was the sweetest, most enchanting companion – and bedfellow – that a man could desire. But when things didn't go just the way she wanted she threw tantrums, and sulked, and generally made his life a misery. It hadn't often happened before they married. But just recently the tantrums had been getting ever more frequent.

Not for the first time he recalled what Valerie, his mother-in-law, had told him just before the wedding. Valerie was a warm outgoing woman whose affable nature concealed a core of steel. Widowed by the war, she had run her own business and single-handedly raised three spirited daughters, of whom Julie was the youngest. 'She's a sweet girl, Dan,' she said, 'and I know she'll make you a good wife. But I'll tell you one thing for free, if you've not discovered it already. She's a headstrong little thing when she wants to be. Likes her own way, does our Julie, and can be as stubborn as a mule about getting it.

'Now what you do about it, Dan, is up to you. Maybe you'll just give in, for the sake of a quiet life. But if you don't mind a word of advice from the mum-in-law – well, I've always found a firm hand works wonders. Surprises you, does it? Oh yes, many's the time I've had to put that young madam over my knee and take a hairbrush to her saucy little backside. Her sisters too, come to that. But it's always Julie who's needed it most. Call me old-fashioned, but I believe you could do worse than likewise. I think you'd be the happier for it, my dear – and so would she, though I bet she wouldn't admit it.'

Dan smiled and nodded politely. Inwardly, he resolved that such primitive methods would have no part in his marriage. But now he found himself wondering if Valerie might not have a point . . .

In the bathroom, Julie moodily admired herself in the full-length mirror, peering over her shoulder to inspect the rear view. She *did* have a sexy bottom, no question of it – she didn't need Dan to tell her that. Pert and lusciously rounded, her ripe young cheeks peeked provocatively out from under the scanty blue triangle, inviting attention. She'd been counting on getting a near-all-over tan she could show off to her girlfriends back home – not to mention the glances, envious or lecherous, she'd attract on the beach. And now Dan thought he could spoil her fun, did he, the rotten old stick-in-the-mud? Well, he couldn't, so *there*!

Julie gave her reflection a secret grin. Then she took off the bikini, put on something more modest and went out to act the dutiful young wife.

The hotel was the smartest in town. At the time they married, Dan's new business had been at a critical stage, and he'd only been able to spare a long weekend for the honeymoon. But things were running smoothly now, he'd landed some lucrative contracts, and to celebrate and make it up to Julie he'd booked them two weeks at the Grand. 'No expense spared, my darling,' he'd told her. 'Terrific food and drink, sun and sand – and a lovely big soft double bed where we can do all the naughty things we like, day and night.'

Julie had giggled delightedly.

As it was their first evening, they went to town on the dinner. The Grand boasted a French chef and a lengthy wine list, and the young couple did full justice to both. They got to bed very drunk and very amorous, and fell asleep fully entwined.

The next morning, despite the drink, Julie woke early. While Dan lay snoring she eased herself out of his arms and crept into the bathroom. There she quickly pulled on some clothes, grabbed the minimal bikini, a towel and a bag and headed for the beach.

It was a beautiful morning, clear and windless and already warm. Julie had hoped the beach would be empty, but though it was early there were quite a few people about. She was starting to have misgivings, but her pride wouldn't let her turn back. Finding herself a secluded spot beyond a breakwater, she changed under her towel. Then, standing up and gazing defiantly out to sea, she revealed her bikini-clad form in all its glory.

A piercing wolf-whistle split the morning air. 'Oi! *Cheeky!*'

Julie swung round in alarm.

Above her on the promenade, three young men were leaning over the railing, grinning lasciviously. 'Careful you don't catch cold, darlin',' shouted one of them.

'Nice dumplings, love!' bawled another.

Julie's first impulse was to make a dash for the sea. But as luck would have it the tide was out, and she quailed at the thought of running fifty yards under the barrage of the yobs' raucous comments. Instead, she lay face-down on her towel, took out a book and affected to ignore them. Surely they'd soon tire of their moronic game and move away?

But her feigned disregard only spurred them on. Their shouts grew more boisterous. 'Nice bit o' rump steak there!' yelled one.

'*Two* nice bits!' his friend chortled. Julie gazed fixedly at her book, feeling her face turning red. Other beach-users stared, or came to see what it was all about. Soon a small crowd had gathered. Some angrily told the lads to move off (which only encouraged them to further subtle witticisms) but others added their own comments on Julie's costume, couched in more genteel terms.

'Disgusting!'

'Might as well be wearing nothing at all!'

'Soon will be, at this rate.'

'Young women these days! No shame!'

'Put her across my knee if she were mine.'

'Not as if this was *Brighton*, after all.'

At last Julie could bear it no longer. She stood up, avoiding anybody's eye, and reached for her things.

Just then a voice called politely, 'Over here please, miss!' Still bent over, she glanced round and saw, to her dismay, a young man taking her picture.

He lowered his camera and smiled amiably. 'Thanks, miss. With luck you'll make today's edition.'

Flustered and dishevelled, Julie regained the shelter of the hotel and stealthily re-entered her room. She breathed a sigh of relief: Dan was still sleeping soundly. Quietly she undressed, hid the bikini in a drawer and slipped in beside him. He half-woke and kissed her sleepily, caressing her breasts. 'Hi, darling,' he murmured and fell back to sleep.

The day passed uneventfully. They took a train to Weymouth for lunch, strolled on the beach, had a swim (Julie in a modest one-piece costume) and returned, tired but happy, in time for dinner. Occasionally the memory of the reporter troubled Julie's mind, but she dismissed it. Even if the picture was published, Dan would never see it. The *Bournemouth Echo* or whatever wasn't his kind of reading matter.

On Saturday nights at the Grand, a small orchestra in the dining room played popular hits of the day. As Julie entered with Dan she glanced over at them, and was taken aback when a trumpeter grinned at her and raised his instrument in ironic salute. It was one of the rowdy lads from the promenade. Still grinning, he got up and whispered to the bandleader who nodded, smiling. Bringing the song they were playing to a swift conclusion, the band segued smartly into a new number – a tune then riding high in the hit parade.

It – was – an
Itsy-bitsy teeny-weeny
Yellow polka-dot bikini
That she wore for the first time that day . . .

Alerted by the change of tune, guests looked up. Several of them noticed Julie and whispered to each other. One or two even tittered and pointed. Julie felt a hot blush of embarrassment flooding her cheeks.

Dan looked round, puzzled and faintly irritated. 'What are they snickering at?' he asked.

'Dunno,' Julie muttered. 'Let's sit down.'

As they sat down the tittering subsided, and Julie thankfully buried her flushed face in the menu. But worse was to come. Conscious of someone standing beside her, she looked up to see a young woman smiling uncertainly and holding out a newspaper.

'Excuse me,' said the stranger, giggling nervously, 'but would you sign it for me?'

THE NEAR-BARE LOOK COMES TO BOURNEMOUTH, read the headline. And there beneath it, right on the front page, was Julie, bending down and peering coquettishly, as it seemed, over her shoulder. Even in black and white the picture had come out well – especially the exposed and temptingly proffered half-moons of Julie's curvy bottom, white beneath the darker fabric in the monochrome picture.

'May I?' said Dan, snatching the paper without ceremony. He studied it briefly, then looked up at Julie. His eyes were expressionless. He glanced from her to the smirking musicians to the grins of their fellow guests, then abruptly stood up, thrusting the paper back at its startled owner. 'I think we'll skip dinner, Julie,' he said quietly. 'Let's go.'

On the way up to their room, Dan maintained a grim silence. Upstairs he locked the door, then swung round on his wife. 'Well?' he demanded. 'And just when was that taken?'

'This morning,' Julie admitted miserably. 'I went out early, while you were still asleep. I thought there'd be nobody about.'

'Your mistake,' Dan retorted. 'But an even bigger mistake, my girl, was wearing that bikini when I told

149

you not to. I *told* you what would happen, didn't I? But did you listen? Did you hell!'

'But I only wanted to get a proper tan,' Julie protested. 'What's so terrible about that?'

'What's so terrible? Oh, nothing at all. Only that you've ruined our holiday. Only that for the rest of this fortnight, wherever we go, not just in the hotel but all over the town, we're going to have people pointing and sniggering and making snide remarks. All because you, young lady, were so set on having your own way that nothing else mattered!'

Julie had never seen Dan angry before – not really angry, not like this. It gave her a strange fluttering in the pit of her stomach. Fear, yes, but something else too – something oddly like excitement. 'I'm sorry, darling,' she said in a small, penitent voice. 'I won't do it again, I promise.'

He glared at her furiously. 'Bit late now, isn't it? You know, I thought it was a bit strange what your mum was telling me just before the wedding. But now I'm beginning to realise she knew what she was talking about.'

A spasm of alarm contracted Julie's bottom-cheeks. *Oh no*, she thought, he couldn't mean – could he? 'What – what did she say?'

'That you were a sight too fond of getting your own way, young lady. And that the best treatment for you was a damn good smacked bottom! Well, I think that's just what you're asking for, my girl.'

'No! Dan – don't you dare!' Julie backed away as her irate young husband advanced on her. She'd intended it to sound defiant, but it came out more like a plaintive yelp. 'You can't! I won't let you!'

But Dan was in no mood to heed her protests. Seizing her by the wrist, he drew her over to the bed, sat down on it and pulled her down across his knee.

'No, Dan! Please! Don't!' Julie cried, putting a protective hand over her bottom, but he secured her slim wrist in his left hand and held it well out of the way while he rucked up the long velvet evening dress.

White nylon knickers, adorned with tiny blue flowers, fitted snugly over Julie's appealingly curved rear end. Held face-down in classic spanking posture, perfectly positioned for stern marital retribution, the petite blonde looked for all the world like a naughty little girl about to receive her just deserts. It was a delicious sight, but right now Dan was too angry to pause and admire it. Gripping the knickers by the waistband, he yanked them down well clear of the target area.

'Ooooh!' wailed Julie, as she felt the last protection stripped from her vulnerable rear. To the apprehension of her forthcoming punishment was added the humiliation of having her bottom bared. Though her mother had spanked her soundly and often, she had usually been allowed to keep her knickers on. This would be her first bare-bottom spanking in years – and, from the determined look on her young husband's face, she suspected he would show scant mercy to her sensitive flesh. 'Oh no, Dan, don't, *please*!' she begged.

But Dan was adamant. 'So you wanted to get a proper tan, did you?' he demanded grimly. 'Well, my sweet, you're about to get tanned better than you've ever been in your young life!'

His hand descended hard and fast, making contact with her rounded left cheek with a crisp clean smack that echoed round the room. Julie gasped and squirmed wildly, then yelped in dismay as his hand came down again, on her right cheek this time. The spanks stung like fury on her defenceless flesh-cushions. 'Owww! No! Dan, that really *hurts*!' she wailed.

'Good,' muttered her husband callously. 'It's meant to.' Rhythmically his vengeful palm rose and fell, now left, now right – each swat stinging vividly, igniting fires on her soft quivering globes. Julie yelped and squealed, kicking her legs and wriggling beneath the remorseless onslaught. But Dan had her pinioned in a firm grip, and there was no escape for the disobedient girl.

Julie had always taken pride in her handsome young husband's sinewy good looks, his broad chest and muscular arms. Now, to her dismay, she realised his strength could have its drawbacks – especially where a naughty teenager's sensitive bottom was concerned. Dan was showing her no mercy, putting the full strength of his anger behind every stroke, and his hard hand was hurting her rear end even worse than her mother's hairbrush used to do. Already her bottom was ablaze, and Dan had settled to a steady relentless rhythm that seemed set to go on for quite some time.

'Owww! Oh, Dan, that's enough! No more, *please*!' she begged. 'I'm sorry – I'll never do it again, I promise! Help! Oh stop, darling, please! You're hurting me!'

But, plead and protest as she might, poor Julie had no choice but to submit until Dan decided she'd had the spanking she deserved. Desperately she squirmed on his lap, trying to evade the steady fusillade of swats assaulting her rearward curves. No such luck; Dan, warming to his task, landed each smack with a sure aim. If, as it seemed, this was the only way to make his wilful young bride behave, then he intended to make a good job of it. This first spanking of Julie's married life would be a memorable experience – for both of them.

Again and again his punishing palm smacked down on Julie's soft pouting bottom, distributing the spanks all across the luscious globes, leaving no part of the target area neglected. Dan put all his anger and exasperation into his vigorous swats, gratified to know from Julie's anguished yelps and wails, and from the radiant blush that mantled her wriggling cheeks, that they were having a suitably chastening effect. Her fair skin marked readily and soon her peachy curves were suffused with a roseate glow that would have piqued the envy of a sunset.

Poor Julie's fears were justified. Dan was a sturdy and robust young man, well fitted to make her punishment long, hard and thorough. Tearfully, she begged for mercy, promising every kind of good behaviour if only he would stop smacking her tormented rear end. But not until every inch of the ripe mounds was bright red and sizzling hot, and her pleas had turned to inarticulate sobs, did he finally let her up and take the whimpering girl in his arms. 'OK, honey,' he murmured, gently stroking the glowing curves of her soundly smacked rear, 'you've had your punishment. I'm sorry I had to do that,' he added, not altogether truthfully, 'but you'll be a good girl from now on, won't you?'

'You're horrid! I hate you!' Julie insisted, pouting at him reproachfully. But she put up no resistance when he bent to kiss her trembling lips and slipped his hand down over her belly, his fingers dabbling in the telltale wetness between her legs. The heat of her spanked bottom was transmitting itself to adjacent parts, swelling her clitoris and filling her cleft with desire. Already the pain was easing, leaving an all-consuming ardent glow that demanded satisfaction. And, for all her complaints, the way her handsome young husband had treated her with such stern loving mastery rendered him irresistible to her.

Dan was feeling equally aroused. His anger had been genuine and his motives – at least to begin with – strictly punitive. But, even while venting his fury, he found that turning his pretty young wife over his lap and spanking her soft bare bottom was one of the most richly erotic pleasures he'd ever known. And now as he held her, murmuring soothing endearments, he relished the thought that this deliciously sexy marital chastisement would surely not be the last.

The prospect of spanking his naughty girl again, soon and often, swelled Dan's erection near to bursting point. Julie responded to his ardour, reaching down to liberate his eager penis and guiding him into her with gasps of passion. So aroused were they both that after only a few deep thrusts they exploded into a simultaneous climax that lifted and took them both to the furthest bounds of ecstasy.

But it took more than a single spanking, however soundly applied, to quell Julie's mutinous spirit. Waking early the next morning while Dan still slumbered beside her, she found herself torn by conflicting emotions. That spanking really hurt, she thought indignantly, sensing a lingering warmth in her rear end. How *dare* he? She, a grown-up married woman, to be spanked on her bare bottom like a naughty child! True, there had been something exciting about being punished across Dan's knee that way: for all the pain, it had felt strangely reassuring. And the sex afterwards had been fantastic, the best ever!

But, then again, just who the hell was he to tell her she couldn't wear her bikini, and to spank her when she chose to ignore his orders? She'd wear what she damn well pleased, *when* she pleased – so put *that* in your pipe, Dan McIntyre!

Quietly Julie slipped out of bed ...

Half an hour later she reclined happily, in all her scantily clad glory, on a remote beach at the far end of town. It was Sunday, so there were even fewer people about; no rowdy yobs this time, she was relieved to note. The sun felt delightfully warm on her skin. She closed her eyes and dozed.

Suddenly she felt a chill. Had the sun gone in? Blearily Julie peered up. A figure was blocking the sun. 'Hey,' she protested, 'could you move, please? I'm cold.'

'Oh, are you?' responded a familiar voice. 'Well, young lady, let's see if we can't warm you up a little.'

Julie gasped. 'Dan! How did you find me?'

'Not difficult,' replied her husband, kneeling down and fixing her with a look that boded no good.

'Beautiful young blondes tend to get noticed. A more interesting question, my sweet, is what are we going to do about you? You see, you just don't learn, do you? I really thought I'd spanked some sense into you last night, but I guess I just didn't spank you hard enough. Well, maybe *this*'ll help you remember.'

'Oh no!' yelped Julie as she realised what was coming. But before she could flee Dan had grabbed her, and to her horror she found herself sprawled over his knee, her bikini-clad bottom poised invitingly uppermost.

'Dan, *no!*' she wailed. 'Not here! People can see! Oh please, Dan, don't!'

'You bet they can,' retorted her husband. 'That's what you wanted, isn't it – lots of people to see you in your skimpy little bikini? To get a good look at this sexy young bottom of yours? Well, now they're going to get a ringside view.'

Julie squirmed frantically. Bad enough that she was going to be spanked again, and on a bottom still tender from last night's session. But to be spanked in public was too humiliating! 'Dan, please!' she begged desperately. 'Take me back to the hotel – you can spank me all you want there! I know I deserve it. But not like this – with people watching! I'll just die!'

But this time Dan was determined to get through to his wilful young wife, and if a public spanking was what it took then so be it. 'You should have thought of that sooner, young lady,' he told her, brushing the sand off his hands, 'before you broke the promise you gave me last night. Think yourself lucky I don't take your bikini down. But, since it leaves so much of your bottom bare, I think I can do a pretty good job just the same.'

Peering apprehensively over her shoulder, Julie gulped in alarm as Dan raised his hand high in the air. The next moment she yelped as it cracked down across her temptingly exposed mounds with a vivid report that rang out across the quiet beach.

'Owww!' Julie wailed. On her still-tender bottom Dan's hard hand stung like fury. 'Oh no, Dan, please!'

She might have saved her breath. Remorselessly her husband's hand rose and fell while Julie yipped and wriggled, uttering heartfelt pleas for forgiveness as the heat built up in her gyrating bottom-cheeks. Dan was in no mood to be forgiving. His errant bride would be spanked just as thoroughly this morning in public, he resolved, as in private the night before. So, for what seemed to poor Julie an eternity, swat after stinging swat fanned the flames on her defenceless rear, each one hurting worse than the last. Her only consolation, as spanks rained down hard and steadily on her tormented hindquarters, was that yesterday's news photographer hadn't shown up. That would have been the ultimate humiliation.

Not that her chastisement lacked for an audience. The spectacle of a pretty girl being spanked on her all-but-bare bottom wasn't so common in 1960s Bournemouth as to pass unnoticed. The beach had seemed almost deserted when Julie's punishment started, but as if from nowhere a small crowd soon gathered to watch the show. It was well worth watching, too. The slim, shapely blonde, her bare legs kicking in the sand and her blonde mane tossing wildly, a deepening blush enhancing the beauty of her lush rearward curves, made a glorious sight in the clear morning sunlight.

One or two of the spectators murmured uneasily, but most of them were clearly enjoying the show. 'That's the little minx who was in the paper yesterday,' remarked one man to his companion, a pretty brunette not much older than Julie. 'Didn't I say she needed a damn good spanking? Glad to see she's getting it, too, flaunting herself like that!' He fixed the brunette with a baleful eye. 'And if I catch you wearing anything like that, young lady . . . !' The girl giggled nervously and chewed her lip, her fascinated gaze fixed on Julie's bouncing reddening rump.

Unfazed by his audience, Dan continued to spank Julie soundly, concentrating his fire on the exposed half-moons of her lower cheeks and especially on the soft sensitive undercurve where bottom meets thigh. If she had ever wondered just how much of her pert globes the ill-fated bikini left uncovered, she was now getting very tangible evidence.

'Oh stop, please, Dan,' she wailed, writhing wildly as the merciless spanks rained down. 'No more, please! I'm sorry! I'll never wear it again, I promise! Oh please, please stop!'

'Too right you won't, honey,' retorted her husband, smacking away with unabated gusto, 'because after we're through here I'm going to take it away and burn it. But, before I do, I'm going to make sure something else is burning!'

So saying, he unleashed a salvo of hard fast smacks that made Julie squeal and kick up her heels. One of her flailing feet kicked over her beach-bag, and – alas, poor Julie! – out fell sun-oil, a paperback novel – and a hairbrush. A black wooden hairbrush with a handle and a flat oval back, just perfect for applying to a naughty girl's already well-warmed bottom.

With a dangerous grin, Dan reached down and picked up the wicked-looking implement. 'Ah,' he said, 'just what I need. How thoughtful of you to bring it, my love.'

Julie gasped in dismay. 'Oh, Dan, no!' she begged plaintively. 'Not the hairbrush, please! It'll really hurt!'

'Oh, will it now?' asked Dan, patting her roseate rump with the back of the brush. 'So my hand-spanking doesn't *really* hurt, then? Seems I haven't been spanking you hard enough, young lady. Well, this should do the trick.'

He raised the brush high in the air, prompting sharp intakes of breath from the rapt spectators. Then down it swept, contacting the tender target area with a sharp crack that elicited a shrill squeal from Julie. And again and again, now right, now left, turning her bouncing behind from bright scarlet to a rich deep crimson.

Frenziedly, Julie squirmed and wriggled, trying to evade the brush's cruel kiss. But Dan had her firmly pinioned and there was no escape. Spankings from her mother, she now realised, were nothing compared to the impact on her vulnerable rear end of a hairbrush wielded by determined male muscles. Each stroke seared her flesh, igniting fresh fires on her sizzling-hot mounds. To poor Julie, it felt as if she'd never sit down in comfort again.

Ceasing to struggle, she lay limply over her husband's lap, her frantic pleas reduced to inarticulate sobs of 'Sorry – sorry – sorry . . .'

But Dan was not to be diverted from his purpose. He felt a fierce protective joy in holding his headstrong young wife over his knee and giving her the spanking she deserved; and to do so in front of others only strengthened his resolve. So for several minutes the crisp sound of hard wooden brush on soft female bottom-flesh, accompanied by remorseful wails, rang out across the sunlit beach. Only when Julie's twin globes were blushing like ripe tomatoes did he at last relent.

'OK, my sweet,' he told her, stroking her soundly spanked curves, 'I think you've learnt your lesson. Up you get.'

With murmurs of amusement and appreciation, the crowd started to disperse as Julie rose painfully and hid her tearstained face in her husband's shoulder, gingerly rubbing her flaming *derrière*.

Dan stroked her hair, murmuring soothing words and feeling a surge of tenderness and desire for his wayward love. 'Come on, bad girl,' he whispered, 'back to the hotel. I've got something here that'll make you feel much better.'

* * *

The scandalous bikini, as Dan had promised, met a premature end in the hotel fireplace. And for the rest of their holiday Julie's behaviour showed a marked improvement. No longer did she throw tantrums, stamp or sulk; no longer did she demand her own way. Mentally Dan raised a glass to his mother-in-law, marvelling what magic could be worked on a stubborn young woman by such a simple – and simply delicious – expedient as toasting her bottom.

Yet, oddly enough, Julie must somehow have contrived to misbehave. How else to explain the fact that, at least half a dozen times before their return home, the pretty little blonde found herself turned over her husband's sturdy knee, her sweetly rounded bare bottom bouncing and reddening beneath his punitive palm? Surely she must have been naughty – what other explanation could there possibly be?

On one of these occasions of marital discipline, it happened that a passing chambermaid, hearing the sound of yelps, gasps and vigorous smacks, couldn't resist putting her eye to the keyhole. And, even in prestigious establishments like the Grand Hotel, Bournemouth, gossip has a way of spreading.

When, on the last day of their holiday, Dan and Julie entered the dining room for dinner, Dan was puzzled to see the orchestra's leader wink at him as they launched into a new tune. Julie, luckily for her potential embarrassment, wasn't familiar with it. But Dan, who knew his Gershwin, permitted himself a quiet grin as he recognised the big chorus number from the second act of *Porgy and Bess*:

'*Oh, I can't sit down . . .*'

12

Tutoring Miss Lillian – An Edwardian Romance

On a crisp clear morning in the spring of 1903, a pony-chaise might have been seen approaching the gates of Cartwright Hall in Lincolnshire. It carried a sole passenger, a young man named Walter Jessop. A few weeks earlier, he had been one of the most promising scholars of Pembroke College in Oxford. But the sudden death of his father, his financial affairs in sad disarray, had obliged Walter to break off his studies. Now the sole support of his widowed mother and young sister, he had bowed to necessity and taken a post as private tutor to the heiress of the Cartwright estate.

As the chaise swung round a bend in the road, the driver pointed with his whip. 'There be the Hall, young sir.'

In the distance Walter saw a handsome Jacobean pile, venerable but still robustly well preserved. The same, he soon found, could not be said of its owner. Mr Merton Cartwright, Walter's employer, proved to be an elderly gentleman who spoke in a whisper so faint the young man had to bend to catch his words. Sunk deep in a huge studded leather armchair in the dusty air of his library, an ancient tome open on his lap, Mr Cartwright seemed so fragile that any sound louder than the turning of a page might loosen his scant hold on life. Only his eyes were fully alive. Startlingly blue, they blazed with an ironic intelligence in the dry parchment-like old face.

'So you have come to tutor my niece, Mr Jessop?' he enquired in his papery whisper. 'D'you think you can?'

'I don't see why not, sir,' responded Walter staunchly. 'At Oxford I was accounted a good scholar.'

The old man gave a thin smile. 'No doubt, else I should not have engaged you. But scholarship may not be enough, young man. My niece is a headstrong creature – what is known, I believe, as a New Woman. She has an excellent mind, as you will discover, but applies it just when and as she feels inclined. Any notion of discipline is wholly foreign to her. Her father died when she was an infant and her mother – my poor dear sister – did not long survive him. I, as you see, am a poor sickly specimen, in no state to impose conduct upon a wilful girl. That, Mr Jessop, will be your task.'

'I shall do my best to prove equal to it, sir.'

Mr Cartwright regarded him quizzically. 'I'm sure you will – do your best, that is. But I should warn you that Lilly has already seen off a whole procession of tutors and governesses, all of whom doubtless strove to do their best.'

Half an hour later, Walter was shown into the room set aside as a schoolroom. Spring sunshine flooded through the high mullioned casements, so that at first he did not see the girl who stood watching him by the window. Her voice, clear and musical, made him start. 'Well, at least you're not positively repellent!'

Peering into the dazzling light, Walter perceived approaching him a strikingly attractive young woman. Lillian Trent, eighteen-year-old heiress to the Cartwright fortune, seemed to blaze with vitality: a mass of red-gold curls framed a lovely face whose fresh beauty was, if anything, enhanced by a hint of stubbornness about the mouth. Her dress, elegantly simple, betrayed a slim and fetchingly nubile figure.

'I'm gratified that I don't repel you at first sight, Miss Trent,' said Walter, bowing slightly. 'I hope you'll think as highly of my teaching methods.'

'Oh, as to that,' she flung back carelessly, 'I'm sure you'll prove an intolerable bore like all the others!'

Boredom, Walter soon found, came readily to Lillian Trent. She had a lively intelligence and rapidly grasped the essential principles of all subjects. But once she reached that point where brilliant intuition no longer sufficed, and a little patient persistence was required, she lost interest. 'Oh! What a *bore*!' she would exclaim, and refuse to study further, demanding a change of subject or tripping scornfully away with a toss of her pretty head.

This could not go on, Walter mused to himself. As long as she was given her head, his pupil was frankly unteachable. He could resign, but what then would become of his mother and sister? Besides, his surroundings were agreeable, his salary not ungenerous – and Lillian, when not in a petulant mood, had a bewitching smile. No, Walter resolved, he would not give up so easily. Something must be done about this sweet seductive and utterly spoilt girl.

The inevitable clash came one morning some ten days after his arrival at Cartwright Hall, while he was attempting a German lesson. Though her pronunciation was excellent, and she sang Schubert *lieder* charmingly, Lillian showed a blithe indifference to the intricacies of German grammar. 'Oh pooh!' she cried, springing to her feet, when Walter pointed out her umpteenth fault in declension. 'The devil take the stupid Germans and their stupid adjectival endings! I shan't waste another second on this idiotic language! I'm off!'

'Miss Trent,' responded Walter, quietly but firmly, 'if you persist in flouncing off at every difficulty, you will never learn anything. You have an excellent brain; all you lack is application, and it's my job to help you

162

acquire it. Now, I must insist that we complete the lesson.'

Lillian's eyes blazed with anger, and she stamped her foot pettishly. 'Oh, you insist, do you? And who are you, a hired tutor, to *insist*? I'm off, and I'd like to see you stop me!'

The insult stung Walter to the quick, the more sharply since he could scarcely refute it. He was indeed a hireling, but it wounded his pride to be reminded of it – especially by a chit of a girl. He still spoke quietly, but there was a dangerous edge to his voice that Lillian would have done well to heed. 'I may be merely a hired tutor, Miss Trent. But one of the duties I was hired to discharge was to instil in you some sense of discipline. And since you persist in acting, not like a well-bred young lady, but like a spoilt brat, I'm tempted to impart that lesson by the most appropriate means.'

Lillian glared in disbelief. 'Are you threatening me with violence?' she cried.

'Yes, Miss Trent, I am. That is, if you include under that heading the treatment you so richly deserve – namely, a good sound spanking.'

The girl's cheeks flushed with indignation. 'How dare you – you wretch!' she exclaimed, and struck Walter hard across the face.

The next moment, to her great surprise, Lillian Trent found herself face-down across Walter's knee, her pretty nose inches from the parquet floor. She kicked and struggled, emitting cries of fury, but he was a well-built young man, and her efforts to escape were in vain.

Walter too was surprised, indeed taken aback by his own temerity. The idea of spanking the girl had been an exasperated impulse, not the fruit of mature consideration; now that he found himself on the point of doing so, he was overwhelmed by alarm. That he, a mere paid tutor, should dare lay violent hands on the heiress to the

Cartwright estate – why, it was outrageous! The consequences would surely be dire.

But his hesitation lasted barely a second. True, he was courting disaster. But simply by putting Lillian across his knee he had already burnt his boats. The outrage was committed: to release her unspanked would gain him nothing. Chastising her would surely relieve his feelings, and in any case a sound spanking was just what she deserved. Besides, she was enchantingly pretty – and the light fabric of her morning gown, clinging close about her rearward curves, revealed that not least of her feminine charms was a deliciously rounded and eminently spankable bottom.

With a sigh that might equally have betokened resignation or pleasure, Walter raised his right hand and spanked. Hard. Lillian gasped, kicking her legs wildly, as Walter's vengeful palm descended again. And again. And again.

It was a brief spanking, but an effective one. For two minutes or so, Walter's arm rose and fell, smacking Lillian hard and fast and igniting on her squirming posterior such a blazing heat as she had never known. Not in all her eighteen years had anyone raised a hand to this headstrong girl, and she had no notion how vividly a determined male palm could sting soft female bottom-flesh. The thin organdie fabric of her gown offered scant protection. Each resounding spank hurt worse than the one before, and her outraged shrieks rang round the room.

When Walter finally let her up, Lillian's face was flushed and she was weeping as much from anger and humiliation as from pain. 'You brute!' she cried, her hands clasped to her smarting *derrière*. 'I shall have you thrown out!' Sobbing, she rushed from the room.

Left alone, Walter found himself seized by confused emotions. He had ruined his newfound career almost before it had started. Mr Cartwright would dismiss him without a reference, and he might never find such another post. Still, it had afforded him huge satisfaction to chastise the lovely impossible girl as she so richly merited. Satisfaction – and, he could not conceal from himself, pleasure. Spanking that sweet young bottom, feeling the tender globes quiver and gyrate beneath his hand, had proved one of the most exquisite erotic experiences he had known. It was with a sense of loss that he reflected he would never have the chance to repeat it.

Within a few minutes there came the expected summons to Mr Cartwright's presence. But, before Walter could blurt out more than a few words, the old man raised his hand. 'One moment, Mr Jessop. Am I to understand from my niece that you took it upon yourself to *spank* her?'

'Well, yes, sir. You see –'

'No explanation is necessary, young man.' The old man's eyes shone with amusement, and he emitted a quiet wheezy chuckle. 'I am delighted to hear it, and I am sure she eminently deserved no less. Were I not so enfeebled, I should have done as much myself years ago. Pray do not think of resigning your post. On the contrary, I am most anxious that you should stay, and to that end I propose to double your salary.'

Lillian Trent did not return to her lessons that morning. Nor did she appear at lunch, sending word that she had a headache. Walter reflected that the discomfort was probably situated quite elsewhere in her anatomy. However, she reappeared for dinner, and he was pleased to note that she took her seat at table somewhat gingerly. She avoided his gaze throughout the meal, but as she rose after dessert their eyes crossed; Lillian blushed charmingly, and hastened from the room.

The next morning, rather to Walter's surprise, his pupil attended her lessons as usual. She made no reference to the previous day's events, but he detected an expression in her eyes that, in a less independent-minded young woman, might almost have been taken for respect.

Whether as a result of the spanking, or of what had passed between her and her uncle, from then on Lillian applied herself to her studies with unwonted diligence. Walter was delighted: with her quick apprehension and acute intelligence, she was a pleasure to teach. True, now and then her attention wandered and the words 'What a *bore!*' rose unbidden to her lips. But Walter had only to murmur, 'Discipline, Miss Trent,' and with a faint blush the girl would readdress herself to the task in hand.

Shorn of her petulant airs, Lillian proved a charming, indeed enchanting, companion. Frequently, she and Walter were thrown together after lessons were over for the day, and it seemed she enjoyed his society. Nor was this for want of any other, for suitors for her hand were never lacking. As the richest heiress in the county, young and beautiful into the bargain, she attracted a constant stream of admirers – none of them, in Walter's wholly unprejudiced view, remotely worthy of her.

Among the most assiduous visitors was Mr Cartwright's nearest neighbour, Sir Hubert Tremayne. A plump ungainly individual in his thirties, he was master of several hundred acres, all heavily mortgaged. But who could doubt that any personal or financial deficiencies were eclipsed by the glory of his title, one of the most ancient baronetcies in the land?

Sir Hubert, Walter was glad to note, received scant encouragement from Lillian in his lumbering courtship. On the contrary, she treated him with open contempt, frequently choosing the hapless baronet as the target of her humour at the dinner table. Most of her shafts being too subtle for his dull wit, Sir Hubert generally responded by smiling uneasily, though not without a certain bovine complacency, perhaps taking her mockery for a mark of affection.

Now and then, though, a satirical thrust would penetrate even Sir Hubert's suety carapace, making him dimly aware of the scorn behind her raillery. 'Oh I say, Miss Lilly,' he protested after one such sally, 'you're a bit hard on a fellah! I'm not a complete fool, y'know.'

'Indeed, Sir Hubert?' enquired Lillian sweetly. 'Then do tell me – just which parts are you missing?'

Walter could not suppress an involuntary snort of mirth. Sir Hubert shot him an irate glance.

Not all Lillian's suitors, by a long way, were as fatuous as Sir Hubert. But, to Walter's gratification, she seemed to prefer the company of her young tutor to that of her admirers, no matter how handsome and well born.

As the weather grew warmer, Lillian took to riding in the afternoons, and Walter often accompanied her. No great horseman, he found in the stables a placid grey mare to suit him. Lillian, who rode superbly, easily outpaced him on her black stallion, and could not resist taunting him for his slowness. More than once, as she cantered ahead of him, Walter found himself studying the jouncing curves of her pretty young bottom, and recalling how they had jounced even more deliciously when he spanked them. One more jibe about his poor horsemanship, he mused, and he would be sorely tempted to repeat the treatment.

One hot afternoon in July, they rode to the furthest reach of the estate, where a hill clothed in ancient woods gave on to a hazy distance of soft rolling countryside. Dismounting by a venerable chestnut tree, whose gnarled roots afforded natural seating, they left their horses to crop the nearby grass.

Lillian was looking her loveliest. Her red-gold hair, tousled from her ride, fell in profusion about her face; her hazel eyes sparkled with vitality; and the close-fitting riding habit made the most of her alluring figure. As they talked, she smiled on Walter so beguilingly that, before he knew what he was doing, he had taken her in his arms and kissed her.

She returned his kiss with enthusiasm. It was a long and fervent embrace, and when Walter finally released the lovely girl it was only to blurt out, without stopping to think what he was saying, 'Dear Lillian – Lilly – will you marry me?'

At these words, the change to Lillian's face was startling. Her expression of dreamy arousal gave way to one of utter contempt. Pushing Walter away so rudely that he almost toppled over, she sprang to her feet.

'Not you as well!' she exclaimed furiously. 'I thought you were different. But you're just another squalid little fortune-hunter, aren't you? Like all the rest! Just like that fat fool Hubert!'

Walter sat thunderstruck as the implications of her words sank in. The ardour of her embrace had been unmistakable; yet his impulsive proposal was rejected with scorn. As for comparing him with the oafish Sir Hubert, that was the last straw. Anger rose in him, and his voice trembled with rage. 'So that's what you think of me, young lady? The humble tutor – good enough to amuse yourself with as a brief fling, but quite unworthy to aspire to your ladyship's hand? I thought better of you, Lillian Trent. You're not just a spoilt brat, you're a conceited little snob to boot! Well, you'll be treated as you deserve!'

Half-rising, he seized her by the wrist. She cried out and made to strike at him with her riding crop, but he grasped that hand as well, pulling her inexorably down towards him. There was fear in her eyes but also, he perceived, a covert hint of excitement.

'Walter! You wouldn't . . . rape me?' she implored.

He grinned sardonically. 'You flatter yourself, my girl. No, I merely mean to complete the treatment I

started a few weeks ago. I thought I'd spanked some
good manners into you, young lady, but it seems I
didn't do the job thoroughly enough. I shan't make the
same mistake this time!'

Ignoring her outraged protests, Walter pulled Lillian
down across his knee and turned her riding skirt up
above her waist. She kicked and struggled wildly, but he
clamped his right leg over both her thighs, pinioning her
in position, and surveyed the tempting target now
revealed to his gaze.

She wore no petticoats, and her raised skirt disclosed
a charming pair of lace-trimmed *directoires* whose
creamy silk fabric clung closely to the delectably
rounded flesh, hugging it like a second skin. Such fine
material would offer little protection; but the temptation
to see, and spank, Lillian's sweet bare bottom was too
great to resist. As well be hung for a sheep as a lamb,
Walter murmured to himself, as, hooking two fingers in
the waistband of her undergarment, he drew the lacy
fabric down over her ripe rearward curves.

As she felt herself denuded of her most intimate
garment, Lillian writhed desperately. 'No! Walter! How
dare you!' she shrieked, and flung one hand back to
shield her naked rump. But Walter captured her wrist in
his left hand, and lowered her drawers until they hung
in a silken tangle around her knees.

Her bottom was soft, full and flawless, its plump
contours the more voluptuous by contrast with the
slimness of her waist. Walter regarded it with delight,
then raised his hand and brought it down with a ringing
smack that echoed through the woods.

'Aaaah!' Lillian gasped in pain and surprise. She
remembered how much her first punishment had stung;
but to be spanked on her bared bottom, she now
realised, would sting considerably more. Another
smack, just as hard, left her in no doubt. 'Oww!' she
wailed. 'Walter! Stop it! That *hurts!*'

'I'm delighted to hear it, young lady,' her tutor responded pitilessly, continuing to spank her quivering mounds with gusto, 'and I can assure you it'll hurt a great deal more before I'm done. Since this may well be the last lesson I shall ever give you, I mean to impress it effectively upon your – memory.'

'Owww! No! Walter! Let me – aahaah! – go at once!' Lillian yelped, but Walter was as good as his word. His arm was strong, his hand was hard and his frustration was enhanced by anger that this lovely girl, whom in many ways he adored, should appear so heartless a minx. He would soon part with her forever, but first he was resolved to give her a chastisement she would remember the rest of her days.

So there in that sunlit glade Walter spanked spoilt young Lillian Trent long and hard on her squirming bare bottom, relishing his task, taking care to cover every inch of her soft girlish roundnesses with resounding smacks. So crisply did they ring through the woods that a gamekeeper half a mile off on the next estate paused to wonder who was chopping trees in the Old Copse. Each stinging spank deepened the blush on Lillian's nether cheeks, turning the luscious young flesh from white to pink, from pink to rosy red, until the full expanse of her lovely orbs was suffused with a rich fiery glow.

Writhing helplessly over Walter's knee, Lillian now heartily repented having treated him with such contempt. Her russet curls tossed and her long legs kicked wildly as the heat built up in her shapely rear, each remorseless spank fanning the flames ever more hotly. She was being punished, humiliated, hurt as she had never been hurt before; yet in some strange fashion she felt assured, protected even – as if she had been found out and known in her most secret place, and was now held firmly there and treated severely but justly. Once before she had provoked this man to anger, and had suffered the consequences. If now he again visited retribution on her, it was no more than her due, and she could find it in herself to respect him for it. But – owww! – would he *never* stop?

As her spanking progressed, her outraged yells gave way to tearful pleas for forgiveness. But Walter felt no pity; rather, a fierce joy possessed him. Lillian was a delight to spank: her gasps and yelps warmed his heart, and her bottom, so soft and sensitive, bouncing beneath his vengeful palm, appeared yet more beautiful now it was blushing bright red. He could happily have gone on spanking her all day.

But at last he paused and Lillian believed her ordeal was over. Then to her horror she saw him pick up the riding crop that had fallen from her hand. 'Oh no, Walter! Please! Not that!' she wailed, but her tutor was merciless.

'You tried to strike me with this, young lady,' he told her, disregarding her frantic pleas. 'I think you may come to regret it.'

Swish-CRACK!

'Yaaa-haaah!' squealed Lillian as the slender crop cracked across her already anguished bottom. A crimson stripe sprang up against the scarlet of the spanked cushions. Walter regarded it with satisfaction, then went on to print two dozen more alongside the original, until the whole expanse of the girl's bottom glowed dark red. Lillian writhed desperately, begging for mercy. 'Owwww! Oh, Walter, no more, I beg you! *Owwww!* Oh stop, please! I'm sorry! Aaaah! Oh, it hurts so!'

After the 25th stroke, Walter stopped and let the sobbing girl slide off his knees to the woodland floor, where she lay whimpering face-down, her blazing mounds on display. Walter leant down and gently stroked her hair. 'Goodbye, Lilly,' he murmured, then mounted his horse and rode off down the valley, his mind seething. He would never see her again, he was sure, and the thought stabbed his heart; yet there was pleasure in knowing that he had chastised her as she so richly merited. What none of her high-born suitors, no matter how provoked, had ever dared do, he – the penniless tutor – had achieved. Of that at least he could be proud, come what may.

It was late in the afternoon by the time Walter regained the Hall. Seeking out Mr Cartwright in the library, he tendered his immediate resignation. The old man received the news with regret but, recognising Walter's resolve, made no attempt to dissuade him.

Loath to spend even another night at the Hall, Walter asked a parlour maid to enquire about trains and arrange for the post-chaise to be brought round, then repaired to his room to pack his things. While he was so engaged, there came a light tap at the door. 'Come in!' he cried, expecting the maid with the train times, and continued to pack without looking round.

'Walter.' The voice behind him was soft and sweet and low.

He swung round. 'Lilly! I thought – I expected never to see you again, after . . .'

'After you'd spanked me so unmercifully?' She smiled ruefully, and her hand strayed involuntarily to her still tender rear. 'Indeed, you were very cruel. But you know –' she moved closer and touched his arm, gazing up at him appealingly '– I think perhaps I deserved it. What you did was quite unforgivable, of course. But what I said was no less so. So may we not forgive each other for our unforgivable faults?'

She was very close now. There was a softness and submissiveness in her expression that he had never seen there before, and a hint of tremulousness about her lower lip. She had never seemed more adorable to him. He held her close and kissed her, and for some time there was silence in the room.

Finally, Walter spoke. 'Lilly – dear, sweet, infuriating Lilly – will you marry me?'

'They will call you a fortune-hunter, Walter,' she responded teasingly.

'Let them call me what they will. I have known what it is to be poor, and have learnt the value of money. With me as your husband your fortune will be far safer than with any of those titled drones. Once more, will you marry me?'

She shot him an enigmatic look. 'Tell me, Walter, if I become your wife, will you still be so cruel as to spank me?'

'Certainly, my darling, with the greatest of pleasure – very soundly, and whenever you deserve it. As a loving and conscientious husband with your best interests at heart, I could do no less. Now, for the third and last time: will you marry me?'

'And what, pray, will you do if I refuse?' she enquired, glancing up at him coquettishly from beneath her lashes.

Walter smiled. 'Then, my beloved, I shall once more put you across my knee, bare your impudent bottom and spank you smartly until you say yes.'

'In that case,' she murmured with a provocative pout, 'I shall *not* say yes – for at least the next five minutes . . .'

13

'Spank Me Baby, Don't Mean Maybe': the Missing Chapter from *Brave New World*

In a recent article on 'Spanking in Literature', I noted that Aldous Huxley often betrayed an interest in the subject, and that 'spanking references, if no actual spankings' showed up in several of his novels. A few months later, I was intrigued to receive a packet from a post-graduate student working at a certain Southwestern US university that holds an extensive collection of Huxley's papers.

Both the post-grad and the college must remain anonymous, since she tells me she found these pages in a file marked EMBARGOED – NOT FOR PUBLICATION. But it's clear that what we have here is a hitherto suppressed episode that Huxley originally intended for his best-known novel, the 1932 satirical futurist classic Brave New World.

The novel's set in a sterile technological 26th-century utopia whose deity is Henry Ford. Bernard Marx, a top-caste 'Alpha' tormented by a sense of dissatisfaction with the supposedly perfect society he lives in, is on vacation in New Mexico with the lovely and 'wonderfully pneumatic' young Lenina Crowne. Though Bernard finds Lenina highly desirable, he's irritated by her mindless tendency to parrot the glib propaganda phrases of this 'brave new world', and to urge 'a gramme of soma' (a euphoric drug) on him every time he expresses unconventional opinions. Eventually his patience wears thin . . .

From their hotel window, on the 65th floor, Bernard Marx gazed moodily out at the towers of Santa Fe. Except for the luminous blue sky overhead, there was little to distinguish them from the familiar multistorey towers of Charing T. He turned back to face the room. Impersonal in its luxury, it offered much the same comforts as his own apartment: liquid air, television, vibro-vacuum massage, boiling caffeine solution, soma dispenser, heated contraceptives, synthetic music vents, multiple-choice scent diffuser. Below him, on the lower floors, his fellow guests were no doubt happily engaged in erotic play, or in games of Escalator-Squash-Racquets or Electro-Magnetic Obstacle Golf, just as at home.

Why bother, Bernard mused morosely to himself, when every place was like every other, all offering the same prospects, the same comforts, the same hazard-free, well-regulated diversions. Even, he reflected bitterly, as Lenina emerged from the bathroom wearing only her shell-pink zippicamiknicks and undulated seductively towards him across the deep-pile carpet, her arms raised to embrace him, even the same lush, flawless, infinitely desirable flesh. Lovely as Lenina undoubtedly was, he could no doubt have found other girls just as lovely, just as unhesitatingly compliant, here in Santa Fe. 'Why bother?' he repeated out loud.

'Oh, Bernard!' Lenina stopped in her tracks. Her arms dropped back to her sides and she gazed at him with a hurt expression in her eyes. 'But I thought you liked me. Everyone says I'm awfully pneumatic.' She regarded her curvaceous person worriedly. 'Am I *too* plump for you? Is that what it is?'

She turned, presenting her rearward charms for Bernard's consideration. Even in his disillusioned mood, he had to admit that they were superb. Lenina's full perky breasts, crowned with rosy nipples, her elegantly turned legs, her moist full-lipped smile, her wide blue eyes and lustrous blonde hair were all in their own way glorious; but her bottom was a triumph of the geneticist's art, honed to perfection over six centuries. Generation after generation of spermatozoa and ova, lovingly selected for the dominant gene of callipygousness, of exceptional posterior beauty, had been painstakingly bred, matched and spliced, nourished and nurtured in optimum laboratory conditions of impeccable sterility; inspected, appraised and approved by team upon team of dedicated biologists; and these delectable twin globes, offered now to Bernard's reluctantly admiring gaze, were the triumphant outcome. Rounded, soft and peachy, a delight to the eye and an irresistible temptation to the hand, Lenina Crowne's hinder parts were the apotheosis of female bottomhood.

Faced with irresistible temptation, who was Bernard to resist? Almost despite himself, his hand reached out to squeeze and fondle the shapely hemispheres, whose succulent flesh the satiny fabric of the zippicamiknicks hugged as intimately as a second skin. Coyly, the twin mounds yielded to his libidinous palping, their tender roundnesses rippling beneath his exploring fingers.

'Thank Ford,' Lenina breathed to herself as she felt Bernard's tactile homage to her nether orbs, 'he's all right again.' And, as she had told her friend Fanny, he did have awfully nice hands.

She remained facing away from him until she judged the moment propitious, then turned and wound her arms about Bernard's neck, completing the interrupted embrace. Feeling his body respond to hers, she purred happily, nibbled his earlobe and began to murmur her favourite erotic incantation:

Hug me till you drug me, honey,
Kiss me till I'm in a coma,
Hug me, honey, snuggly bunny,
Love's as good as *soma* . . .

Disgusted, Bernard pushed her brutally away. 'Oh, for Ford's sake,' he snapped, 'don't you have a single original thought in your head?'

Lenina gaped at him, confused by this unfamiliar concept. 'I don't know what you mean,' she stammered, tears filling her blue eyes. 'Oh, Bernard, I just wanted us to have fun.'

'Fun? Oh, of course, by all means. Ford forbid that we should fail to have fun when the opportunity presents itself! And then, after we've had fun – what then? More fun, no doubt, and then more, and more. Fun unlimited, fun without end – fun to the furthest reaches of eternity!'

'But what's wrong with that?' protested Lenina helplessly.

'Oh, nothing – nothing whatsoever,' Bernard retorted. 'But if fun's all we want, then we might as well be Gammas, mightn't we? Or even Deltas or Epsilons. They have fun too, don't they?'

'Well, yes, but not as good. I mean – well, it's wonderful to be an Alpha, isn't it? Especially an Alpha-Plus like you, Bernard. You should be happy about it.'

'Oh, I am. Deliriously, stupidly happy. How could I not be? A hundred and twenty repetitions three times a week for thirty months, right through my infant sleeping hours, telling me how happy I was. So, inevitably, I am. But, you see, so are the Betas. "I'm really awfully glad I'm a Beta," they'll tell you brightly, for all the world as if they'd worked it out for their own stupid selves. And the Gammas are awfully glad too, and so are the Deltas and the Epsilons. All of them awfully, marvellously, damnably glad!'

'A gramme is better than a damn,' Lenina responded automatically.

Bernard groaned. '*Soma*. That's all you know, isn't it? Every time I try to talk to you, to express ideas of my own, all you can suggest is *soma*. Or fun, of course.'

'But your ideas are so dreadful, Bernard. They make me feel uncomfortable, and I'm sure they're what's making you so miserable. And if you'd just take *soma* you'd forget all about them. Remember,' she added, reaching for another reassuring nugget of infant-learnt wisdom, 'one cubic centimetre cures ten gloomy sentiments. Oh, do let me give you some!'

Without waiting for Bernard's response, Lenina turned and bent over the *soma* dispenser, once more presenting him with a fine prospect of her delectable rump; indeed, an even finer prospect than before, since her semi-inclined posture enhanced the lush curvature of her buttocks, jutting them invitingly towards him. As she operated the dispenser, her movements caused the soft mounds to tremble appealingly.

The impulse seemed beyond Bernard's control. All his irritation at Lenina, his disgust with himself, his frustration, anger and resentment collected together, coalesced and flowed down his right arm into his open hand. The hand rose of its own accord.

The noise of that prodigious slap rang round the room like a pistol shot.

'Ow!' Lenina shot upright, gazing over her shoulder with huge horrified eyes. She clapped one hand to her injured bottom-cheek.

Bernard gazed back, feeling the power and vibrant impact of the smack swell to possess his whole being. Suddenly he knew what, at that moment, he wanted to do more than anything else in the world.

Reaching out, he grasped the astonished girl by the wrist. 'Come here, Lenina,' he said. 'I'm going to spank you.'

'But – what – why – oh, Bernard, please, no!'

But her protests were in vain. Filled with determination and a fierce glee, Bernard drew her inexorably towards the bed, sat down on it and pulled her face-down over his lap, positioning her so that the voluptuous contours of her bottom curved uppermost. Encased in the skin-tight zippicamiknicks, whose sheer pink fabric moulded itself lovingly to the dimpled flesh, the beautifully rounded twin globes presented themselves alluringly ripe for smacking.

Bernard paused for a moment, savouring the exquisite sense of anticipation, then brought his hand down in a resounding spank.

Lenina wailed as it stung her sensitive flesh. 'Oww! Oh no, don't –'

But again the hand descended, swiftly and implacably; again and again and again. Desperately Lenina squealed and writhed as the heat built up in her gyrating rear; pitifully she implored him to stop. To no avail. Not until several dozen vigorous smacks had made their impact smartingly felt did Bernard pause; and then, Lenina realised with dismay, it was only to remove the scant protection of her zippicamiknicks.

Zip! The garment, helpfully designed for speedy and trouble-free access, fell obligingly apart and slid down the girl's thighs to hang deflated at her knees. Its passing revealed a delectable sight. Roused by the reiterated assault of Bernard's palm, Lenina's blood had rushed defensively into the thousands of tiny capillary veins that wound their delicate tracery through the subcutaneous layer of the lovely buttocks, heating and engorging the tender flesh, suffusing the flawless epidermis. Like a bright flag of submission, a tribute to the effectiveness of his chastisement, a rich warm blush now mantled the whole glorious expanse of her behind, the roseate curves offering an exquisite contrast with the pearly whiteness of her back and thighs. To Bernard, this rosy hue only enhanced the natural beauty of Lenina's bottom, making it seem even more enticingly spankable.

Delighted, he resumed her chastisement with increased vigour, relishing the feel of her soft flesh bouncing and quivering beneath his smacks, the crisp clean sound of bare hand meeting bare bottom. With every spank the rubescent glow deepened on the defenceless globes, and Lenina's tearful wails increased in urgency. Her bottom felt as though it were on fire, swollen to twice its normal size, and still the merciless punishment continued.

If Bernard had been asked why he was spanking Lenina, he would have been hard put to frame a coherent reply. He felt no dislike for the girl; on the contrary, he felt fonder of her now than ever before. Nor did he believe that this chastisement would effect any significant change in her behaviour, or that she seriously deserved punishment for mouthing sentiments over which she had little control. His irritation towards her had vanished with the first few strokes, and ever since he had been spanking her for the sheer radiant joy of it.

It felt right. It felt better than right; it felt fulfilling. To hold this lovely girl wriggling and squirming across his lap; to see her hair tossing and her long legs kicking; to spank her hard and steadily, covering every inch of her gratifyingly plump bottom (for she was indeed, as she'd said, awfully pneumatic) with stinging smacks, and hear her gasp and yelp at each stroke; all this felt not just arousing but infinitely satisfying, as satisfying as anything he had ever done.

He could scarcely have guessed that Lenina too, for all her pleas and protests, would come to find it strangely satisfying; nor that, well before her punishment was over, she would start to feel the stirrings of erotic excitement.

So when at last, reluctantly, he stopped spanking her and released her, expecting an outburst of grief or anger or both, he was surprised at her reaction. True, tears stood in her blue eyes and she rubbed ruefully at her richly encrimsoned bottom-cheeks. 'Oh, Bernard, that was horrid of you! Horrid!' she said, but her tone carried little reproach; and when she knelt unbidden to embrace him there was more passion in her kisses, more intimacy in her caresses, than she had ever shown before.

Some hours later, Bernard once again stood at the hotel window and gazed out at the towers of Santa Fe, now glowing golden like bejewelled rods beneath a sky darkening to indigo. How beautiful they were, he thought. How beautiful everything was.

He and Lenina had made love several times. Twice more, during the course of their play, he had turned her over his lap and spanked her again, reviving the glow that had scarcely faded from her luscious mounds. Each time her protests had seemed less indignant, her pleas for mercy less sincere. Her squeals seemed more an expression of excitement than of pain. On the last occasion, as the spanking mounted in intensity, she had unmistakably started to arch her bottom upwards to meet his hand, as if inciting him to administer further and more severe chastisement.

Now, sated and content, he contemplated the evening sky and listened to Lenina singing in the shower. Bernard smiled as he recognised her favourite erotic ditty. But wasn't there something unfamiliar about the words? He stole over to the bathroom door and listened more closely. A look of astonishment crossed his face.

Something remarkable was occurring. For the first time in her snugly well-ordered life, Lenina Crowne found herself moved to independent thought – and independent creative thought, at that. Unprompted, uncoerced, quite unaided by sleep-teaching, she had composed a new verse for her favourite song, and was now happily singing it to herself as the hot water trickled amorously over the curves of her still-smarting rump.

'Spank me, baby, don't mean maybe,
Spank me till my bottom's glowing,
Turn it red then let's to bed,
Spanking gets me going.'

Smiling, Bernard moved away and lay down on the bed. Putting his hands behind his head, he stretched luxuriously, relishing a new sense of sheer animal well-being. 'I'm so glad,' he murmured to himself with an ironic grin, 'I'm so glad I'm a beater.'

14

Heads and Tails

'Denise Black!' Helen Peters's voice rang out across the classroom, shrill with exasperation. 'Denise, I have *had* it with you! Go and report to the Principal's study – *now!*'

'*Me*, miss?' Wide-eyed, Denise adopted her most insolent tone of phony innocence. 'What did *I* do, miss?'

'You know damn well what you did!' To Denise's delight, the young teacher's voice was close to hysteria. Several of the class giggled audibly. 'You've been disrupting this class all morning! Now go! Go! NOW!!'

Sighing loudly and theatrically, the pretty blonde sixteen-year-old rose from her desk and slouched slowly towards the door.

'Stand up straight, girl!' snapped Helen Peters. 'And get going, will you!'

Denise swapped her slouch for an exaggeratedly sexy slink, wiggling her bottom outrageously. Her classmates responded with more giggles, and a few ironic wolf-whistles. Helen half-rose from her chair. Not for the first time, she regretted that corporal punishment had been banished from the British education system. She longed to land a stinging smack on that impudently gyrating young behind, but contented herself with glaring furiously as Denise left the classroom. The door closed; then the girl's face reappeared in the glass door-panes, squinting and tongue stuck out. Squeals of laughter from the class. The teacher made an angry gesture, and the face vanished.

Denise strolled casually along the corridor towards the Principal's study. She was in no hurry. In fact, she was delighted to have been ejected from the class; history was an utter bore, and she'd been trying all morning to provoke Miss Peters into chucking her out.

As for her forthcoming interview with the Head, she felt not the least apprehension. Here at Grove End Sixth Form College, discipline was even more lax than it had been at her secondary school. Dr McMullen was a well-meaning liberal type who believed 'sympathetic understanding' could work wonders. He'd tut sadly over Denise's misdemeanours, enquire kindly how things were going at home and send her away with a minimal punishment and an exhortation to behave better in future.

I can handle the old fart, no trouble, she thought to herself. He's a pushover. Besides, on the rare occasions when even Dr McMullen's patience had been tried too far, she'd always found that crossing her legs to give him a quick flash of her knickers worked wonders. Well aware of her own adolescent charms, Denise invariably opened an extra button or two on her blouse and wore her dark-blue pleated school skirts at least three inches shorter than the regulations allowed.

Arriving at the Principal's study, she knocked briskly, pushed the door open – and stopped in surprise. In place of the balding bespectacled figure of Dr McMullen, another man altogether was seated behind the desk: a much younger well-built individual who fixed her with a piercing dark-eyed stare.

'Did I tell you to come in?' he enquired sternly.

'No – that is – I – n-no, sir,' responded Denise in confusion. 'I – I was looking for the Head.'

184

'I am the Head, for the time being. Dr McMullen was called away earlier. He may not be back for some time. So, in the meantime, I've been asked to stand in for him. My name is Michael Philips; you may call me Mr Philips, or sir. And you are – ?'

'Denise Black, sir,' answered the girl in a respectful voice that she scarcely recognised as her own. There was something disconcerting about this man, with his rugged good looks and confident air, that robbed her of her usual cheekiness. His direct gaze inspired in her a thrill that might have been excitement, or apprehension – or both.

'Well, Denise, I *didn't* tell you to enter. So now you can go out again, and wait outside until I call you in.'

'Yes, sir,' she murmured meekly, and obeyed.

Outside in the anteroom she sat down on an upholstered bench. Its cold leather made her very conscious of her bare thighs. For some reason that she couldn't fathom, Denise found herself regretting that her skirt was quite so short. She recalled those cool dark eyes, calmly appraising her. Michael Philips, she suspected, would be anything but a pushover.

In the study, Mike Philips swivelled round and pulled open a filing cabinet. He extracted a file and flicked through it. His lips pursed as he read the contents. Checking back to the first page, he found a number and picked up the phone.

'Mrs Black? This is Mike Philips, Acting Principal at Denise's college. Yes, that's right: Dr McMullen has been called away. Can you spare me a moment? Thank you.'

Outside, kicking her heels, Denise was regaining her usual cockiness. OK, so this guy was younger and, by the look of him, a lot more clued in than poor dopey old Mullibum. But he was still a man, wasn't he? Standing up, she regarded herself complacently in the mirror, admiring the long coltish legs and fetchingly nubile figure. She undid another button on her blouse, then half-turned, noting how the skirt jutted temptingly out over the curves of her cute little bottom. That'll get him, she thought – then jumped as she heard his voice through the study door.

'Denise, you may come in now!'

He was standing behind his desk, a file in his hand. 'Close the door, Denise. Sit down. Well, young lady, you're quite the troublemaker, aren't you?' He brandished the file at her.

'Oh, well, sir, Miss Peters –'

'Yes, I've read what Miss Peters notes in your file. I've also read what your other teachers have to say. It seems pretty consistent. You're not stupid, Denise – far from it. But you're lazy, impertinent, disobedient, a constant disruptive influence throughout the college. What's more, there are quite a few other girls silly enough to admire you for all this, so you've got your little group of followers and imitators. In fact, the whole thing's getting seriously out of hand. You're sixteen, at a sixth-form college – you should be outgrowing this kind of juvenile idiocy. But it seems you're getting worse. This is the fifth time in two weeks you've been sent to see the Head. Well?'

Too bad he's standing up, Denise thought. He won't get anything like such a good view. Still, what the hell. 'Oh, sir, it's not fair,' she breathed, dropping her voice half an octave and gazing boldly into his eyes. Slowly, deliberately, she crossed her legs. 'The teachers pick on me. I think they're just jealous.' Holding his gaze, she pouted appealingly.

At this point, Dr McMullen would have got all flustered and tongue-tied. But Mike Philips simply smiled. It was a smile that said, I know that trick you're pulling, little girl, and it's not going to work; not this time. To her annoyance, Denise found her gaze wavering, then falling, before his cool ironic glance. What's

186

the matter with me? she thought – what kind of wimp am I turning into? But there was something scary about this man, with his calm, level tones. Excitingly scary, even – but scary.

'Jealous, you think? Somehow, Denise, I doubt it. I think they were just doing their best to instil some sense of discipline into you. And discipline, young lady, is what you sorely need. Tell me, what did Dr McMullen do on the many occasions you were sent to see him?'

'He – he talked to me, sir. Sometimes he gave me detention.'

'I see. Well, young lady, Dr McMullen's methods may have been admirable in their way – but mine are rather different. While I'm in charge here, there are going to be some radical changes in the way miscreants are dealt with. And you, Denise, will now have the honour of being the first pupil to experience them. Stand up, please.'

Moving round the desk, Mike Philips came and sat down on the upright chair Denise had just vacated. Puzzled, she stood before him. What the hell was he getting at? Suddenly an image flashed into her mind: herself, some years younger, standing in front of her seated father just before he – oh no! A spasm of alarm tingled across her rear end. No, surely he couldn't be meaning to – ?

Mike Philips read the girl's expression, the flash of fear in her blue eyes. 'That's right, Denise,' he said quietly. 'As from today, I'm reintroducing corporal punishment in this college for cases of serious misbehaviour. You, young lady, are going to be put across my knee and spanked. *Hard*.'

Denise gasped in disbelief. 'You can't do that!' she exclaimed.

'Oh, can't I? Well, my girl, you're about to learn otherwise.'

Denise tried to back away, but the desk impeded her path. 'I'll tell my mother!' she blurted desperately.

Mike Philips smiled. 'I've just spoken to your mother,' he informed her. 'She tells me you've been utterly out of control since your father left, and that she can't handle you any longer. She added that, before they split up, your father had a very effective way of dealing with you when you were naughty. Remember what that was?'

'No!' cried Denise wildly.

'Really? I think you do, Denise.' His voice slowed, becoming almost hypnotic. 'I think you remember very well – that when you'd been naughty he used to turn you over his knee, take down your knickers, and spank you. Didn't he, Denise? Spank you long and hard on your bare bottom; spank you until your bottom was bright red and burning hot; spank you until you were a very sore and sorry little girl indeed. Isn't that right?'

A hot blush of embarrassment flooded Denise's face at the shameful memory. Standing there in her school-girl uniform she felt as though she was ten years old again, a naughty little girl about to receive her just deserts from a stern but loving father. She hung her head, unable to meet the man's steady amused gaze. 'Yes,' she mumbled.

'Good. And I'm glad to see that you retain enough sense of shame to blush for your misdeeds. Though, believe me, young lady, that's nothing to the way you'll be blushing very shortly on a rather different portion of your anatomy. OK, Denise, it's time for your punishment. Come here, please.'

Reaching out and taking her by the wrist, he drew the petite blonde inexorably towards him. Denise wanted to scream, to struggle, to run, but she seemed strangely unable to resist. The next thing she knew, she found herself lying face-down across Mike's broad lap with her pert little bottom uppermost, its arched curves perfectly presented for spanking. She gasped with horror. 'Oh no, sir, please don't spank me!' she wailed. 'Please! I'm sorry, I'm really sorry!'

'A bit late for sorry, my girl,' Mike observed, rolling up his right shirt-sleeve. 'But you'll soon have plenty to be sorry about, I can assure you. In fact, Denise, I think you'll soon be sorrier than you've ever been in your life before. This, young lady, is going to be a spanking to remember.'

With a pleasing sense of anticipation, he grasped the hem of the girl's blue pleated skirt and lifted it back above her waist. There were revealed to his gaze rounded twin mounds clad in tight white cotton panties, fitting snugly as a second skin over the contours of the pretty teenager's girlish hindquarters. Mike regarded them appreciatively. 'Very becoming,' he commented, 'but I think we'll have these down. A good hard bare-bottom spanking is what you deserve, young lady, and that's just what you're going to get.'

'Oh no!' yelped Denise, dismayed. She flung back a protective hand, but Mike captured it easily and held it in the small of her back. Then he hooked his finger into the waistband of her panties and peeled them slowly down over the girl's ripe young rearward curves, down to dangle around her thighs, well clear of the now very bare and unprotected target area.

And, as target areas went, this one was a peach. Denise's bottom was small but shapely – soft, sweet and just begging to be spanked. Deliberately prolonging the joy of anticipation, Mike stroked the chubby young hemispheres, relishing the way the tender flesh quivered beneath his fingers as if trembling at the prospect of the punishment it would soon be suffering.

'You have a very pretty bottom, Denise,' he told her. 'But it's a bottom that's in dire need of a good spanking – and I reckon it hasn't been spanked nearly enough just recently. So I intend to make up for some of that sad neglect. Unluckily for you, my girl, there's nothing

189

requiring my urgent attention for the next half-hour; so I can devote most of that time to giving this cheeky young rear end the roasting it so sorely needs.'

Prone and pinioned across his lap, Denise waited in an agony of apprehension. Mike Philips was a powerfully built man, and a determined one: if he said she was in for a long hard spanking, she felt sure he meant it. Bared and defenceless, her soft young bottom felt horribly vulnerable to what, she knew, was going to be a very painful punishment indeed.

Almost worse, though, was the humiliation of it. She, a sophisticated sixteen-year-old, virtually an adult, one of the prettiest girls in the college, being taken across a man's knee, having her panties pulled down to be spanked on her bare bottom like a naughty child! It was indecent – it was shameful! If her friends ever found out, she would just *die*!

Yet in some strange way it felt right, almost comforting – as if this was where she truly belonged. Memories flooded back of the spankings she had received from her beloved father. They had hurt, all right – he had never gone easy on her – but along with the pain had come a sense of being warmly held and protected, as though the spanking was just another aspect of his all-enveloping love for his adored wayward daughter. Since he left, no one had spanked her until today; and now, as she lay helpless across this stranger's lap, dreading the first stinging smack on her trembling bottom-flesh, it was as though she had come home.

Mike's voice broke her reverie. 'OK, Denise: this is what you've been asking for, and now you're going to get it.'

Taking a firm grip on the girl's slim waist, he brought his hand down hard on her rounded deliciously bare little bottom.

'Aaah!' Denise gave a sharp intake of breath as Mike's hand stung her defenceless rear. She'd forgotten just how much a spanking could sting – and now she was getting a sharp reminder. 'Owww!' she yelped. 'Oh, sir, please, that really *hurts*!'

Mike paused to enjoy the effects of his handiwork. Like many young blondes, Denise had pale delicate skin that marked readily; and after only half a dozen spanks a warm pink blush already suffused her pretty bottom-cheeks, making them look even prettier – and promising a yet richer hue in due course.

'Of course it hurts, silly girl,' he retorted callously. 'It's a spanking; it's meant to hurt. But, believe me, it's going to hurt an awful lot more before I'm through with this saucy young bottom.'

So saying, he resumed her punishment, spanking her hard and steadily, right and left, covering every inch of the quivering bouncing globes, and paying special attention to his favourite spank spot, the soft sensitive undercurve where bottom meets thigh. Each spank, laid on with vigour, rang round the room like a pistol shot, making the plump young flesh bounce and jiggle; at each one Denise yelped and gasped, her long legs kicking wildly and her blonde mane tossing. Frantically she wailed and begged for mercy as the stinging heat built up in her spanked rear end.

But all her heartfelt pleas were in vain. Mike had no intention of stopping just yet. This insolent pert-bottomed little minx was a sweet delight to spank, and furthermore richly deserved it; and, since his pleasure and her well-earned punishment so happily coincided, he intended to take full advantage of it and spank her to his heart's content. So for ten minutes or more his hand rose and fell, deepening the roseate blush on her ripe young bottom, turning it from white to pink, from pink to red, and from red to a rich fiery scarlet that contrasted exquisitely with the whiteness of her back and thighs.

Desperately Denise writhed on Mike's lap, vainly trying to evade the remorseless chastisement. But he had her securely pinioned, and there was no escape for the wailing sixteen-year-old. Spank after stinging hand-spank rained down on her girlish rump, until it felt swollen to twice its normal size, and still her punisher showed no sign of relenting. And when at last he paused, it was only to reach over to the desk and pick up a broad wooden ruler that lay there.

'Right, my girl,' he remarked, 'that should have warmed you up nicely. That was for persistent misbehaviour in class and being a disruptive influence – and I very much hope, for your sake, that you've learnt your lesson.

'But we've another little matter to settle, Denise: your impudent attempt to vamp me just now. Do you think I didn't know what you were up to with all that pouting and fluttering your eyelashes, and flashing your knickers at me? And where's it got you, young lady? Across my knee, that's where – with those same knickers taken down to have your saucy little bare bottom soundly spanked.

'So now, Denise, just to remind you not to try those jailbait tactics on your teachers again, a little supplementary punishment: sixty good hard swats with this.'

Peering over her shoulder, Denise caught a glimpse of the ruler in his hand and let out a wail of dismay. 'Oh no, sir! Please don't! I'll be good, honestly I will! Oh, no more, sir, please! My poor bottom's so sore – it'll hurt awfully!'

'I'm sure it will,' responded Mike callously, swishing the ruler through the air. It felt nicely weighted, ideal for applying to a naughty girl's already well-spanked bare bottom. 'That's exactly why I'm going to use it. I promised you a spanking to remember, Denise, and I think this is going to impress itself quite lastingly upon your – memory.'

'Ooooh!' wailed Denise as she saw the broad wooden ruler poised high in the air – and then come flashing down.

Denise squealed as a band of fire seared across her tender young curves. Mike's hand-spanking had hurt like hell, but she now realised it was nothing compared to this. Only one stroke, and already she felt as if she'd never sit down again. 'Oh please, please, no more!' she begged.

But Mike Philips was merciless. Again and again the cruel wood cracked down across the squirming twin globes, paddling the fiery cheeks a rich deep crimson. Five dozen hard stinging spanks, and Denise squealed and sobbed at each one, begging to be let off.

What a surprise Denise's friends and classmates would have, Mike reflected, if they could see her now. Where now was the cocky young madam who'd sashayed into his office with her provocative pout and her can't-touch-me air, flaunting her long legs and her pert little rump? Cool conceited young Denise, terror of her teachers, envy of her fellow pupils, lay wriggling over his lap with her blonde hair tossing and her legs kicking wildly, tearfully begging for mercy just like any naughty teenage miss receiving her long-deserved come-uppance, with her skirt up round her waist, her panties down round her thighs and, framed between them, her soft round bottom bouncing, blushing and quivering beneath the finest spanking of her young life. It was a delicious spectacle, and his only regret was that it would soon be over.

So he took his time, pausing after each crisp smack of the ruler to let the sting sink in and admire the vivid blush mantling the girl's squirming bottom-cheeks, which now glowed like two ripe tomatoes. And when at last the final spank (shrewdly aimed across his favourite undercurve) had elicited a last shrill squeal from the now very penitent teenager, he helped her up off his lap, handed her a pack of tissues and tactfully turned his back to let her compose herself.

'Ooooh! Owwww! Oh my poor bum!' Denise whimpered to herself, gingerly rubbing her anguished rear. She peered over her shoulder, catching a glimpse of her blazing cheeks. 'God, I shan't be able to sit down for a week!' But she felt no resentment towards the man who had punished her so severely. On the contrary, she felt every last stinging spank had been fully deserved. He had treated her justly, and she respected him for it. 'Mr Philips?' she said softly.

Mike turned.

Denise's face was still flushed and wet with tears, but she smiled tremulously at him. 'Thank you,' she whispered. 'I know I deserved that, and I'm sorry I was such a brat. Please, would you give me a hug? That's what my dad always did after . . . after he'd spanked me.'

'Sure,' said Mike. He took the slim teenager in his arms and hugged her warmly. 'You're a brave girl, Denise,' he told her, 'and you took your punishment very well. You can skip the rest of this morning's classes – I doubt you'd be able to sit at your desk anyway.' He held her at arm's length and regarded her seriously. 'I think maybe you've learnt your lesson, young lady. But remember this: if I hear of you causing any more trouble, I won't have you sent here to my study. I'll come to your classroom, put you over my knee right then and there and spank you just like I did today, on your bare bottom – in front of the whole class!' He grinned at her horrified expression. 'You know I mean it, don't you?'

Denise gulped. 'Yes, sir.'

'Yes, sir, is right. And, as for those silly young friends of yours who think acting up is so funny, tell them just what any girl who's sent to me can expect – across my knee, knickers down, and a long hot hard spanking on her cute little bare bottom. OK?'

Denise gulped again, and nodded.

'Good. OK, Denise, off you go.' He propelled the pretty teen towards the door with a farewell smack – not hard, but on her freshly spanked bottom it was enough to make her yip and scamper hastily out.

As the door closed behind the chastened Denise, Mike Philips sat down at the desk and stretched luxuriously, grinning to himself. He sighed with contentment, then took a folder out of his briefcase and skimmed through it. The topmost document was a letter on formal notepaper, headed in Gothic script 'The Wetherington Academy for Girls, Highbury, Vermont. Founded 1905. Old-fashioned Excellence – Old-fashioned Discipline'. The letter began, 'Dear Mr Philips, We are truly delighted that you have agreed our terms, and look forward to welcoming you here in the capacity of Dean of Discipline ...' Mike's grin broadened, and a look of pleasurable anticipation crossed his face.

After a while there were sounds outside the door, and a balding middle-aged man in spectacles bustled agitatedly in, breathing heavily. 'Ah, Mike! Everything all right?' panted Dr James McMullen. 'No problems while I was away?'

'Nothing I couldn't handle, thanks, Jim. But how's your mother?'

'Oh, she's OK. Just bruised her leg slightly. But she's in such a state about the damage to the car.' McMullen collapsed on to the chair where Mike had so recently sat to spank Denise, and mopped his brow. 'She really shouldn't still be driving at her age. Maybe this will convince her. Blessing in disguise if it does. But, Mike, I can't tell you how grateful I am to you for holding the fort. I just had to go and help mother, and with the Deputy Principal away sick – well, it was providential that you happened to drop by.'

'No trouble – I was glad to help.'

'No, but really, it was so good of you to help out an old colleague like this. Especially when you're off to this new job in the States next week.' Leaning forward, McMullen glanced at the letter in the folder. 'Old-fashioned discipline, eh? Wouldn't do here, I'm afraid. Counter-productive. Not our style at all.'

'No, I suppose not. Well, better be going.' Mike collected his papers and shook McMullen's hand. 'Bye then, Jim. Good to see you.'

'Bye, Mike, and good luck with the new job. And thanks again for standing in for me. I really appreciate it.'

Mike Philips smiled cheerfully. 'Believe me, Jim, it was a pleasure. A real pleasure.'

15

Corrective Measures

I'm an accountant. Instant conversation-killer, that.
Polite people say, 'Oh . . . that must be very interesting,'
and hastily change the subject. Less polite ones snigger,
or mutter 'Get a life' and dredge up the punchline of
some ancient *Monty Python* sketch. Either way, the
reaction's much the same: accountancy equals grey,
boring and duller than a wet Sunday in Grimsby. Right?

Well, as it happens, no. Wrong. Dead wrong.

OK, if you work for one of the big traditional firms, it
must be pretty monotonous, stuck in the same old office
day after day. I'm more by way of a troubleshooter: a
travelling freelance who firms call in to vet their books
when annual meetings are due. And some of them aren't
above cutting a few corners. That's when the job really
grips – when you first sense that someone's trying to con
you, and that somewhere in those sober columns of
figures there lurks, like a wily old fish in a deep dark
pool, the scam they've hidden so carefully. Then you get
all the joy of the chase, the blind alleys, the battle of wits
– and at last, as you catch the first glimpse of a telltale
glitch, the sheer adrenalin rush: got you, you bugger!
Think figures are dull? You'd be amazed.

Of course, the majority of firms are anything but
crooked. But, even when they're straight as a die, I'm
mostly dealing with smallish, ambitious outfits that tend

to be run by lively people, interesting to meet. *Very* interesting, sometimes.

Wainwright Design were based in Somerset, near Taunton, an up-and-coming outfit just starting to make their name in the design world. I was shown in to see the MD, Robin Wainwright, an amiable, slightly distracted guy in his thirties.

'Mr Lewis? Mr Jeff Lewis?'

I always enjoy that glance of involuntary surprise. They think, 'Accountant? Where's the grey suit?' With me it's more likely to be an open-necked shirt and chinos. Who needs a uniform? I'm known for the quality of my work, not my sartorial conformity.

That small hurdle over, we got down to business. 'I'll take you in to see my sister Katie,' said Robin Wainwright. 'She acts as the company secretary, though she's also one hell of a designer in her own right. She'll have all you need ready for you.'

In the next office, a chestnut-haired woman was standing at a design slope with her back to us. She wore jeans, which she filled to perfection. Long legs and a slim waist accentuated the lush swell of her deliciously rounded bottom.

'Katie?' said her brother. 'This is Jeff Lewis. He's come to audit the books.'

Katie Wainwright turned. I liked the front view as much as the rear (which, coming from a dedicated bottoms man, is quite some tribute). She was about thirty, and beautiful rather than pretty in a refreshingly unconventional style. She favoured me with a frank direct gaze from grey-green eyes, and a firm handshake.

'Thanks, Rob,' she said. 'All the stuff's in the next office, Mr Lewis. I'll take you through.'

Next door, a desk was piled with invoices, bills, print-outs and account books, along with a computer. Katie switched it on and accessed the spreadsheets. 'I ought to warn you, Mr Lewis –' she began.

'Jeff, if it's OK with you?'

'Fine by me. OK, Jeff – I should warn you that I'm a designer first and company secretary very much second. So, if you find the odd cock-up in the accounts, put it down to incompetence.'

I grinned. 'Don't worry,' I said, appraising the methodical heaps of documents. 'Compared to some companies I've seen, this looks like a pretty well-organised job.'

She grinned back. 'Better not speak too soon. Like a coffee? OK, I'll leave you to it. I'll be right next door if you need anything.'

As -she left I cast another appreciative glance at that superb rear end, then settled down to work. Despite what she'd said, Katie had done an excellent job, especially for someone without training, and the accounts were clean and systematic. By midday I was well advanced, and felt sure I'd have it all finished that day. I'd found just one or two minor discrepancies – nothing in the least dishonest, simply the kind of small error in presentation that a non-professional would make. I mentioned as much to Katie when she came in to see how I was getting on.

'Nothing to worry about,' I added. 'I'll just take corrective measures.'

Unthinkingly, I'd used the accountant's jargon term for this kind of tidying-up process. Katie's reaction, though, was unexpected. She gave me a quizzical look from her grey-eyes, then held out her hand, palm upwards, like a schoolgirl expecting punishment.

I smiled and slapped the proffered hand, just hard enough to sting slightly.

'Ow!' said Katie, shaking her hand with an exaggerated grimace, then laughed. 'We're just going to lunch,' she said. 'The local pub – food's not bad. Like to join us?'

Besides Katie and Robin, four other designers came along, two male and two female. They were young and bright and the atmosphere was relaxed, with plenty of friendly teasing. No one deferred to Robin as the boss. Wainwright Design was evidently a good place to work.

From some of the joshing, I gathered that Katie was currently between boyfriends – 'playing the field', as one of the young men flirtatiously put it.

She gave a dismissive shrug. 'Field? More like a sodding mud-slide round here, I reckon.'

Back at the office I got back to work. It still went pretty smoothly. I was all but through when Katie came in again around five o'clock.

'All OK, Jeff?' She came and stood beside me, close enough that I could smell the scent of her.

'Fine. Just one or two small details again.'

'Ah. More corrective measures needed?'

I glanced up. She was looking at me meaningfully, with an enigmatic half-smile. Her lips were slightly parted. Have I mentioned that she had a temptingly full sensual mouth?

Did she mean what I thought she meant? I wondered. Could I really be that lucky? Keeping my tone light and jokey, I responded, 'Yeah, maybe so. Your place or mine?'

'Well, most people leave here by six. But I could always stay later . . .'

This time there was no mistaking her meaning. I reached out and stroked her arm. 'My pleasure, Katie.'

She stooped and kissed me lightly on the lips. 'Mine too, I hope. Till then.'

Over the next hour I finished off the accounts, trying hard to keep my mind on my work and ignore the visions of Katie's denimed curves that swam before my eyes.

Just before six Robin Wainwright popped his head round the door. 'All in order, Jeff?'

'Fine, thanks, Robin. Katie's done a grand job. I'm just finishing off.'

200

'Great – thanks. Send us your invoice. Katie will see you out.'

I heard the last people leave. Silence descended. Then Katie's voice came: 'In here, Jeff.'

I went into the next office. Katie was sitting on a plans chest, swinging one leg. She indicated a nearby couch.

'OK, Jeff,' she said when I'd sat down, 'just what corrective measures did you have in mind for me?'

'Well, I couldn't help noticing that you have an exceptionally lovely bottom . . .'

'Why, thank you, kind sir.'

'So I thought I'd rather like to give you a spanking.'

'Mmmmm,' said Katie. The sound came from somewhere deep in her throat, pitched between a purr and a growl. 'Would you now? And were you planning to put me across your knee like a naughty girl?'

'Of course.'

'Take down my knickers?'

'Absolutely.'

'And spank me on my bare bottom?'

'You bet.'

'Hard?'

'*Very* hard.'

'Oooh!' she said in mock-terror, giving a coquettish little wriggle. 'And if I told you I was awfully sorry, and promised to be very careful about the accounts from now on, and begged to be let off – that wouldn't help a bit, would it?'

'Not a bit,' I responded cheerfully.

'Mmm, that's rather what I thought. Well, in that case there's no help for it, is there? I guess I'll just have to resign myself to being spanked.'

'Yes, I guess you will. So over here with you, please, my girl.'

With a dramatic sigh she slipped down off the plans chest and came and stood beside me, close to my right knee. In the warm sunset light flooding the room she looked even lovelier. Her eyes were sparkling, and a flush of anticipation coloured her cheeks. I'd noticed before that she didn't wear a bra; her breasts were small and firm, and now the nipples stood out against her shirt, erect with excitement. But, then, so was I.

I reached round and patted that glorious bottom. It felt just as spankable as it looked. My throat was dry. 'OK, Katie,' I said, 'let's have these jeans down, shall we?'

Obediently she unfastened the belt, unzipped the front and slid the jeans down over her hips, letting them fall around her ankles. Taking her by the hand, I drew her down across my lap in the classic spanking posture, and lifted the tail of her shirt, pushing it up to expose the small of her back.

Black nylon panties, fringed with lace, covered less than half the expanse of Katie's delectable rump. The luscious mounds curved invitingly upwards, perfectly placed for my hand. I lightly twanged the elastic on the panties. 'Nice,' I said. 'But even nicer with them down, I think. Such a lovely bottom deserves to be spanked on the bare.'

'Cruel beast!' murmured Katie, but she helpfully lifted her hips as I slid the flimsy garment down over her ripe rearward curves and left it dangling around her thighs. As she felt her most intimate covering being removed she wriggled nervously on my lap, making the soft globes of her bottom quiver enticingly.

Full, flawless and voluptuously rounded, Katie's bottom was a joy to the eye – and to the touch. Enchanted, I rested my hand on the cool smooth hemispheres, squeezing them gently, prolonging the exquisite moment of anticipation. 'You do have the most gorgeously spankable bottom, my sweet,' I told her. 'Ever been spanked before?'

'Oh yes,' said Katie. 'My last-but-one boyfriend used to spank me a lot.'

'I hope that wasn't why you left him?'

'No, on the contrary, I think that's what got us together. I chucked him because he was a two-timing shit.'

'And your last boyfriend?' I asked, still stroking the lush orbs, relishing their yielding softness.

She laughed. 'Oh, he was a nice guy. Too nice. Wouldn't spank me, however hard I tried. Said he was afraid he'd hurt me. I told him, "That's the whole point," but he just didn't get it.'

'More fool him,' I said. 'Still, I'm glad to know such a superb bottom hasn't been entirely neglected. OK, young lady, prepare for corrective measures!'

With a feeling of sensuous delight, I began to smack the tender trembling mounds of Katie's shapely bottom. She gave a swift intake of breath as she felt the first strokes sting her soft rump, then relaxed over my lap, giving herself up entirely to the sweet sharp pleasure of being spanked.

At first I spanked her quite lightly, just hard enough to sting, revelling in the feel of the plump flesh as it wobbled and flattened beneath each smack. Her pale skin coloured readily, and after only a few spanks a delicate pink blush suffused the lovely cheeks, making them look even lovelier. Gradually I increased the force of my strokes until I was spanking her lustily, landing hard ringing slaps left and right on the lush quivering globes. As the heat and sting built up in her soundly spanked rear end Katie began to yip and squirm, but she made no attempt to escape, or to put a protective hand over the target area.

Even the distant traffic noises had faded, and all was quiet in the room except for the sweet music of spanking: the crisp clean sound of hand smacking down on soft bare female bottom-flesh, and the yelps of mingled pain and excitement from the spanked girl. Once I thought I heard a sound by the door and glanced that way, but after that there was nothing to distract me from the joyous task of reddening Katie's adorable bottom.

Since she was clearly deriving as much pleasure (or maybe even more, who knows?) from this supposed punishment, I felt no compunction about spanking her long and hard, taking my time and enjoying myself to the full. By the time I finally paused and stroked the well-warmed mounds, the sunset glow outside had faded from the sky; but it was emulated by the radiant glow that now adorned the whole expanse of Katie's delectable rearward curves.

'Ow-ooooh!' said Katie, reaching back and gingerly rubbing her fiery cheeks. 'Jeff, you certainly know how to spank a girl! Is your hand sore?'

'A little. But nothing like as sore as your bottom, I bet.'

'Mmm, I think you're right. But you know, if you wanted to –' She peered over her shoulder with a provocative little grin.

'Wanted to what, exactly, young lady?'

'Well – there's a hairbrush in my desk. Top left-hand drawer.'

'You *are* a glutton for punishment, aren't you? OK, on your own head – or, rather, your own bottom – be it.' I helped her up off my lap. 'While I'm getting it, why don't you go and stand over there by that plans chest with your back to me? Tuck your shirt up, so I can admire my handiwork.'

Katie grinned. 'Whatever you say, O Master.'

In the desk drawer I found the hairbrush. It was a classic oval-backed Mason & Pearson, solidly crafted of broad black wood – a perfect spanking implement.

When I looked up, Katie was leaning over the plans chest just as I'd suggested. But she'd stepped out of her jeans, stripped off her shirt and stood there completely naked but for the erotic tangle of black knickers around one ankle. Her glossy chestnut hair hung loose down her back, and the whiteness of her long legs and slim back enhanced the beauty of her full blushing bottom. It was a glorious sight, worthy of the brush of a Degas or a Renoir.

Coming up behind her, I stroked the roseate twin globes, savouring the tender warmth and weight of them, then slipped my hand down between her legs. Her cleft was hot and sopping wet, and she moaned softly at the touch of my fingers.

She half-turned and we kissed deeply, while her hand slid down to caress the bulge in my trousers. I reached for my zip but she stopped my hand, smiling impudently into my face. 'All in good time, Jeff,' she breathed. 'First I'd like to feel that hairbrush.'

I smacked her bottom smartly, making her yip. 'OK, my girl, you asked for it.' I led her back to the couch and once again put her in position. Lying there in all her naked beauty, her rosy bottom upturned and ready for further punishment, she fitted perfectly over my lap. It all felt so right, so natural, as if I'd been spanking her for years.

Teasingly, I rubbed the back of the hairbrush over her hot cheeks, making her tremble with anticipation. 'Right, young Katie,' I said with assumed severity, 'now you're really for it.'

'Ooooh,' said Katie, gripping my leg as I brought the brush sharply down on the rosy curve of her right bottom-cheek. It made contact with a fine juicy smack. She yelped, tossing her chestnut mane, and yelped again a moment later as her left cheek received equally smart treatment. She went on to yelp quite a lot more over the next few minutes, wriggling and kicking her legs, as the hard wooden brush rose and fell, colouring her flaming cheeks a yet more flagrant red.

Relishing my task, I paddled her hard and steadily, pausing now and then to rub the tender mounds, and to slip my hand down between her legs, making her wriggle and moan. As her spanking continued, Katie began to arch her bottom up as if to meet my strokes, and her yelps turned to gasps as her excitement mounted. I paused again, but she gasped, 'Oh, God, no! Don't stop! Harder! Harder!'

So I spanked her right through her orgasm; and when it was over she lay limply over my thighs, giving little gasps and whimpers as the final tremors died away. I caressed the blazing curves, then raised her up off my lap and our mouths met in a long deep kiss. She reached down and unzipped me, releasing my eager erection from the confinement it had strained against ever since I first took her over my knee.

A few moments later, Katie was once again bending naked over that conveniently positioned plans chest as I took her from the rear. The feel of her fiery cheeks, hot against my belly as I drove deep into her, increased my already rampant excitement, and after only a few thrusts we reached a gasping simultaneous climax.

We had dinner in a pleasant little Italian restaurant in the town, sharing secret smiles whenever Katie squirmed ruefully on her chair. What would the other diners have thought, I wondered, if they'd known that the beautiful sophisticated young woman opposite me was sitting on a bottom still blushing and tender from having just been soundly spanked?

And afterwards, back at her apartment, I once again put her across my knee, lowered her knickers and spent several joyous minutes rekindling the glow on that succulent bare bottom, before we eagerly fell into bed together.

'Do you know,' I asked as we lay entwined in a sated drowse, her hand caressing her still-fiery rear, 'that you called me Daddy just now while I was spanking you?'

'I didn't, did I? Oh shit, what a giveaway.'

'Did your dad spank you when you were a kid?'

'Yes – though I'm sure he never guessed what a kick I got from it. Poor Dad – I adored him, but I used to provoke him deliberately so he'd give me a spanking. I remember lying across his knee yelling blue murder – and loving every second of it.'

'Did he spank your brother, too?'

'Never needed to. Rob was the good little boy. I was the rebel, always up for a dare.'

I gave her bottom a light slap. 'Still are, too, aren't you?' A thought crossed my mind. 'Did Robin ever watch you getting spanked?'

'Don't think so, no – though he'd have heard it all right. The house wasn't that big. Why d'you ask?' Before I could reply she continued, 'Come to think of it, he did spank me himself a couple of times, before I got big enough to put up a fight. Funny, I'd forgotten that. Don't get the idea I had this brutalised abused childhood, though. It was pretty happy, all in all.'

The talk drifted to other matters, and we soon fell asleep.

Next morning, Katie fixed me breakfast before I headed for my train. She looked so gorgeous, wafting about in a T-shirt that scarcely covered her bare rump, that I couldn't resist hauling her over my knee right there at the breakfast table. She giggled and squealed with delight, calling me all kinds of rude names – which earned her a few extra spanks for impertinence. And one thing led to another, so I missed the early train. Not that I minded a bit.

We parted with a warm embrace, making plans for her to visit me in London that weekend. 'You know you'll get spanked some more, don't you?' I teased her.

She laughed happily. 'I should damn well hope so!'

The London train was full, and I found myself stuck opposite a thrusting young executive type, very pleased with himself. In between braying inanities into his mobile phone, he favoured me with tales of how much he was earning, how he'd pulled fast ones on all his colleagues, and so on. Finally, he dropped his favourite subject just long enough to ask, 'What d'you do, then?'

I told him. A look of pitying contempt crossed his brash features. 'Sounds pretty dull.'

I had a mental image of Katie, naked, her glorious rear end aflame, bent over the plans chest and moaning with pleasure as I thrust into her. I recalled another image too, that I'd glimpsed earlier in a mirror reflecting the dark alcove outside her office: Robin Wainwright, his eyes gleaming in the twilight, his gaze fixed on his sister's squirming spanked bare bottom.

'Oh, it is,' I told pushy young Mr Mobile. 'Dull as ditchwater.'

16

First Class Training

Being an Excerpt from the Unpublished Memoirs of Victor Manning, Gentleman of Leisure and Student of the Erotic Arts.

It was on a fine day in the summer of 1887 that I found myself on the platform of the railway station at Shrewsbury, looking for a pretty girl. I should at once explain that I was not merely seeking some chance romantic encounter, diverting though that might have been. No, it was a specific young lady, a distant cousin, who was the object of my search. My task was to meet her and escort her back to her guardian in London; but, since I had never set eyes on her in person, I was casting about on the bustling concourse, wondering how I should recognise my charge.

The young lady's guardian, my uncle Jenner, had assured me with his usual benevolent vagueness that I should have 'no trouble knowing the girl'. 'To begin with,' added he, twinkling roguishly at me, 'the young minx is extremely pretty – and I know, Victor, that you have quite an eye for a pretty face. Then, she has the family features; indeed, she often reminds me of your poor dear mother at the same age. Finally, she will be in the charge of the Academy's matron, who will doubtless prove a female of advanced age, stout build and forbidding aspect, for what school matron is not? Taken together, all these factors should make recognition no very onerous task.'

Yet it transpired that my uncle, not for the first time, had adopted a somewhat simplified view of matters. Since the school term had just ended, the Shrewsbury concourse was positively seething with young ladies of every age from twelve to nineteen, many of them delightful to look at – a charming prospect in itself, but one hardly calculated to facilitate my search. Furthermore, many of these girls were accompanied by older ladies, some of them indeed of so forbidding an aspect that I shrank from accosting them with even the most courteous enquiry.

As I hesitated, gazing about me, my eye fell on a girl of some seventeen summers standing not far away. Not only was she strikingly pretty, but her resemblance to my beloved late mother was remarkable. Thinking that this must surely be my cousin Lucy, I was on the point of approaching her when I noted that her companion, far from being elderly or unprepossessing, was a young woman of comely bucolic aspect scarcely older than herself, surely not old enough to be matron of an academy.

But, while I was still hesitating, this same young woman resolved my doubts by approaching me and enquiring, in a lilting Welsh accent, whether I were 'the gentleman that is come to meet Miss Danvers'.

'Yes, I am,' I responded. 'But are you Mrs Huskinson?'

'Oh no, sir, indeed,' she replied. 'I am Gwyneth Price, head parlourmaid at the Academy, at your service, sir. Mrs Huskinson, I am sorry to say –' although she did not look in the least sorry, but seemed rather to be experiencing some secret amusement '– Mrs Huskinson is indisposed today. But your cousin, I am thinking, can be telling you more about that matter.'

While Gwyneth was speaking, Lucy had joined us and I greeted her with a cousinly kiss on the cheek. To tell the truth, I should have been happy to bestow my kiss on any part of her sweet anatomy that might offer itself, for she was indeed a very pretty girl. She had dark curly hair, sparkling brown eyes with more than a hint of mischief about them, a charmingly retroussé nose and full lips. Her light summer costume revealed a petite but deliciously shapely figure.

'So you are my cousin Victor!' she cried, favouring me with a bewitching smile. 'Dear Uncle has told me so much about you, but he forgot to mention that you were so handsome. I am sure we shall be the best of friends!' With which she impulsively flung her arms about me and returned my kiss, this time full on the lips.

Deciding that it might be as well, before my new-met cousin proceeded to further intimacies, to gain at least some degree of privacy, I suggested that we secure our seats in the London express, just then pulling into the station. Having installed Lucy and myself in a first-class compartment, I took my leave of Gwyneth, thanking her for her trouble and bestowing two sovereigns upon her. She bobbed a delighted curtsey, with a glance suggesting that, had circumstances permitted, she would readily have demonstrated her gratitude in more tangible form.

I had greatly hoped that Lucy and I might have the compartment to ourselves. But just as the train was starting a portly gentleman, somewhat out of breath, wrenched open the door and flung himself in, almost overbalancing in his haste. Having righted himself, he cast us both a suspicious glance and sat down in the furthest corner, where he retired from view behind a copy of *The Times*.

At first his presence inhibited us a little, and we conversed on neutral topics. But such was Lucy's frankness and girlish ebullience that before long we came to disregard the intruder, and chatted like old friends. She was an enchanting girl, open and unaffected in her naive sensuality, and I sensed that our relationship might soon be placed on a most intimate footing. Even I, though, could scarcely have foreseen just how soon that would transpire.

'Tell me, Lucy,' I asked, recalling our conversation on the platform, 'what did Gwyneth mean when she said you would know more about Mrs Huskinson's absence?'

'Oh,' said Lucy, suppressing a giggle, 'yes, I am afraid that was my fault. You see, Matron has been *very* mean to me. She told Dr Natesby I was giggling during his sermon.'

'And were you?' I enquired, trying to look suitably shocked.

'Well, yes – but only a little! And she didn't have to tell him, the rotten sneak. So I got spanked, *awfully* hard.' She pouted appealingly at the memory of this unjust chastisement. 'On my bare bottom,' she added, regarding me slyly from beneath her lashes, as if to see how this revelation would affect me.

I could not deny that the image conjured up by my cousin's words was most beguiling. The mental picture of this succulent young creature face-down across a male lap, her soft bottom bare and blushing beneath ringing smacks, caused me a distinct stirring in the loins.

'But, Lucy,' I hastily interjected, hoping to distract her attention from my stiffening member, 'how are these events connected with Mrs Huskinson's incapacity?'

Lucy giggled again, casting a provocative glance towards my crotch. 'Dear Victor, I am so pleased that my girlish prattle is arousing your – interest. Well, you see, I knew that each evening before assembly Matron liked to enjoy a mug of porter. So . . .' She paused tantalisingly, grinning at me.

'Yes?' I asked. 'So?'

'Well – yesterday I got my friend Alice to keep *cave*, while I sneaked into Matron's parlour and put castor oil – quite a lot of castor oil – into her porter. Then, during assembly, she suddenly made such a funny noise, and clutched her tummy, and scuttled out sort of sideways, with all the school watching! And then –' Lucy was by now near helpless with giggles '– then we could hear all these groans and – and – and squelchy sounds from outside in the corridor! Victor, it was *so* funny! And this morning she didn't come down at all! So Gwyneth had to – had to . . .' She dissolved into incoherence, spluttering helplessly.

I must confess that, despite my efforts to remain dignified, I too was having great trouble restraining my laughter. The portly gentleman, however, had abandoned all pretence at reading *The Times*, and was listening to Lucy's story with evident outrage.

'That was shocking!' he exclaimed. 'Quite shameful, miss! You might easily have caused the poor woman some lasting internal harm! Furthermore, I cannot forbear to observe that she was wholly justified in reporting you for such irreverence. I am sure you heartily deserved your punishment, and I am only glad to hear that it was suitably severe!'

Lucy at once assumed a face of the most demure contrition. 'Oh,' said she, 'I do beg your pardon, sir; pray forgive me! I know that I am indeed a *very* bad girl, and that I should be soundly chastised for my wickedness!'

Crossing the compartment, she seated herself very close to the disconcerted gentleman, placing one hand trustingly on his knee and gazing up into his face with an expression of wide-eyed submission. 'Oh please, sir,' she cried beseechingly, 'you are a good man, an upright man, I am sure of it! Will you not punish me yourself? I have but recently been the pupil of that virtuous clergyman, the Rev Dr Natesby, of whom you have no

213

doubt heard, and surely I derived great benefit from the corrections he bestowed upon me. He would often spank me most diligently upon my bare bottom, from no other motive than to ensure my moral improvement. I beseech you, good sir, will you not do likewise? My cousin, I am certain, will quite concur in such well-deserved treatment. You are so stern and righteous; I am sure it would do me much good!'

With this she stood up and, turning her back upon the alarmed gentleman, raised her skirts as if to bare the appropriate part of her anatomy for his benefit. His expression of horror (not unmixed, be it said, with a certain covert fascination) was wonderful to behold. But at this moment providence came to his rescue and delivered him from further temptation. The train began to slow as it approached Leominster.

'I – I must change here!' cried he, leaping up and feverishly collecting his belongings. 'I – you – you are a most shameless young woman! Sir,' he gasped, addressing me, 'you bear a grave responsibility. May God grant you grace to discharge it! I – I bid you good day!'

After tearing the door open, he leapt from the train before it had fully come to a halt, and precipitately vanished from sight. A startled shriek from without indicated that he had probably, in his headlong flight, collided violently with some unsuspecting female traveller.

Lucy collapsed on the seat in peals of wicked laughter. I too could scarcely forbear to laugh, so droll had been the wretched man's discomfiture. But since, as her senior by some eight years and, at least *pro tem*, her guardian, it was incumbent on me to set this wayward girl a good example, I restrained myself with difficulty and chided her in the gravest manner I could command.

'Lucy,' I said, 'you are a wicked girl. Your behaviour towards that poor gentleman was deliberately provocative. You were fortunate that he had to leave us just at this moment, else I am sure he would have liberally availed himself of your invitation to smack your bottom. And rightly so, since you most richly deserved it.'

'I am heartily sorry,' said Lucy demurely, checking her laughter. 'Perhaps, Victor, you would like to chastise me in his place? If so, I shall readily submit to your just correction since, as you say, it is no more than I deserve.'

The suggestion was too good to pass up. The glimpse I had just received of Lucy's deliciously rounded bottom, clad in lacy white drawers, had been most enticing, and the idea of lowering those drawers and administering a sound spanking to her soft young globes was irresistibly seductive. It was quite evident, too, that Lucy herself was by no means averse to having her bottom smacked. For all the pretence of guilt and retribution, the chastisement would surely bring pleasure to us both.

'Very well,' I said, feigning sternness. 'Since you have been placed in my trust by your guardian, young lady, I stand somewhat *in loco parentis*. And you have indeed been very naughty. So it's clearly no more than my quasi-parental duty – however reluctant I may be to fulfil it – to put you over my knee and give you a good sound spanking on your saucy bottom.'

'Indeed it is,' responded my pretty cousin, 'and I am sure your distaste for the task will be tempered by the satisfaction of a duty well discharged, for I have been assured by an expert in these matters that my bottom is particularly well formed for such chastisement. I assume you intend to spank me on the bare?'

'Why, er – of course.'

'In that case,' she observed with a sly smile, 'I suggest that my punishment should be administered without further delay, since the train is now pulling out and we have the compartment to ourselves. After all, the sooner I am corrected, the sooner my conduct will start to improve. I believe we have nearly half an hour before our next stop at Worcester. Will that allow you time to discipline me as thoroughly as I deserve?'

'I think so – just,' I replied solemnly.

'Good,' said Lucy, 'as I am sure I shall derive great benefit from it. Indeed,' she added, with a meaningful glance at my crotch, where a substantial erection was visibly straining at my trousers, 'I am sure we both shall.'

'Your guardian warned me that you were a forward little minx, Lucy,' I said, taking her by the hand and drawing her face-down across my lap, a procedure to which she offered not the least resistance, 'and you certainly are. Still, I suspect that you may prove to be more modest than you seem, for I can assure you that in a few minutes you will be blushing most vividly for your shameless behaviour.'

While I spoke I turned up Lucy's dress and petticoats to reveal a pair of white lace-trimmed linen drawers clinging lovingly around her ripe rearward curves. Hooking my finger in the waistband, I drew them slowly down, exposing to my gaze as pretty a pair of girlish bottom-cheeks as one could wish to see – plump, pale, perfectly rounded and altogether enticingly spankable. Framed, as if on tempting display, by the snowy whiteness of her underlinen, they seemed to swell upwards as if inviting the strokes that would soon descend upon them.

'You have a most delicious bottom, my sweet cousin,' I said, squeezing and fondling the soft globes, which trembled delectably beneath my hand.

'So I have been told,' responded Lucy, wriggling saucily on my lap – a movement which caused her to rub excitingly against my already stimulated manhood. 'I am sure Dr Natesby thought so, since he never neglected an occasion to chastise me. Of course, he used to spank all the girls, especially the pretty ones, very frequently – and always on our bare bottoms. Every night at least half-a-dozen of us would be sent to bed with warm and tingling behinds, and we often used to raise our nightgowns and compare the rosiness of our cheeks. But I think I was turned over his knee more often, and smacked harder and longer, than any other girl in the school.'

'Perhaps it was because you were the naughtiest,' I suggested.

'Perhaps so. But I'm sure the shapeliness of my bottom had a great deal to do with it. On one occasion, as Dr Natesby was lowering my drawers prior to punishing me, he quoted Shakespeare (for he was a most cultured gentleman, as well as a dedicated disciplinarian), saying, "There's a Divinity that shapes our ends". He added that, since mine had been so ideally shaped to receive chastisement, it was his duty to fulfil the designs of Providence by spanking it vigorously and often.'

'I can quite see that the reverend gentleman might feel the need to invoke a lofty religious purpose,' I responded. 'But for my part, I feel the fact that you are such an impudent girl, and endowed with so exquisitely spankable a bottom, is quite sufficient reason that you should be punished in this fashion. But enough of this talk, young lady,' I added, raising my hand. 'Despite Dr Natesby's laudable attentions, your wanton behaviour indicates that far too long has elapsed since your last chastisement. It is high time, my dear cousin, that you were spanked as you so richly deserve!'

Lucy gasped as my hand connected with the ripe curve of her right bottom-cheek with a smack that rang round the compartment; then yelped as her left cheek received equally smart treatment. I paused to admire the twin pink hand-shapes that now adorned the creamy mounds, then settled down to spanking the saucy little minx hard and steadily, relishing the way her soft young cheeks jiggled and quivered as I smacked them.

'Ooh! Ow!' At each spank, Lucy emitted little yelps and squeals of mingled pain and excitement. 'Help! Oh that *hurts*! Oh, no more, Victor, I beg you! I'm sorry! Ow! I'll be good, I promise! Oh, not so hard, I beg you! Help! I'm sorry, truly I am! Oh no more, pleeease!' But for all her cries, and her wriggling and kicking, she made no real attempt to escape, and it was clear that she was enjoying her chastisement just as much as I was.

So I spanked away to my heart's content, smacking Lucy's peachy bottom both left and right, and taking good care to cover every inch of the luscious target area, from flank to flank of her cheeks, and down to the sweet tender undercurve where bottom meets thigh. Ere long a warm blush suffused the full expanse of her bouncing bare bottom-cheeks, steadily deepening through pink and red to a rich glowing crimson. It was a beautiful sight, and one to gladden the heart – and stiffen the prick – of any devotee of the gentle art of chastising deserving young ladies.

'Well now, my girl,' I said, pausing briefly in my task to stroke her fiery mounds and admire the delicious spectacle, 'you are truly blushing for your misbehaviour. This saucy bottom is turning very rosy indeed, and looks all the prettier for it. In fact, I think it should often be tinged this fine roseate colour, and, while you remain in my care, my dear cousin, I shall see to it that you get well spanked every day. Meanwhile, we shall not reach Worcester for over ten minutes, so I have ample time to make these naughty cheeks blush yet more vividly.' So saying, I resumed my delightful task.

'Oooh! Victor, you are a rotten beast!' wailed Lucy. 'Help! My poor bum is on fire! I promise to behave! Oww! Oh stop, *please*!'

But I was in no hurry to stop. Poised as she was on the very cusp of adulthood, Lucy's bottom presented an irresistible combination: yielding, girlish softness along with the lush fullness of maturity. Can there be any

218

more delectably spankable a creature than a pretty, shapely seventeen-year-old girl? So, as the Worcester-shire countryside sped by, I continued joyfully to smack her plump squirming globes, their radiant blush contrasting exquisitely with the whiteness of her waist and thighs. Not until we were within five minutes of Worcester did I relent, pausing to relish the rich crimson hue that now mantled Lucy's trembling, soundly-spanked bottom.

'Now, young lady,' I told her, 'this shameless bottom has had the spanking it so richly deserved. Consider yourself lucky, though, that there was no hairbrush to hand. After a naughty girl has been soundly hand-spanked, I find a good hard smacking with a wooden hairbrush adds the perfect finishing touch. At home I have the very article, and I shall take pleasure in acquainting you with it at the earliest opportunity. But for now I'll let you off with just one dozen more good hard spanks, and your punishment will be over – for now, at least.'

'Owww-ooooh!' squealed Lucy, as five ringing smacks landed in rapid succession on the roseate curve of her right bottom-cheek. 'Waaa-haaah!'

Five on the left, to even the score. Finally, to round things off nicely, I placed one farewell stinger, laid on with full force, on each tender undercurve. These final spanks, much to my satisfaction, elicited the shrillest squeals yet from my pretty young cousin.

Her spanking over, Lucy lay limp and gasping over my lap. I caressed her hot tender bottom-cheeks before letting her slide off my knee to the floor, where she lay gingerly rubbing her flaming orbs.

'Oooh! Owww! Oh my poor bottom!' she complained, pouting up at me reproachfully. 'Victor, how *could* you, you beast? You spank even harder than old Natey! Oww, I'm on fire! That was *most* severe – you're very cruel!' But her eyes were sparkling, and her lascivious

219

wrigglings were clearly not caused solely by the smarting of her rear. I too felt exceedingly randy, and was sorely tempted to join her where she lay and roger her vigorously there and then. But the countryside through which we had been passing was giving way to urban streets as we neared Worcester. Raising my cousin from the floor, I helped her pull her drawers back up over her rosy curves and rearrange her dress.

As the train drew into Worcester station, I was in a fever of apprehension that our solitude might be intruded upon by other travellers. If that were the case, my frustration would be almost intolerable. The train slowed, and I saw to my dismay that the concourse was busy. However, I had counted without Lucy's resourcefulness. Opening the window and leaning out, the shameless child blandly enquired of those who approached our compartment whether or not they had been inoculated against the malaria. 'My poor cousin,' said she, 'has but recently recovered from a serious bout, though we *trust* he is no longer infectious –'

So efficacious was this ruse that, when the train pulled out, we still had the compartment wholly to ourselves. Lucy, quite unabashed, pulled her head in and turned to me with a delighted grin. 'Now, dear Victor,' she exclaimed, embracing me ardently, 'pray do not delay! The warmth of my bottom is communicating itself to my pussy, and I am eager to feel your prick plunging into me!'

I was far too aroused to chide her for the immodesty of her language. Instead, I hastened to release my rampant penis from its confinement.

Lucy viewed it with unalloyed delight. 'Oh! what a beauty!' she exclaimed. 'Does he stand so proudly because you so enjoyed spanking my bottom?'

'I am sure that has contributed to his stiffness,' I responded. 'But you are a lovely girl, Lucy, and I think the prospect of fucking you would cause many a man to stand proud – even had he not had the pleasure of spanking your soft bottom beforehand.'

'Dear Victor,' cried Lucy, 'you say the sweetest things!' Leaning forwards, she gave me a long kiss, while grasping the shaft of my prick and squeezing it gently. 'Oh, how hard he is! If this is what comes of your spanking me, dear cousin, you may spank me just as often as you like! Now quickly, Victor, quickly,' she breathed, bending to kiss the head of my engorged manhood, 'I long to have you inside me!'

I needed no further urging. As her bottom was too sore for her to lie under me she turned and, resting her upper torso on the seat, presented her roseate rump that I might take her *a tergo*. I was delighted to do so, and thrust joyfully into her tight wet little cunny. As I entered her fully, it enhanced my ardour to feel the blazing mounds of her tender bottom against my belly. So aroused were we both by this stage that, very quickly, we came together in an ecstatic climax. I only hope that the first-class compartments of the Great North-Western Railway were well sound-proofed, or our fellow travellers on either side may have been a trifle alarmed.

Afterwards, we reclined together on the seat, and I held the sweet girl in my arms, kissing her firm young breasts and gently caressing the still-glowing curves of her well-spanked bottom. 'Who would have thought,' I mused, 'that the trick you played on Mrs Huskinson would lead to so delightful a consequence?'

'Oh, as to that,' she replied with a mischievous smile, 'that wasn't entirely true.'

'What? But Gwyneth said . . .'

Lucy giggled. 'Oh, yes, it's true that Matron wasn't well this morning. But that was due to her overindulgence in porter the night before. What I told you about the laxative was just wishful thinking.'

I gazed at her in bewilderment. 'But why on earth did you concoct such a tale?'

'Why? Dear Victor, can't you guess? To induce you to spank me, of course. From the moment I first saw you, on the platform at Shrewsbury, I was resolved to have you. Few men, I've found, can resist spanking my bottom if given the least excuse; and from spanking to fucking I knew would be an easy transition.'

To say I was flabbergasted would fall far short of the truth. 'Why,' I gasped, 'you artful little minx! Lucy, I have a good mind to put you back across my knee here and now. Clearly, I failed to spank you nearly hard enough. Think yourself very lucky, my girl, that I have no hairbrush with me.'

'Oh, but I have a hairbrush in my case,' Lucy announced with her most demure smile. 'Shall I retrieve it for you, dear cousin?'

17

Wilde Times – The Missing Spanking Scene from *The Importance of Being Earnest*

Oscar Wilde is usually pegged as gay. But his status as gay icon and martyr obscures the fact that for a long time he was happily, and very physically, married. And during his first American tour, it's said, he took full and vigorous advantage of the facilities when invited to a cathouse in Colorado. So, bisexual at the least. But was he into spanking? A recent discovery by the tireless researchers of the Camden Institute for Disciplinary Studies suggests that maybe he was.

The find consists of several sheets of pale-mauve vellum writing paper that still, after all these years, retain a faint fleeting odour of patchouli oil. On them, in emerald-green ink, is what appears to be an early version of the opening of Act III of Wilde's most famous play, The Importance of Being Earnest. *Leading Wilde scholars have pronounced the handwriting to be indubitably Oscar's.*

Preceding events: Act II of the play is set in the garden of Mr Jack Worthing's country house, where Cecily Cardew, Jack's young ward, and Gwendolen Fairfax, daughter of the formidable Lady Bracknell, meet for the first time. Each girl believes herself engaged to a certain Ernest Worthing. It emerges that Gwendolen's fiancé is, in fact, Jack, while Cecily's fiancé is really Jack's friend (and Gwendolen's cousin) Algernon Moncrieff. Both men, for reasons far too complicated to go into, have been calling themselves Ernest Worthing. Shocked at this revelation, the two girls flounce scornfully off into the house, leaving Jack and Algernon to discuss the situation as Act II ends.

ACT THREE

SCENE I: *Drawing room at the Manor House, Woolton. GWENDOLEN and CECILY are at the window, looking out into the garden.*

GWENDOLEN: The fact that they did not follow us at once into the house, as anyone else would have done, seems to me to show that they have some sense of shame left.

CECILY: They have been eating muffins. That looks like repentance.

GWENDOLEN: And tea-cake. That looks like inconsolable grief. Oh! They're looking at us. What effrontery!

CECILY: I do believe they're talking about us. That least shows a proper sense of priorities.

GWENDOLEN: They seem to have reached a decision.

CECILY: They're approaching. They appear very resolute.

GWENDOLEN: When one man is resolute, that may indicate strength of character. When two men are united in resolve, their purpose is usually deplorable. Let us preserve a dignified silence.

CECILY: Certainly. It's the only thing to do.

Enter JACK and ALGERNON. JACK looks serious; ALGERNON is grinning.

224

JACK: We are agreed. Between you, you have utterly exposed our respective subterfuges. We find this most inconsiderate of you.

GWENDOLEN and CECILY (*together*): Oh!

ALGERNON: Deception is the essence of civilised society. If we all went around demolishing one another's deceptions, what would become of polite conversation?

JACK: Or of sound business practice?

ALGERNON: Or of political principles?

JACK: Or of the Church of England? Besides, behaviour such as yours sets a most pernicious example to your elders.

ALGERNON: Young ladies have no business setting bad examples. There will be plenty of time for that once you are married.

CECILY (*indignantly*): But what of the bad example you have set us, in misleading us as to your names and characters?

JACK: Young gentlemen are supposed to mislead young ladies. That is what courtship is all about. There is no place in it for brutal honesty.

ALGERNON: There will be plenty of time for that once *we* are married.

JACK: Besides, you have done us an even more unforgivable injury.

GWENDOLEN (*haughtily*): And what was that, pray?

ALGERNON: By retiring so abruptly from the tea-table, you left us with no alternative but to finish all the muffins.

JACK: And the tea-cake.

ALGERNON: Our constitutions may never recover. We shall probably live out wretchedly blighted lives as martyrs to indigestion. And martyrs are notoriously unwelcome in good society. They expect to be persecuted, and sulk intolerably if they are not.

JACK: In short, we feel that your conduct has been quite unforgivable.

GWENDOLEN: Then why have you followed us indoors?

ALGERNON: In order to forgive you.

CECILY: Oh, that shows generosity of spirit. I admire that in a man.

GWENDOLEN: And a total absence of logic. I admire that even more.

ALGERNON: However, we feel that we cannot forgive you –

GWENDOLEN: Oh!

CECILY: How vexing!

ALGERNON: Until we have spanked you for behaving so badly.

GWENDOLEN and CECILY (*horrified*): Spanked us!

JACK: Decidedly. Do I take it that you object?

GWENDOLEN: Of course I object. I have never been spanked – or, at least, not recently. I should find it most humiliating.

CECILY: I have never been spanked at all. I should find it most exciting – I mean, outrageous.

ALGERNON: Your objections are cogent, and deserve to be considered at length. Accordingly, we shall postpone consideration of them until you've been spanked. Action is always improved by a little thought after the event.

ALGERNON advances on CECILY, who backs away, her eyes shining with excitement. JACK advances purposefully on GWENDOLEN.

GWENDOLEN: Mr Worthing! Are you offering violence to my person?

JACK: Offering? Certainly not. You might decline, and think how humiliating that would be. I intend to bestow it, which bespeaks generosity on my part, and furthermore relieves you of the tiresome burden of choice. You may express your gratitude in due course.

He takes her by the wrist and sits down on an upright chair, drawing her down over his lap.

GWENDOLEN: Oh! How dare you! Let me go at once! This is shameful!

JACK: Surely not. Punishment is recommended by the best authorities as a means of making people better, and indeed I feel better already. In a few minutes' time I'm sure I shall feel positively seraphic. (*He begins to turn up her skirts.*)

ALGERNON has captured CECILY, who puts up an unconvincing show of resistance. He leads her over to an upholstered pouffe, sits down upon it and puts her across his knee.

CECILY: No, Algy! Don't! Do you take me for a child?

ALGERNON: Oh, by no means, darling. Spanking is far too good to be wasted on children. (*He flips up her skirt and slip, revealing a neat but sweetly rounded bottom clad in white linen drawers. He strokes it delightedly.*) Dear Cecily, I always said that your person was absolute perfection. Here is further proof of my discernment. You are quite perfectly, adorably spankable.

CECILY: Darling, you say the sweetest things! But then why has Uncle Jack never spanked me?

ALGERNON: Quite clearly, the deficiency of his taste regarding neckties extends also to the spankability of girls. (*He starts to lower her drawers.*)

GWENDOLEN (*attempting a withering glare, which is not easy from a prone position*): Algy, that is most offensive! Jack is about to spank *me*. And no one has ever accused me of not being spankable.

JACK (*caressing the voluptuous curves of her silk-clad bottom*): Indeed you are, my darling – deliciously spankable. I am about to prove it to my complete satisfaction – and yours, I hope. Algy, you wretch, apologise to your cousin at once!

ALGERNON: Later, perhaps. At present I should find the unaccustomed effort quite distracting. And to give anything less than my full attention to Cecily's first spanking would be inexcusable. She would have cause to doubt my utter devotion to her.

ALGERNON starts to spank CECILY soundly on her bare bottom. She squeals and kicks her legs.

CECILY: Aah! Ohh! It stings so! Algy, do all spankings hurt so much? Ow-oww!

ALGERNON: Only when they're done properly, my darling.

CECILY: Oww! Oooh! And is it proper for you to spank me on my – aa-aah! – bare bottom?

ALGERNON: It's a matter of aesthetic appreciation, dear child. Would a connoisseur hang a veil before his most cherished painting?

JACK: Yes – because the charms of mystery are inexhaustible, while those of disclosure are finite. Besides, fine sheer silk, if it's tightly stretched, can feel (*he administers a sharp spank to GWEN-DOLEN's bottom*) quite exquisite!

GWENDOLEN (*squirming wildly*): Aaah-oww! Er-nest – I mean, Jack – I am already convinced of your ardour! (*JACK applies several more ringing spanks.*) Ohh! Oww! There is no need – aa-haah! – to give me such vivid proof!

JACK (*continuing to spank her vigorously*): But, as yet, dearest one, so much of the proof has been bestowed in the form of kisses. The other end of your person, though equally lovely, has remained neglected. I merely aim to redress the balance.

The double spanking proceeds unabated for some time.

CECILY: Oww! Ohh! Aah! Oh, darling Algernon, please stop a moment! Oww! I want to ask you something, and it's impossible to think – oww! – while one's having one's bottom smacked.

ALGERNON (*pausing*): What is it, my angel?

CECILY: Will you still be so cruel as to spank me when we are married?

ALGERNON: Of course, darling.

CECILY: Then you may continue.

ALGERNON: With pleasure, sweet girl. (*He does so.*)

GWENDOLEN: Aa-haah! Oww! Dear Jack, please stop – I also have a question. (*JACK pauses, caressing her bottom.*) Should the obstacles to our marriage prove insuperable, will you ever spank another girl?

JACK: Only out of a sense of duty, darling.

GWENDOLEN: Then you too may continue. (*He does so.*)

Enter MERRIMAN, the butler. He betrays not the least surprise at the situation, but coughs loudly.

MERRIMAN: Ahem! Ahem! Lady Bracknell!

Enter LADY BRACKNELL. She stops short in the doorway, astounded by the sight that meets her eyes. Exit MERRIMAN.

ALGERNON: Good heavens! Aunt Augusta!

JACK: Lady Bracknell! I hope you will forgive us if we do not rise. As you see, Algernon and I are somewhat encumbered.

LADY BRACKNELL: So I perceive. Is this chastisement intended to improve the young ladies' conduct, or is it purely for recreational purposes?

JACK: Both, I hope, Lady Bracknell.

LADY BRACKNELL: I am sorry to hear it. Pleasure and moral instruction should never mix. The results are invariably disastrous, especially in France. (*She raises her lorgnette.*) That bottom looks strangely familiar. Gwendolen! Is that you?

GWENDOLEN: Yes, Mamma.

LADY BRACKNELL: Why is Mr Worthing spanking you? Yesterday I found him on his knees before you, and today I find you over his knees before him. I shudder to think what yet more indecorous posture may be in prospect for tomorrow.

JACK: Miss Fairfax came here to see me, Lady Bracknell, against your express prohibition. I was shocked by such shameless disobedience. Knowing that Lord Bracknell was not in the best of health, I thought it no more than my duty to stand *in loco parentis* and administer a suitably paternal correction.

LADY BRACKNELL: I see. What your explanation lacks in credibility, Mr Worthing, it makes up for in ingenuity. (*She advances into the room.*) Algernon, I fail to recognise this young lady – from either end. Who, may I ask, is she?

ALGERNON: This is Miss Cecily Cardew, Aunt Augusta, Mr Worthing's ward. We met this afternoon and have become very fond of each other.

LADY BRACKNELL: So it would appear. Why are you spanking her?

ALGERNON: For the fun of it, Aunt Augusta.

LADY BRACKNELL: Good. I greatly prefer your answer to Mr Worthing's. It is entirely selfish, and thus has the ring of truth. (*She sits down in a chair affording a good view of both chastisements.*) Very well, you may both proceed.

JACK: Do I gather that you approve of our spanking these young ladies, Lady Bracknell?

LADY BRACKNELL: Certainly I approve. Girls should be spanked regularly. It discourages them from too much sitting, which may lead to reading and other undesirable pursuits. Far better to make a girl's bottom smart, than her head. It also ensures care over the more intimate items of apparel. A girl who knows she may be spanked at any moment will be sure to choose her most becoming undergarments.

GWENDOLEN: But, Mamma, won't you rescue me?

LADY BRACKNELL: Rescue you, Gwendolen? Really, you have a very strange sense of priorities. Yesterday you were eager to marry Mr Worthing, an action which would have entailed lasting consequences to your social standing – to say nothing of my own. Today you want me to dissuade him from giving you a spanking, whose effects will last no longer than tomorrow. Or perhaps the day after, since he appears to be a vigorous and resolute young man. The request is scarcely consistent. Mr Worthing, pray proceed. You too, Algernon.

JACK: Thank you, Lady Bracknell.

ALGERNON: Thank you, Aunt Augusta.

The double spanking recommences, giving rise to much yelping and wriggling from the young ladies. LADY BRACKNELL levels her lorgnette and looks on with an air of satisfaction. Enter MERRIMAN, bearing two wooden hairbrushes on a silver salver. He offers one to each of the men. The girls gasp in dismay.

GWENDOLEN: Oh no! Jack, please – not the hairbrush!

CECILY: Algy! You wouldn't!

ALGERNON (*brandishing his hairbrush with relish*): In the circumstances, Jack, I feel the least we can do is make sure –

JACK: Quite so, Algy: that both these darling girls are spanked – in earnest!

CURTAIN

18

The Pirate's Bride – A Swashbuckling Romance

'But, my dear,' said Lady Pamela, in what she hoped were tones of persuasive reason, 'at least meet the young man. Surely there can be no harm in that?'

Her daughter gave a heavily theatrical sigh. 'Mama, how many times must I tell you? I have already met him. Five years ago, at Lady Porchester's ball in Berkeley Square. A pasty-faced tongue-tied youth of no distinction whatsoever. I thought little of him then, and have no desire to meet him again now.'

'But five years is a long time, my dear. During that interval, may the young man not have changed a good deal for the better?'

'Indeed – or for the worse. You tell me he has become an excellent businessman, and has transformed the fortunes of his father's sugar plantations here on the island. Most impressive, I'm sure. But, Mama, if I wished to die of boredom, no doubt there are quicker ways of doing so than by marrying "an excellent businessman".'

Lady Pamela cast her eyes to the heavens. 'Isabel, I declare I sometimes despair of you. John, help me, for pity's sake! Can you do nothing to persuade your daughter?'

Lord Abercrombie turned reluctantly away from the window, where he had been contemplating the lush Barbadian scenery and the azure sea that lay beyond. In truth, he was a little in awe of his fiery-natured daughter, and rarely tried to oppose her wishes. Contemplating her now, her dark-haired beauty enhanced by the flush on her cheek and the sparkle of indignation in her eye, and mentally contrasting his own pale sandy-haired looks, he wondered, not for the first time, how he could have sired such a girl. Indeed, there had been rumours: Lady Pamela in her youth was not averse to the pleasures of Regency London, and a certain Castilian grandee from the Spanish Embassy had been much in her company . . . Still, why waste time on such fruitless musings?

'Come, my dear,' he murmured soothingly, 'is it so much to ask that you meet this young man for an hour or so at dinner? And, you know, if by chance you like him, it could be a most advantageous match for you.'

'For *me*!' Lady Isabel laughed scornfully. 'Father, let's at least be candid with each other. You choose to gamble and fritter away our family inheritance, and now you hope that an alliance with a rich trader of the Indies may restore your fortunes – or at least stake you again at the gaming tables. Advantageous, you say? I don't doubt it!'

'Isabel!' protested her mother. 'How can you speak so disrespectfully to your father? For shame!'

'Mother,' retorted the young woman, 'had my father wished me to honour him with the deference due from a daughter, he might have bestowed on me a little more of the care and affection expected of a father. It's a trifle late now to establish conventional family ties. Besides, might I remind you that you brought me out here – both of you – under deceitful false pretences? This journey, you told me, was intended to restore my father's health. Now it transpires that your true aim was to barter your

234

only child for a bag of gold.' Anger and contempt flashed from her eyes. 'And *you* dare ask respect of *me*?'

With these words Lady Isabel flounced from the room, leaving her parents to gaze at each other in dismay. Eventually, Lord John shrugged helplessly. 'We are expected at dinner, m'dear. We'd better go, and give the Trevelyans what excuse we may for Isabel's absence. A touch of tropical fever, perhaps?'

But news travels fast in the Caribbean. Long before Lord and Lady Abercrombie, graciously apologetic, had presented themselves at their hosts' dining table, sharp-eared and quick-tongued Barbadian servants had conveyed from one household to the other – not without much laughter – the true reasons for Lady Isabel's non-appearance.

Three days later, that headstrong young lady was strolling on the beach below the villa her parents had leased. The beach, a perfect crescent of pristine white sand fringed with palm trees and lapped by gentle blue waves, offered irresistible appeal to her romantic nature, and she had taken to walking there early each morning before the day grew too hot. It was a lovely spot, and she found herself thinking that, all told, there might be many worse places to live. Only not – she shuddered – as the wife of some sugar-growing *commerçant*, a dullard preoccupied with yields and harvests and market prices. No, what the wild beauty of the island suggested to her was a companion altogether more dashing, more spirited – a man whose bold nature would relish meeting the challenge of a woman worthy of his mettle . . .

Lost in her reverie, she unconsciously rounded the small headland of the bay, only to pause at an unexpected sight. There in the next cove a ship lay at anchor: an old-fashioned square-rigged galleon, all but motionless on the calm sea. And nearer at hand, drawn up on the shore, a longboat with its oars berthed.

With instinctive caution, Isabel turned to retreat. But before she could retrace a single step, a voice spoke behind her. 'Well, here's a pretty surprise for a fine morning. Where did you spring from, my beauty?'

Isabel swung round. Five paces away a man was reclining on a rock, smiling lazily at her. His skin was brown and his hair was long and tousled; he was bearded and a golden earring hung from his left earlobe. Though he was young – scarcely older, Isabel guessed, than herself – there was an air of authority about him that belied his casual, even ragged, attire and his bare feet. He was, she acknowledged with an involuntary tremor, very handsome, but at the same time there was something dangerous about him. Strangely, Isabel found herself recalling a puma she had once seen at the Zoological Gardens in Regent's Park. Though this man's body was utterly relaxed, it was as though he might pounce at any moment.

Yet more puzzling to Isabel was an odd feeling that his face was somehow familiar, though just why she was unable to recall. 'Have – have we met?' she asked absurdly, for all the world as if they were conversing in some genteel Mayfair drawing room.

The man smiled all the more broadly. 'Now is that likely?' he asked. 'You, a fine young lady from London, and I – well –' with a gesture he indicated his tattered shirt and breeches '– as you see me.'

'How do you know I'm from London?'

'Oh, my lady, this is a small island, and word gets around. Especially to someone like me, who make it my affair to know things. So, yes, I know who you are, Lady Isabel, and who has brought you here – and why.'

'Well, in that case,' responded Isabel, her temper rising, 'you will also know that it's none of your damned business! Now, if you will kindly excuse me.' She turned to go.

The man whistled. It was a brief whistle and not loud, but within seconds half-a-dozen men had appeared as if from nowhere and blocked Isabel's path. 'How dare you! Let me go!' she cried, and struck out with her fists, but at once she found herself held, gently but firmly, quite unable to move.

'Ah, but you see,' purred the voice behind her, 'I intend to *make* it my business. And the first order of business today, my lady, is that you make a short sea voyage with me and my companions.'

'No! Help!' screamed Isabel, struggling wildly, but to no avail.

The largest of the men, a broad-chested grinning bald giant of a fellow with a striped jersey and red neckerchief, slung her unceremoniously over his shoulder like a sack of potatoes and marched off with her towards the longboat. She kicked furiously and thumped his back with her fists, but she might as well have assaulted a mountain.

After a brief ride in the longboat, Isabel was toted up a rope ladder in the same undignified style and set upright upon the galleon's deck. The boat's crew were joined by a dozen more assorted ruffians, some black, some brown, some white, but all rakishly attired and regarding her with unconcealed curiosity, while the man who had first accosted her seated himself on an upturned cask and gazed at her coolly. 'Welcome, my lady, aboard our humble vessel,' he remarked ironically.

Isabel stared around her in mounting alarm. 'You're – you're pirates!' she gasped.

'Pirates? Oh, come, Lady Isabel, that's a crude, ill-favoured word. We prefer to call ourselves – freebooters.'

The crew chuckled. 'Aye, freebooters,' they repeated, seemingly much taken with the term.

Isabel drew herself up with all the haughtiness she could muster. 'Call yourselves what you will, but you had best let me go at once, before this kidnapping brings the Royal Navy about your ears! My father is a British peer, and my fiancé one of the richest men on the island.'

'Your fiancé? And who might that be, pray?'

'Mr Henry Trevelyan.'

The self-styled freebooter threw back his head and laughed lustily. 'Mr Henry Trevelyan, indeed? Ah, that's rich, my lady!'

'Why do you laugh, you villain?'

'Why, because first of all he's not your fiancé. How can he be, when you refuse so much as to meet him? Second, because that poor milksop is my father's son.'

Isabel stared. 'You lie! Henry Trevelyan has no brother.'

'Oh, not officially, perhaps. But, as you must know, Lady Isabel, these things may happen in the most respectable of families. Wrong side o' the blanket I may be, but a Trevelyan nonetheless.' Rising, he swept her a low bow. 'Charles Trevelyan Esquire, my lady, at your service.'

He settled himself back on the cask. 'Which brings us handily to the second order of business. You were brought to Barbados, Lady Isabel, to marry a scion of the Trevelyan family. And so you shall. Me.'

'You presumptuous wretch!' Isabel's eyes flashed fury; she stepped forwards and dealt him a ringing slap across the face. 'I marry a bastard! How dare you?'

Several of the crew started forwards, but Charles waved them back. Rubbing his injured cheek, he grinned wolfishly at Isabel. 'Bastard maybe, my girl, but even bastards don't take kindly to being struck. I would strongly advise you not to do that again.'

'I scorn your threats,' stated Isabel proudly. 'As for marrying you, I'd die first!'

'Oh, I doubt that will be necessary. I'm sure you'll find marriage a preferable alternative. You see, I've made all due respectable provision.' He gestured, and a trembling clergyman was pushed forwards from among the crew. 'A genuine pastor, I assure you. We abducted him only last night. I hope, sir, your congregation will not be too discommoded by your absence.'

'Were he the Bishop himself, I should still refuse!' stormed Isabel.

'As you wish, my lady. I merely thought that, as a well-brought-up girl of good family, you would prefer the more honourable option. But, believe me, my beauty, when I tell you that, with or without benefit of clergy, you shall grace my bed tonight.'

'Why, you unspeakable blackguard!'

This time, the slap was even harder. It was followed by a deathly hush. Isabel, seeing the look in Charles's eyes, backed away as he rose and advanced purposefully upon her.

'You wouldn't hit a woman!' she pleaded, raising a protective hand to her face.

Charles smiled. 'Oh, I shan't smack your face, my lady. It's much too pretty for that. But you must learn that, daughter of an English peer or no, you can't go about hitting whomsoever you wish. And Mother Nature in her wisdom has furnished, elsewhere about the female anatomy, parts far more pleasingly shaped for smacking.'

'No!' cried Isabel as she divined his meaning. She turned to flee, but she felt her waist encircled by a strong arm. Before she knew what was happening, she found herself lifted bodily off the deck and deposited face-down across Charles Trevelyan's sturdy lap as he sat back down on the cask.

'You wretch! Let me go at once!' she cried, struggling wildly, but Charles had her firmly pinioned with an arm across the small of her back, while with his free hand he rucked her dress up above her waist.

In that tropical clime Isabel had attired herself as lightly as was consonant with modesty. The lifting of her dress revealed that only drawers of fine white silk veiled the lush curves of her bottom. The clergyman gave an ineffectual bleat of protest, drowned by lusty roars of approval from Charles's crew.

'That's the way of it, Cap'n!'

'Warm her pretty arse for her!'

'Give it her hot and strong!'

Ignoring Isabel's cries of fury, Charles coolly stroked the soft silken mounds that lay so invitingly at his mercy. 'You have a lovely bottom, my lady,' he observed pleasantly, 'but I'll wager it's not been spanked near as often as its shapeliness invites, nor indeed as often as the conduct of its owner deserves. A regime of sound and regular chastisement might have done much to curb that wayward temper; but I doubt your lazy wastrel of a father ever troubled to tan this spoilt young backside for you.'

'Certainly not!' exclaimed Isabel indignantly. 'How dare you! Let me go, you brute!'

'As I thought,' returned her captor. 'And doubtless no one else did, either. More's the pity. A sound spanking once a week or so, my fine lady, might have improved your manners beyond all recognition. Still, better late than never: and once we are joined in blissful matrimony, my sweet, I shall have ample occasion to make up for your father's neglect of his parental duties in this regard.'

Peering over her shoulder, Isabel saw Charles raise his right arm high in the air.

'No! Don't!' she yelped, reaching back to protect her vulnerable rear.

But Charles merely captured her wrist in his left hand, holding it well clear of the target area, while his right hand descended hard and fast. The ringing slap echoed across the calm waters of the bay.

Isabel gasped, as much from surprise as from pain. She had not lied; not since infancy had anyone physical-

240

ly punished her, and never would she have credited how sharply a hard male hand could sting a soft pampered female bottom. 'Oww!' she yelped angrily. 'You brute! That hurt!'

'No doubt,' retorted Charles calmly. 'That was the intention. But, believe me, my sweet, it will hurt a lot more before I'm finished. You need to be taught a lesson, my lady Isabel, and I mean to impress this one firmly upon your memory.'

Once again his hand swept down with a resounding smack, making Isabel gasp again as he stung her other cheek. He paused a moment to let the sting sink in; then, settling to a steady rhythm, he proceeded to administer several dozen hearty spanks to Isabel's squirming rearward curves, much to the amusement and approbation of his crew.

Charles too could scarce forbear to grin, such was the pleasure he experienced in spanking this lovely wilful girl. At 22, Lady Isabel Abercrombie was at the height of her beauty, and her posterior was by no means the least of her charms. Full and superbly rounded, it seemed as if made for just such intimate chastisement; the lush mounds quivered and jounced at every smack, offering irresistible targets to his punishing palm. Beneath its silken veil the girlish flesh felt deliciously soft and sensitive, and he could tell from her yelps and kickings that his exertions were having the desired effect. Already a delicate pink tinge was making itself visible through the sheer fabric, testifying to the rosy blush burgeoning beneath.

In due course he paused, stroking the trembling globes. 'Well, my lady,' he asked, 'have you learnt your lesson? Can we expect better behaviour of you?'

'I'll see you hanged first!' came the defiant response. 'Hanged and damned, you pirate bastard!' She attempted to wriggle free, but Charles held her fast.

'Evidently not,' he observed calmly. 'It seems this lovely bottom needs more spanking yet.'

'Haul down her drawers, Cap'n,' called the bald giant who had lugged Isabel aboard. 'Let's see her pretty red arse.'

'Shame on you, Jem,' chided Charles. 'This is a lady, gently born, not one of your tavern wenches. Spanking she may deserve, but not the shame of having her virgin modesty exposed to your coarse gaze. Besides,' he added, with a crisp spank to Isabel's bottom that made her yip, 'I suspect these elegant drawers can be affording her hindquarters precious little protection.'

He was right in that. Indeed, if anything the thin silk, tightly stretched across the rounded contours of Isabel's rump, only enhanced the sting of each smack. Already her bottom felt as though it were on fire, and as Charles, taking a firmer grip on the girl's torso, resumed her punishment Isabel began to fear she would never sit down in comfort again.

At first the humiliation of finding herself so ignominiously chastised before so many lustful male eyes had seemed worse than the pain of the spanking itself. But now, as spank after merciless spank cracked down across her tender globes, she forgot her ribald audience, forgot her injured pride, as her attention focused ever more intently on the discomfort being meted out to her anguished rear end. Charles, she felt sure, was spanking her harder than ever. The sting of his hand was all but unbearable, and she found herself near to weeping.

Yet at the same time she felt gripped by strangely contradictory instincts. There was, she couldn't deny, a certain excitement in being thus forced to submit to the first real spanking of her life, and at the hands of a man so strong and masterful, so utterly different from the effete overbred fashion-plates of polite London society. The pain inflicted on her sensitive hinder parts hurt worse than anything she had ever known, yet at the same time it was arousing passions whose urgency left her bewildered. Torn by these cross-currents of emotion, Isabel, to her intense shame, burst into tears.

Charles paused, stroking the burning mounds. 'Well, well,' he murmured, 'can this be a sign of penitence? Let's be merciful and suppose so.' After replacing Isabel's dress, he helped her to her feet and held her while she sobbed, her face hidden on his shoulder. When her tears had abated he offered her a moderately clean handkerchief and beckoned over the trembling cleric. 'Come, parson,' he ordered, 'do your duty and be brisk about it, ere the young lady changes her mind.'

As the clergyman gabbled his way through the ritual of the marriage service, Isabel consoled herself with the reflection that her union, even if consummated, would be of but short duration; the forces of British justice, she felt confident, would soon overtake her pirate groom. But in any case she had devised a plan, and as the ceremony concluded she saw her chance.

No doubt the pirates assumed that so fashionable a young lady would scarce know how to swim. They miscalculated. Growing up on the Abercrombie estate on the Devon coast (long since lost to her father's creditors), Isabel had swum almost before she could walk. Now, as the buccaneers crowded round to congratulate their chief, leaving her momentarily unobserved, she sprang to the ship's rail, stripped off her dress and dived into the sea.

The cool water came as a benison to her glowing bottom. She struck out for the shore, hearing behind her shouts of surprise and alarm, followed by a splash. Glancing over her shoulder she saw that Charles had dived after her, while a boat was being lowered from the galleon. She redoubled her efforts. But, though she was a strong swimmer, Charles was stronger. Fifty yards from the shore he caught her and, laughingly evading her blows, gripped her fast until the boat reached them. A few minutes later, to her fury and despair, Isabel found herself back on the galleon's deck, the object of amused interest from the crew. Her wet bodice and drawers, she was uncomfortably aware, left few of her bodily charms to the imagination.

'A blanket there, you gawping numbskulls!' snapped Charles, stripping off his wet shirt. 'Dammit, you knaves, some consideration for a lady and my new-wedded bride!' Taking a proffered blanket, he draped it around her. 'And now –' he beckoned two of the less ruffianly-looking crew members '– Paul, Barnaby, escort the lady to my cabin with all due courtesy. But I think you had best bind her, to prevent any further bids for freedom. Pinion her gently but securely. Apologies, my dear,' he added with a bow. 'I shall join you very shortly.'

Charles's cabin proved to be snug and singularly well appointed. Paul and Barnaby followed their captain's instructions to the letter, and Isabel found herself skilfully bound, in such a way that the ropes held her firmly but without cutting into her flesh. Then, with ironic bows and grins, they left her.

From above, she could hear Charles's voice as he gave orders to the crew. Otherwise, the only sound was the soft lap of the waves and the distant cry of sea-birds. Since for the moment escape was impossible, Isabel took stock of her surroundings. They included, she was intrigued to note, several shelves of books. Of more interest to her, though, was a heavy brass compass upon the desk, and the fact that the cabin boasted portholes broad enough to allow egress.

After a while she heard steps descending the companion-way, and Charles entered the cabin. He was still stripped to the waist and Isabel couldn't but admire his muscular torso. As a lover, she had to admit, he cut a fine figure of a man. Nonetheless, she reminded herself, this was the villain who had kidnapped her, forced her into marriage under duress – and, most unforgivably of all, put her over his knee and publicly *spanked* her, the brute! (At this memory she experienced an involuntary spasm of excitement, but resolutely suppressed it.)

'Your pardon, my sweet bride,' said Charles with a winning smile, 'for neglecting you like this on our wedding day. From now on, I assure you, you may count on my most devoted attention. I regret too that I had to have you bound. But really, we couldn't have you leaving us again so abruptly, now could we?'

Taking a dagger from his belt, he severed the cord that bound Isabel's wrists to her waist and the cord binding her ankles together. 'And now, off with that wet linen, my sweet,' he commanded. 'Ladies' finery, I regret to say, is in short supply on this ship, but I have a cambric shirt or two – and well laundered, I assure you – that may suffice you at a pinch.'

'Turn away, then, sir,' responded Isabel. 'Even a woman-beater like you can surely assume the outward semblance of common courtesy.'

Amused, Charles turned his back and began to rummage in a closet. At once Isabel snatched up the compass. One good blow to the back of his head, and she would be out the porthole and away before the crew were alerted. This time, she should be certain of reaching the shore and finding help. Stepping soundlessly behind the oblivious buccaneer, she aimed a vigorous swing at his head.

But luck was not with Lady Isabel that day. At the very last second Charles turned, and the compass caught him a glancing blow on the ear. 'Ow!' he roared, grabbing her arm. For a moment he glared at her in rage and she thought he might kill her, but then his face relaxed and he laughed.

'A fine spitfire I've yoked myself to! Well, I admire your spirit, sweet bride, but braining your lord and master is no foundation for a good marriage. It seems to me you yet need a touch more husbandly discipline, my girl.'

'No! Let me go, you monster!' cried Isabel, but her protests were in vain. A moment later she found herself, for the second time in less than half an hour, draped ignominiously face-down across Charles's knee, her shapely nether regions upturned for further attention.

Alas, poor Isabel! Cruel enough, in all conscience, that a second spanking should follow so hard upon the first, to be inflicted on a bottom still tender from its recent chastisement; but worse was yet to come. 'Well, my dear,' remarked Charles, 'since we now find ourselves relieved of an audience, I think I may avail myself of the privilege of a husband and relieve these delectable orbs of their last protecting veil.'

'No! Oh no!' shrieked Isabel, struggling wildly, but her captor took not the slightest notice. To her horror she felt the damp drawers being peeled slowly down until they hung in a moist tangle around her thighs, leaving her rearward curves naked and defenceless. Charles gazed with delight on the prospect before him. 'A spitfire, but a lovely one,' he murmured. 'Rarely, my sweet girl, have I seen a bottom more truly made to be spanked.' Gently he stroked the lush bare cheeks, their beauty enhanced by the delicate blush still visible from his earlier efforts.

That blush was soon revived in all its roseate glory. Isabel, yelping and squirming, learnt that a spanking applied to a bared wet bottom stung yet more sharply. The effort of the watery pursuit and capture had robbed Charles's arm of none of its vigour, and for what seemed to her like hours spank after resounding spank descended upon her quivering mounds.

It was agonising to be thus mercilessly chastised, it was deeply shameful; yet once again, despite her wounded pride, she felt a strange secret pleasure in submitting to this man's mastery. Furthermore, the fires ignited on her rear end were arousing new, disturbing sensations in adjacent parts, and her writhings, she

246

realised, were not occasioned exclusively by pain. The spanking was hurting her exceedingly and she could surely take no more; yet she found herself lasciviously arching her bottom as if to invite further strokes.

At long last Charles paused, caressing the ripe rosy contours of his bride's radiant bottom. How lovely she looked, he thought, all but naked across his lap, her luscious rear curves mantled by a sunset glow that contrasted so exquisitely with the whiteness of her back and thighs. Gently he raised her up and she clung to him, whimpering despite herself. There were tears in her eyes, but when he kissed her she responded with melting passion, writhing her body against his.

It was a long deep kiss, but at length Charles drew back and gazed into Isabel's eyes. 'My sweet,' he said softly, 'the thought that you might be about to knock me unconscious would prove a sad distraction from the joys of our wedding night. So let me propose a pact. If you give me your word that you will make no further attempt to escape tonight, I promise that tomorrow I shall restore you to your liberty. Is it agreed?'

'Agreed,' she breathed, and kissed him fiercely again.

So throughout that long languorous tropical afternoon and deep into the night, Lady Isabel Abercrombie learnt the ways of love from her pirate bridegroom. To his delight, she proved an apt and eager pupil. Her warm young blood, stirred by the fires he had kindled on her bottom, was further heated by her lover's dexterous hands and tongue, arousing her passions to such a pitch that when his rampant manhood forced its way into her virgin cleft she welcomed the transient pain, crying out in a rush of overwhelming joy.

And it was with no less joy that, a few moments later, she knelt over her recumbent lover and tasted her own virgin blood as she licked and teased his wilted member back into hardness, until he groaned aloud and pulled her down on top of him, re-entering her as his hand smacked her still glowing bottom-cheeks. Then, turning her over and positioning her on hands and knees, Charles applied several more brisk slaps before driving into her from the rear, savouring the warmth of her well-spanked bottom against his belly and thighs.

Nor was this Isabel's last chastisement of the night. The next morning, just before dawn, Charles woke her with a tender kiss. Then, before she knew what was happening, she found herself turned naked over his lap while he proceeded to treat her to a sound bare-bottomed spanking.

'Oww!' protested the surprised girl. 'Charles! Stop it! I've done nothing wrong! Why are you spanking me?'

'Oh, chiefly for the fun of it, my sweet,' he retorted, happily smacking her plump soft mounds until they blushed pinker than the Caribbean dawn that was breaking outside the porthole. 'Though for a few other reasons as well. To wit, because you're an exceedingly spoilt young woman who deserves henceforth to be soundly spanked at least once a day – and, whenever possible, more often than that. Because you have such a lovely deliciously spankable bottom. Because I thoroughly enjoy it. And because, my wilful darling, I rather suspect that you do too.'

'Oww! You brute! No I don't!' Isabel cried indignantly. But, when at last he released her, her passionate embrace told a different story.

A hour or two later, the galleon's longboat beached in the same bay Isabel had left barely twenty-four hours before. Charles and Isabel, the sole passengers, disembarked while the bald giant Jem rested on his oars and grinned at them. 'Hope you wasn't too uncomfortable, m'lady, a-settin' on these hard seats.' He chortled.

Isabel blushed. The boat's wooden seat had indeed reminded her very tangibly that she was sitting on a bottom still rosy and tender from her most recent

248

spanking. Her uneasy shiftings, it seemed, had been more evident than she thought.

'Enough of your impudence, Jem,' ordered Charles, pushing off the boat. 'Get yourself back to the ship. I'll signal you later.'

'Aye, Cap'n,' said Jem, and rowed off singing cheerily to himself. The words were none too clear, but they seemed to be his own personal version of the old ballad 'Cherry Ripe'.

Charles laughed. 'A rough fellow, but good hearted,' he observed, and led the way along the beach, in the opposite direction to the Abercrombies' villa.

'Where are we going?' enquired Isabel. 'Do you not risk being captured?'

'Oh, I think I may hazard that for your sake, my sweet,' said Charles carelessly. 'As for where we are bound, you'll learn that soon enough.'

At the far end of the beach a path led through the trees. In a few moments a fine colonial villa with a pillared portico came in view. Showing no caution, Charles marched up to the front door and entered boldly. Bewildered, Isabel followed at his heels.

They found themselves in a spacious hall, flagged with black-and-white tiles. A grand double staircase curved before them. No one was to be seen.

'Hullo there!' called Charles, setting the echoes ringing. 'Is nobody at home, dammit?'

In response, a portly middle-aged woman came bustling out of a doorway. 'Why, there you are, Master Henry!' she exclaimed. 'A fine time to be off playing your pirate games, with the whole island in an uproar! Lady Isabel Abercrombie has vanished – kidnapped, it's feared! And who, may I ask, is this young lady?'

But Isabel was staring open-mouthed at her companion. 'Henry? But you said you were –'

'Charles? Why, so I am, my love.' He made her a low bow. 'Charles Henry Trevelyan at your service, my lady.

This is Martha, our trusty housekeeper. And Martha, this is – or, rather, was – Lady Isabel Abercrombie.'

'Was? What on earth do you mean, Master Henry?'

'What I mean, Martha, is that she is now, and has been since yesterday, Lady Isabel Trevelyan – my wedded wife.'

'Your wife?' Martha's jaw dropped. 'Master Henry, if this is another of your pranks . . . Oh my Lord sake's, I must tell the mistress!' She turned to go, then dropped Isabel a flustered curtsey. 'Begging your pardon, m'lady – if you really are m'lady, that is – oh, mercy me!' She scuttled off calling frantically, 'Madam! Madam!'

Grinning, Charles turned to confront Isabel's furious glare. 'Disappointed, my sweet?' he enquired.

'You tricked me, you – you mountebank!'

'True, so I did. But since it seemed you were loath to accept a "pasty-faced tongue-tied youth of no distinction whatever", or indeed an "excellent businessman", for your husband, I thought you might find a pirate chieftain more to your taste. For you must admit, my sweet, that our nuptials were anything but dull – as, I hope you'll agree, was our wedding night.'

To her annoyance, Isabel found herself blushing.

'I see you concur, my love. Well then, I trust you'll believe me that I intend our life together to continue as it's begun. No less romantic, no less exciting, no less filled with love and adventure. But, if you doubt me, sweet Isabel, then your freedom is yours to take this instant.'

He smiled winningly at her. But there was a note of unease in his voice that made her realise he genuinely feared to lose her, and it was that hint of uncertainty that won the day for him. Besides, he was without question devilishly handsome. Still, she could not resist the chance of coquetry. So she kept him on tenterhooks for several moments before saying, 'Very well, then, I agree – but on three conditions.'

'And they are?'

'First, that henceforth you will always be known as Charles.'

'Agreed.'

'Second, that I shall be far less a businessman's wife than a pirate's bride.'

'Agreed.'

'And third that, as pirate or businessman alike, you faithfully keep the promise you made me.'

'Which promise was that?'

The sound of approaching agitated voices could be heard. She leant forwards and whispered in his ear.

He laughed delightedly. 'Agreed, with all my heart!' he cried, and embraced her warmly just as his mother and father and a gaggle of excited servants poured into the hall.

A second wedding followed hard on these events – a rather more formal affair, with a genuine bishop officiating – followed in turn by a long and happy marriage. Not least of the sources of their happiness was that Charles Trevelyan faithfully observed the promise made by the pirate to his bride: that Lady Isabel, that lovely and exceedingly spoilt young woman, should henceforth be soundly spanked at least once a day. And, whenever possible, more often than that.